The Devil Gets Divorced

Angela Corbett writing as
Destiny Ford

The Devil Gets Divorced

Angela Corbett writing as
Destiny Ford

Copyright © 2025 by Angela Corbett

Cover design by Kat Tallon at Ink and Circuit Designs

All rights reserved. No part of this publication may be reproduced, distributed, or transmitted in any form or by any means, including photocopying, recording, or other electronic or mechanical methods, without the prior written permission of the publisher, except in the case of brief quotations embodied in critical reviews and certain other noncommercial uses permitted by copyright law.

This is a work of fiction. Names, characters, places, and incidents either are the product of the author's imagination or are used fictitiously, and any resemblance to actual persons, living or dead, business establishments, events, or locales is entirely coincidental.

ISBN 978-1-965228-00-5

Published in the United States of America by Midnight Sands Publishing, Utah

Printed in the United States of America

Dedication

For the unstoppable small army of women growing larger every day.

Chapter One

My name is Kate Saxee, and as the editor for *The Branson Tribune,* I have at least one unexpected thing happen in my life every day. I looked up at the sky and sent a tiny ask to the universe that this was today's only offering.

A white sedan was stopped in the middle of the road, covered in what appeared to be a thick, sticky substance that had been applied over the car like a Jackson Pollock painting. The abstract art was sprinkled with pieces of what appeared to be bread. Two oval hashbrown patties were sticking straight up from the windshield wipers like shredded potato devil horns.

A large red truck that appeared to be cosplaying as a semi was parked sideways across from the sedan. Liquid that looked like it had once been a dirty soda—a Utah staple full of caffeine, but not coffee, so it was still legal by Mormon/LDS Church standards—was splattered all over the passenger side door of the truck. It was slowly dripping off the running board, though it was so cold outside that the soda was starting to ice over. The truck's window was open, which seemed strange given the frigid temperatures. Two groups of angry people, who I assumed had once been in the vehicles, were standing about fifty feet apart, shooting daggers at each other with their eyes.

I pulled my coat tighter around my neck. It was the first of February and freezing. I'd been at the scene less than five minutes and had more questions than the notes app on my phone could hold.

I snapped some photos as Bobby, or Officer Bob to people who were being a bit more proper, trudged over to me through the snow. I'd had a rough go of it with Bobby when I first returned to my hometown of Branson Falls, Utah, last year, but I'd known him since high school when he had spiky hair with frosted tips and drove a rusted-out puke green station wagon, so that kind of history and humiliation creates a bond. Since it was apparent we'd both have to work together a lot for our jobs, we'd developed a rapport that was mostly friendly and only a little hostile some of the time. We'd even given each other Christmas gifts.

"The police scanner indicated this was a road rage situation," I said to Bobby, gesturing between the car and semi-truck wannabe. "This looks like a fast-food fight."

Bobby angled his head, thinking. "That's not a bad explanation. It started as road rage and escalated."

I stared at him for a few seconds. "When I said it looked like a food fight, I was joking. They really threw food at each other?"

Bobby pulled his hat more tightly over his ears to block the wind that was whipping the snow into tiny frozen tornadoes. "Yep. The sedan driver slammed on the brakes. The truck owner got mad, rolled down his window, and threw his breakfast at 'em. His meal deal landed on the car."

"With the hashbrowns sticking straight up?"

"That was done after the fact by one of the vehicle passengers."

I raised one brow as Bobby continued, "The driver of the car retaliated by throwin' her soda. She used to play softball and was picked for the All-State team, so she had good aim."

I looked at the truck, the soda dripping down the side, and the open window above it. I could practically see the replay in my head. "She launched it into the truck through the open window?"

Bobby's eyes sparkled a bit and he was trying hard not to sound as impressed as he seemed. "I probably shouldn't have an opinion about it, but it was an impressive shot. The lid came off on its way to the window, but the bulk of the drink exploded in the truck driver's car, so he pulled sideways and cut the sedan off to confront 'em. We got here right before they started throwin' punches."

I shook my head, stunned. "Let's hope she never teams up with Mrs. Olsen," I said, remembering the situation at the grocery store a few months ago. "The two of them together could be unstoppable at food assaults."

Bobby snorted. "Seriously. I hope they don't ever meet."

"Can I talk to the vehicle owners?"

"Yeah," Bobby said. "The sedan owner is over there." He pointed to a man with a red face, and a woman with pursed lips, her arms folded tightly across her chest. They didn't seem to be talking to each other. "The truck owner is over there." Bobby pointed to a big guy wearing a trucker's hat, sunglasses, jeans, and a blue t-shirt with a bear on it. His shirt looked like he'd been hit with the dirty soda version of birdshot.

The truck driver was closer so I went there first. I didn't recognize him, so I didn't think he was local, but so many people had moved into town in the past year that I couldn't keep track of everyone. I put my hand out as I said, "Hi, I'm Kate Saxee with *The Branson Tribune.* Can I ask you some questions?"

His eyes met mine before deliberately trailing down my body and back up. Given the current weather, the only thing he could ascertain from his unwanted perusal was that I had dressed adequately for snow. He gave me a slow smile and shook my hand. "Sure, sweetheart."

I paused at the pet name he'd felt entitled to assign to a stranger, and gave him a smile that let him know I was tolerating him and nothing more. "What's your name?"

"Boyd Hollow."

I didn't recognize it. "Can you tell me what happened?"

He pointed at the woman and man across the road from him. "I was drivin' and that idiot slammed on her brakes. I almost hit her, but swerved out of the way. It's a good thing, too, because my truck could've driven right over the top of that puny little car."

He was probably right about that. His truck was a blood red monster with custom suspension and tires as tall as the door handle on my Jeep. It would give Drake's Hummer a run for its money in the height and absurdity department.

"How did the breakfast food end up on the car?"

He lifted a shoulder. "I rolled down my window and threw it."

Of course he did.

The corners of his lips turned down. "I'm pretty pissed about that actually. Now it's after eleven in the mornin' so I can't go get more French toast sticks and hashbrowns, and they have the best in town."

I watched him for several seconds to see if he'd puzzle out the fact that he was mad he'd wasted the breakfast food he'd willingly thrown. Choices have consequences. "Lessons learned, I guess. Don't assault other motorists with breakfast food you want to eat."

He grinned and bit his bottom lip in a move I think he meant to be alluring, but instead bore a strong resemblance to a rabbit chewing on a carrot. "You're feisty. I think I like you."

The feeling was definitely not mutual. "So, you launched your French toast sticks and hashbrowns, and then the other vehicle's passengers retaliated by throwing their drink in response?"

I could see the muscles working in his jaw before he answered through his teeth, "Straight through my open window. Damn thing splattered everywhere."

I gave a pointed look at his shirt. "I can see that."

His eyes followed mine down, his nostrils flaring slightly at the reminder. "I pulled over in front of 'em and we had words."

"What caused her to slam on her brakes?"

"Hell if I know! Crazy women drivers. Don't know why her boyfriend, or whoever he is, wasn't behind the wheel instead of her."

I took a very deep breath and told myself I would not start a fist fight with this dude over his sexist and antiquated opinions.

When I was capable of talking without verbally flaying

him, I thanked him for his time, then walked over to the couple.

They were standing with several feet between them, and were turned away from each other. I'd taken a body language class, and could see they were both screaming at each other silently. I introduced myself to them. The woman was blonde, tall, and had the build of an athlete. She said her name was Brexley Burns. The man had brown hair, cut in a short missionary haircut, a wide nose, and was rail thin. His name was Ray Poll. They'd recently gotten engaged after dating for only a month, which wasn't uncommon in Utah, and also a good way to spend the rest of your life and eternity with someone you didn't really know, or like.

"Can you tell me what happened?" I asked.

Brexley took a deep breath and looked at me, her face lined with worry. "I was driving and hit the brakes too hard. The guy in the truck got mad, blocked us, and threw his breakfast at my car. Ray was already angry before the truck blocked our lane, and told me to throw my dirty soda at the truck. The guy's window was down from where he flung his breakfast at me like an enraged chimpanzee. I used to play softball and have a good arm. My drink went through his window and exploded. I felt bad after the fact, and told him I'd pay for his car to be detailed."

I typed all of that in my notes and then asked, "Why did you slam on your brakes?"

Color rose in Brexley's cheeks. "I got a little distracted."

"By what?" I asked, thinking it was her phone, or maybe something on the radio.

She pressed her lips together and her fiancé, Ray, red-faced and still far beyond angry, answered for her, "By that," he said through clenched teeth, and pointed at the billboard on the side of the road.

It was a giant, and very attractive man wrapped up in the blanket being advertised. He was only wrapped from the waist down, and wasn't wearing anything but abs on top. He did have jeans on, but they were hard to locate and barely peeked out from the blanket. I'd seen the billboard before and had noticed it, but not to the point of preventing concentration. Then again, I had two men in my life who looked like that for real, and were distracting enough all on their own. Ray did not look anything like the billboard, so I could understand why Brexley was a bit flustered.

"Was it your first time seeing the billboard?" I asked Brexley?

She nodded and her tongue went over her lips like she was thinking about what billboard abs might taste like. "Yes. It surprised me a bit, that's all. I've never seen a guy like that."

"With abs?" I asked genuinely. I didn't intend for it to come out as an insult to Ray, but realized too late that it probably did.

She pursed her lips for a few seconds like she was trying not to laugh. Then answered, "Without a shirt."

Ah yes. Mormons aren't supposed to have sex before marriage, and women aren't even really supposed to think about it. Purity culture, especially related to women, has always been strong in the Mormon faith. I'd been Mormon in my youth and had once been in the room with a date when he changed the sweater he was wearing over his shirt. I'd seen the bottom part of his stomach and the abs that came with it, and thought I'd have to confess to my bishop. I'd been on my way out of the religion in high school, but I'd officially left the church as soon as I'd moved away from home, and had since done a great many things that would require much broader confessions and repentance if I were still part of the faith. Some of them I'd even done recently.

Brexley's attention shifted back to the billboard and held, almost glazing over. Ray noticed and fisted his hands as his red face got redder and he bellowed, "This kind of immoral advertising is nothing more than temptation and it shouldn't be allowed!"

I tilted my head and pushed my brows together. "But that's okay?" I asked, pointing to the billboard across the street with a stunning woman wearing a deeply low-cut pink shirt, with cleavage up to her chin. It was an ad for breast augmentation —a very popular procedure in Utah.

Ray was getting madder by the second. "That's different," he bit out.

Brexley, who had caught onto my questions and realized I might have opened the door for her to win the argument they'd clearly been having, had torn her eyes away from the abs-vertisement and was staring at Ray. "*How* is that different?"

He glanced at the billboard boobs before answering, "Because it's a woman, and it's normal."

Brexley bristled so hard I could practically see the hair rise on the back of her neck. "You mean it's normal to sexualize women, but not men?"

"Yes! I mean, no!" Ray said, trying and failing to defend himself.

"Then why is the boob billboard okay, but the billboard of the guy without a shirt isn't?" she asked.

"Because! You're a woman, and a member of the church,

and you're supposed to be sweet and innocent. This," he said, waving at the abs billboard, "isn't helping that!"

Their argument was about far more than billboards, abs, and boobs, and was about to turn into a much bigger discussion that might end up being a deal breaker for them both. I was just glad they'd found this out before they got married.

I had enough information for my story so I excused myself to give them some privacy.

I got a few more photos and then bundled up against the wind, my wavy brown hair that fell to my mid-back whipped at my face. On my walk back to my Jeep, I passed some witnesses, some local older men, and heard them talking.

"I ain't never seen anythin' like it," one of them said.

"Well, maybe in movies," the other said. "Or on TV. Or in the big cities, but those cities are basically Sodom and Gomorrah anyway. I sure didn't think we'd get it here."

"It started with the coffee shop, tattoo shop, and now this. Just another sign of the times!" the first man said.

"The Second Comin' will be here any day!"

I hadn't heard of attractive shirtless men on billboards as a precursor to the End Times, but this was Utah, where anything could be used to justify belief. I got in my Jeep and went back to the *Tribune* office.

I pulled into my parking space behind the *Tribune* and walked in the back door. A wave of blissful warm air hit me and I sighed as I unbuttoned my coat and walked across the black carpet speckled with green dots. The office sits in a row of other buildings on Main Street. It has an archive room in the back, and a large open space with my desk, and desks for correspondents. A counter at the front separates the waiting area with customers from the staff.

A woman with shoulder length brown hair was standing at the counter, her voice raised, as she argued with our office assistant, Madison.

"What do you mean I can't place the ad?" The woman's voice was getting louder with each word. "My money's the same as everyone else's!"

I put my bag on my desk and hung my coat and scarf over the back of the chair as I listened to their discussion to see if I needed to intervene.

Madison was holding her ground, but I wondered how long they'd been at this. "It goes against our publishing standards," she answered calmly.

The woman slapped her hands on the desk in front of Madison. "What standards? You publish crap!"

Ah, so she was one of *those* people. Angry about everything because they didn't get their way. I walked up to stand next to Madison, who looked at me with relief and stepped to the side.

"Hi, I'm Kate Saxee, the editor of the *Tribune*. What's your name?" I asked, trying to diffuse the situation.

She glared at me as she ground out, "Shasta Wentworth."

I'd also be mad if I'd been named after a bargain soda.

I gave her a disarming smile. "It's nice to meet you, Shasta. Can you show me the ad you want to run?"

Shasta took a piece of paper she'd been holding and pushed it toward me. It was a photo of a beautiful woman with long blonde hair, blue eyes, long black eyelashes, full lips, and the picture-perfect illustration of what every Mormon man is told to want, and what every Mormon woman is told she's supposed to become: perfection. Above the picture, the word "Liar" was written. Below it, her name was spelled out in big, bold letters: Whitney Hatch. Under her name were the words: SL,UT Cheater.

I pressed my lips together trying not to let the words I was thinking come out of my mouth. It took several seconds but when I was capable of speaking without swears, I said, "Madison was correct in denying your ad. That definitely violates our publishing standards."

"Why?" Shasta demanded.

"Because it's defamatory and if we publish it, it becomes libelous. Beyond that, the word "slut" is unacceptable, as well as the accusations."

"It's not *slut*, you dummy. There's a comma."

SL,UT was sometimes used to cleverly refer to Salt Lake, Utah. It was really an excuse to use the derogatory word. Again, Utahns are excellent at justification. I gave her a knowing look. "Just because you're trying to disguise your slur doesn't mean it's still not a slur."

Her fists were clenched so hard her knuckles had gone white. "It's not an accusation, either," Shasta seethed. "Everything I wrote about Whitney is true. I know, because I'm her sister-in-law."

I had to fight hard not to let my grimace show. Shasta was not a friend, enemy, or relative I would want to have, even by marriage. "Regardless, it's not acceptable for our newspaper, and Whitney could sue you, and us, for placing the ad."

Shasta snorted. "She can't sue anyone if she's not here."

My brows came together. That was a weird thing to say. I

wasn't sure if it was a statement, or a threat, and wasn't sure how seriously to take it.

Shasta grabbed her purse off the counter. "I got rights and I'll find some other, more reputable place, to post my ad."

The *Tribune* was the only newspaper in town, so I wasn't sure who else would publish it for her unless she posted it on social media, which was a real possibility, and could also get her sued.

She started to stalk to the front door and then turned and pointed her finger at me. "I've seen the coverage of you on the podcasts, and heard plenty about you from The Ladies. I know *exactly* who you are. No wonder you're on Whitney's side. You're just as much of a hussy, sleepin' with two men."

The Ladies were the female equivalent of an STI—irritating, hard to get rid of, and most were no friends of mine.

I gave her a curious look. "My personal life really isn't any of your business." I didn't even bother to correct her because she'd already decided her opinion and it wasn't worth my energy. Ever since the combined Murderoonies and *Branson Tribune* event a couple of months ago where I'd been caught on social media live stream cameras with both Hawke and Drake, people had taken even more of an interest in my love life—on a much broader scale. Sometimes we were even recognized in public outside of Branson Falls. It was strange, and beyond irritating.

Shasta turned dramatically like she should have a villainous cape trailing her, stomped out of the office, and slammed the door on her way out.

"Well, that was dramatic," I said, turning to Madison and taking a deep breath. "Are you okay?"

Madison moved some stuff around on the counter and

smiled. "I'm fine. Everyone has issues—some more than others."

I chuckled. "That's the truth."

Madison went back to work, listening to voicemails and returning calls.

"I thought she was gonna lose her mind," Ella said, coming into the main office area and picking up a donut from the treat table. Ella James was the *Tribune's* volunteer archivist. She was an outspoken, pint-sized widow in her seventies, and she drove a convertible sports car that some might say made her a menace. Like my mom, she bribed the police with treats to get out of tickets.

"I didn't even know you were here," I said to Ella.

"I was hidin' in the back. I didn't wanna get her wrath. Shasta's known for explodin' like a can of soda full of rage and bubbles." Ella took a bite of her maple donut and shook her shoulders happily at the sugar.

"She was a bit unstable," I agreed, going over to grab a donut for myself.

Ella pointed her donut at me. "She did have a good observation about your love life, though."

I rolled my eyes as I picked up a white frosted cake donut with nuts. "I'm not sleeping with two men." Not yet, I added silently in my head.

"I've heard you might be," Ella said, taking another bite of her donut.

"You've heard wrong. People have been saying that since I moved back to Branson eight months ago."

She watched me closely to see if my expression would betray my words. "I don't know what you're waitin' for," she said. "If I had Hawke and Drake interested in me, I would've hidden all their pants a long time ago."

"I'm surprised you haven't broken into their houses to do that anyway," I said, taking a bite of my donut.

Ella's eyes sparkled like she'd considered it, and was still coming up with a way to make it happen. I thought I should maybe warn Drake and Hawke. Then again, Drake had security cameras, and she wouldn't make it within a thousand feet of Hawke's property line without him knowing she was there —and his property line was an entire mountain.

She licked some frosting from her fingers. "You still haven't said who ya went away with after the Murderoonies' event."

I had to work to compose my expression into something neutral before I answered, "I did tell you. I went on a trip with a friend."

And that friend was named Hawke. Somehow, we'd managed to keep our short getaway a secret. However, I'd been gone from town for several days and thanks to The Ladies constant surveillance of my house, they knew it. So, there'd been a lot of theories about where I went, who I might have gone with, and complete certainty about what we'd been doing. I'd heard some of the rumors about that last part and they weren't entirely wrong.

Hawke was with me, and Drake had conveniently been gone at the same time, so I knew the speculation was rampant. Drake had asked about my trip and where I'd been, but I'd told him I needed a break after the land development investigation, and went away with a friend. He'd accepted that and hadn't pushed, but other people in town were treating the trip like a true crime of its own. I had no interest in feeding the gossip machine I'd unwillingly become part of, and I was trying to keep the trip information private.

Ella got a soda from the fridge in the corner. "You know someone's gonna figure it out at some point, right?"

I lifted my shoulder in a non-committal shrug like I didn't care. "They can try, but there's nothing to find out."

A spark of determination took up residence on Ella's face and I'm not gonna lie, it scared me a little.

"I'll be watchin' you," Ella said, making a V with her index and middle fingers and pointing them at her eyes and then mine. She made her way back to the archive room with her drink.

I grabbed a glass of water to calm myself, and then sat at my desk and opened my laptop to write the "breakfast billboard abs brawl" story.

The rest of the day went by uneventfully and I was packing up my stuff to go home when I noticed I had a voicemail. I picked up my phone and listened to the message. It was a muffled male voice I didn't recognize. "This message is for Kate. There's a story you should cover. Witches. Go to 111 Healing and Crystals before nine o'clock tonight."

Given that my mom had recently turned her front yard into an inflatable coven, I hoped she didn't have something to do with this. I jotted down the address and left to find out what in the witch was going on.

Chapter Two

Branson Falls is a small, rural Utah community that's growing, despite opposition by people in town. It sits at the base of the beautiful Rocky Mountains, where summers are warm, winters are frigid, and few things are more important than high school sports. A majority of people in town are members of the Mormon Church, also known as The Church of Jesus Christ of Latter-day Saints...or The Church of Jesus Christ, or whatever other name they were branding themselves with lately that made them seem mainstream Christian and not cult-y. Because of church teachings, most people in town didn't drink coffee, watch R-rated movies, or indulge in any alcohol. The religion came with a lot of rules, and membership and weekly church attendance was scrutinized and judged. Anything that could be considered evil, Satanic, or from the adversary was looked down on, and witches definitely fit that category.

By the time I got to 111 Healing and Crystals, smoke was rising from an area behind a large, modern, white barn with black trim that had been converted into a store. The number

111 was painted on the side of the barn in a black, thin, contemporary font, and Healing and Crystals was written in smaller text under it. The barn sat in the middle of nowhere and considering Branson Falls was already in the middle of nowhere, that's saying something. There weren't any houses for miles.

I followed the smoke and walked around to the back where I saw a group of about twenty-five women sitting cross-legged on large poofy circular pillows, around a sizable concrete fire pit. Outdoor heaters were spaced around the women keeping the area toasty even with the chill of the winter night. The women had their eyes closed, and they were chanting, "I release all things that do not serve me."

The good news was, I didn't see my mom anywhere so this was one witch-related event she wasn't linked to...at the moment. Though, she would be jealous of their fire pit.

There was a woman standing behind the circle, her long brown hair cascading down her back in waves. She wore a white coat over her flowy pale pink dress. The dress wrapped around her booted legs as she walked around the women, guiding them through the mantra.

"You're holding the paper with the thing you want to release in your hand. Think about that paper, and what's written on it. Think of how it has affected you. Do you have it? Now I want you to picture it burning up, the ashes rising into the air and leaving you." She paused, giving the women a chance to consider what she'd said. The fire crackled and embers pulsed with glowing heat. "You are the only person who gets to decide what you will accept. You can choose to no longer allow something to hold power over you." Several of the women took deep breaths and some even had tears running down their cheeks. "Now open your eyes, take the paper, and throw it in the fire."

One-by-one, they opened their eyes and looked at their papers. Some folded the papers, some crumpled them up, and others tore the papers to pieces. They took turns getting up and putting the papers in the fire. The papers went up in flames of all different colors, almost like a rainbow, and every piece of paper became nothing but ashes floating into the sky. It was actually kind of beautiful.

The peaceful atmosphere was interrupted by the screaming sounds of sirens and an onslaught of police officers and firefighters who came charging around the barn. They skidded to a stop when they saw the women all sitting peacefully on their poofs, not bothering a soul.

"What's goin' on here?" Bobby asked breathlessly. He'd been the one leading the charge.

The woman who had been leading the meditation answered, "We're having a full moon release ceremony and sound bath." She seemed calm, and not the least bit worried about the entire Branson Falls police force and fire department invading the space. "Would you like to join us?"

Bobby narrowed his eyes. "We had concerned citizens callin' in sayin' there was a séance goin' on, and some kinda witch coven."

The woman leading the ceremony widened her eyes in surprise and laughed. "I assure you that's not the case, Officer. We're just enjoying some girl time, breath work, and nervous system regulation."

Bobby studied her and then the other women like he was trying to decide if they were about to turn him into a bat. "No one here's doing anythin' evil or woo-woo-ee?"

The woman laughed. "No, not even anything illegal."

Bobby didn't seem convinced but went over to talk to the fire chief. After a few minutes, he came up to me. "How did you hear about this?" he asked, crossing his arms over his chest. He deliberately lowered his head, tracking the scene like he was still expecting the fire pit, and women around it, to start birthing demons. "You got here before we did."

"I got a call from someone telling me I should get to 111 Healing and Crystals for a story about witches. I came to check it out—calmly, I might add."

Bobby's features tightened in irritation. "Hell, Kate! We were told there were witches! Burnin' stuff!"

"You guys came in, guns and fire hoses blazing, like you'd been tipped off about a mass murder happening," I pointed out.

Bobby's eye started twitching. "There coulda been! We got calls!"

I tilted my head toward him in disappointment. "Those kinds of rumors are what started the witch accusations in Europe in the fifteenth century, too, Bobby. Then continued in America thanks to lies, and ended with tens of thousands of innocent women dead in multiple countries."

Bobby pulled his lips into a thin line. "I don't mess with Satanic stuff, Kate."

"You know the Satanic Panic was fabricated, right?" Though similar fear-based accusations seemed to be having a resurgence in popularity lately with all the focus on religious hype.

Bobby adjusted his belt and gave me a look like he knew something I didn't. "Some people say that, but I wouldn't believe 'em." He started to walk away.

"It's kind of a problem when you're a police officer who doesn't believe facts," I yelled after him.

He gave me a look over his shoulder and I just shrugged with disappointment.

The group of women who had been participating in the meditation and sound bath started to disperse, some of them I recognized from around town and they smiled and waved in my direction. I smiled and waved back. The woman who had been leading the mantra walked over to me. "I'm Clarissa Hope. I saw you walk in during the release ceremony."

"Hi, Clarissa." I held out my hand and she shook it. "I'm Kate Saxee with *The Branson Tribune*. The ceremony was really beautiful—what I saw of it, at least."

She gave me a kind smile. "You should come back. We do events on the full moon, the new moon, and we have daily meditation sessions and sound baths in our salt cave."

I had no idea. "I've never been here before." Branson Falls was a small town where everyone knew everyone, but there were a lot of smaller communities around it, and they'd all been growing. New people had moved in, and new businesses had started. "How long have you been open?"

"A few years," she said. "We took private clients and used to work out of my basement, but we kept getting bigger and moved into this space recently to better accommodate customers. We're not in a populated location, so most people find us by word of mouth—or when they're meant to."

"Do you own it with someone else?" She'd said "we" so I thought she must have a business partner.

"I own it with a friend. Whitney Hatch."

My eyes widened at the name. She was the woman

featured on the horrible ad that Shasta Wentworth had wanted to place.

Clarissa continued, "Whit started out doing sound baths and meditations, and I was doing reiki and crystals, so we came together to build something using both of our talents."

I'd heard the Hatch family name before. I hadn't met Whitney, but knew her sister-in-law didn't like her much.

"That's great it's grown enough that you're able to move to a bigger space."

She nodded, turning off the outdoor heaters. "So many people, especially women, are going through transitions and searching for community, hope, and help. That's what we try to provide here. I think it's made a difference, and that means a lot to me."

She had a calming energy, and this was the kind of business I liked to highlight for the *Tribune*. "When I got the call about witches, I didn't realize I was coming for a feature story on a new business, but I'd like to write an article about 111 Healing and Crystals, and your work."

The corners of her lips lifted. "That would be wonderful." Her expression turned curious. "I overheard you talking to the police officer. You said someone called to tell you about witches and gave you the name of our business?"

I nodded. "It was a male voice and they said there was a story I might want to cover regarding witches."

She took a deep breath and let go of a sigh. "We knew we'd get some pushback from people locally so I'm not surprised. Women using their power is terrifying for some people."

That was the truth. "It's why the witch trials happened. Men needed someone to blame for their impotence centuries ago, and they were afraid of women healers." I'd read *Witches,*

Midwives and Nurses, and was simultaneously fascinated and horrified by how much blame women had taken in society since the beginning of time.

Her eyes sparkled at my knowledge. "Exactly."

"Have you had other issues with locals?"

"Some. A lot of people feel that work like ours is taking the place of their religion, and they believe we're doing something unholy."

I'd like to say I was surprised, but I wasn't. I'd had an LDS Sunday School lesson once where they brought in a guest who played some popular rock songs backwards and tried to convince us the bands had made deals with the devil in exchange for fame. The songs didn't even say things backwards, and I think I was the only one in the room who questioned their logic. The "suspicious reporter" in me had started young.

I realized that day that religion liked to use fear as a means of control. For Mormons, nothing was scarier than Satan, and sin that could threaten your place in the afterlife: Celestial, which was actually divided into three tiers; Terrestrial; Telestial; and Outer Darkness—the Mormon version of Hell. Devout Mormons wouldn't accept ending up anywhere except top-tier Celestial. A business like this one sat solidly in Terrestrial, maybe even Telestial, and definitely would not be considered LDS temple-worthy. I'd seen cracks in the Mormon Church membership recently though, and thought some people were changing their minds so I tried to be encouraging to Clarissa. "It's hard to break through the mind-set, especially in a place like Branson Falls, but clearly, you're doing it. Do you mind if I stop by tomorrow and get some photos inside the store for the article?"

She smiled widely. "That would be great! Come by any time!"

"Thanks! It was nice to meet you, and I'll see you soon." I put my hands in my pockets and tucked my shoulders up to my ears to try and keep warm as I walked away from the fire and back to my Jeep.

I pulled into the driveway of my mom and dad's grey, brick house. When there wasn't snow on the ground, the yard was covered in flowers of various shades of red, and Redrock stone provided a contrast to the grey brick. My mom's witches, a Halloween decoration she'd left up to annoy one especially irritating neighbor, Gladys, were still standing. I was surprised Gladys still hadn't snuck over to stab the inflatables, or steal them.

I went inside the house to pick up my sweet little black and grey pup, Gandalf, and found my mom busy in her craft room. Shelves of fabric, ribbon, and lace lined two walls. Sewing machines and sergers were against one wall, and a cutting table with a measurement cutting mat, rotary blades, and special sewing scissors sat in the middle of the room. I'd made the mistake of using my mom's sewing scissors for paper once as a kid. I was building a castle out of construction paper and the scissors were so sharp they cut through the thick textured paper like a hot knife through butter. My mom found me mid-cut and to this day, I don't think I've ever feared for my life more than that—and I've been in some pretty scary situations as an adult, including being shot at.

"Hi, Mom," I said, walking in the room and surveying the

boning, ribbon, sequins, and hot pink, black, and red lace spread across her fabric table. This seemed a little more "Red Light District" than I was used to from my mom, and I had questions. "What are you working on?" I picked up a piece of the black boning that seemed entirely capable of also being used as a weapon.

My mom threaded some ribbon through the lace as Gandalf ran up to say hello. I crouched to pet him, and mumbled words about him being my best good boy while I rubbed his ears and head. He gave me some licks, jumped on my leg to tag me like we were about to play a game, then ran off to find a toy to facilitate his plans.

"Just some costumes for the witches," my mom answered nonchalantly.

I raised a brow. "Have the witches joined a sex club?"

She looked at me like she was trying to be horrified because it was the reaction expected of her, but she really wasn't. "Don't be silly, Kate. Valentine's Day is coming up and they need to be dressed appropriately! People drive by the house all the time to look at my display, and they've really come to enjoy seeing how my witches are celebrating each holiday."

I rubbed some of the flimsy lace between my fingers. "Well, if the outfits are any indication, it looks like they're going to need some condoms for this particular celebration."

She pressed her lips together and hummed a little tune to herself like she hadn't heard me. She did that sometimes when she was thinking something she didn't want to say out loud.

Gandalf came running in with his new favorite toy, a bird that chirped. My parents' neighbors' dog, Pocket, was blind and often came over to play with Gandalf. My mom got the toy so Pocket and Gandalf could play together and Pocket could find the toy, too. It was really a cat toy, but Gandalf liked it more than any cat, and even more than Pocket did. I threw the bird and it chirped down the hall as Gandalf ran after it.

I stood and grabbed my purse. "Alright, I'm going home for the night." I leaned in to give her a hug and since her hands were occupied with her sewing, she gave me half a hug back, sequins wrapping around my shoulders. "Thanks for taking care of Gandalf," I said, digging in my bag for my keys, "and have fun with your naughty crafting. No need to tell me if you're really just making something for yourself."

She mumbled something that didn't seem complimentary as I left the room. Gandalf followed me out the door to my Jeep, and I picked up some cheesy breadsticks with extra cheese from Sticks and Pie for dinner on my way home. Gandalf followed me into the house and watched with complete focus as I prepared our food. He gave me the saddest little disappointed eyes when he got regular dog food instead of the cheese he was smelling, so I gave him some shredded cheese from the fridge. I'm a sucker for cute animals. Then we cuddled up on the couch and relaxed.

Chapter Three

I stopped by Beans and Things on my way to work the next morning and ordered a brown butter caramel coffee. It was my new obsession. My drinks were still being paid for by someone, and the Beans and Things staff still wouldn't tell me who. I strongly suspected it was Hawke because while Drake occasionally brought me my favorite chocolate covered espresso beans from Salt Lake City, I didn't think he would pay for the devil's drink on a consistent basis.

Speaking of Drake, I had a bone to pick with him and the Utah State Legislature, which had just started their session and was currently considering a rule that would place even more restrictions on the press. They'd already banned reporters from the Utah State House and Senate floors before the session began, but now they were trying to exclude independent journalists, bloggers, and freelance media from receiving credentials. I called his office.

His assistant answered, "Representative Drake's office, this is Greycie."

"Hi, Greycie. This is Kate Saxee, a constituent calling from

Branson Falls. Can you tell Representative Dylan Drake that I expect him to stand up for independent journalists. That means I don't want him to support the new rule banning independent journalists, and restricting media access in certain areas of the Capitol."

"Sure, I will let him know."

"Thank you, Greycie."

I hung up, feeling like I'd done something good for the day, and would probably have to do the same thing tomorrow as well because I knew Drake would get a list of top concerns at the end of each day and those were the ones he'd focus on.

I walked into the *Tribune* office and unwrapped myself. It had been freezing when I'd left this morning. Even Gandalf had been wearing his coat and boots—which he was still mad at me about.

Spence was already there, relaxing in his office wearing a light blue sweater that perfectly complimented his brown skin tone, and jeans. I stood in the doorway and was hit with a warm breeze that almost made his room balmy.

"You brought in a space heater?"

He glanced up. "Damn straight, I did. I'm from much warmer climes. We don't get stupid weather like this, and I'm not going to just accept it."

I smirked and moved closer to get the benefits of the heat. "It's a bold choice to choose snow as your enemy in northern Utah."

He gestured to the space heater. "I'm winning. Now I just need a heated driveway."

I whistled in a way that sounded like a warning. "They aren't cheap."

"I know. I got a quote." His phone buzzed with a text and he picked it up, a smile lifting his cheeks.

I had a feeling I knew who the text was from. "How was your night out with Xander?" I asked. They'd gone to a concert out of town where it was safer for them to be seen together. Utah wasn't known for tolerance and acceptance—see the Pride flag ban legislation for proof—and that was especially true in a place as religious as Branson Falls. Spence was gay and his relationship with Xander was kind of new, but he seemed happy and I was thrilled for them both. I was also happy because Xander was an excellent cook, and made sure I got salad and vegetables occasionally. It made me sad that they couldn't be open about their relationship in a place like Branson. I hoped that one day, they would be able to. Until then, I would keep advocating for safe spaces and support for their community.

"It was great! The concert was really nice and we tried a new restaurant that Xander suggested. We both loved it."

I couldn't stop my grin. "You're glowing."

Spence blushed. "He makes me happy. What about you? I heard there was a witch situation."

"Not witches. Meditations, sound baths, and crystals." I gave him a quick summary of what had happened, and 111 Healing and Crystals.

When I finished, he blew out a long whistle. "I imagine people around here are going to think a business like that is a problem."

I couldn't disagree with him. "I talked to Clarissa about that. She said they've been in business for three years, but were working out of her basement and expanding through word-of-mouth. We'll have to wait and see how it goes now that they're more public. I'm going out there today to get photos for a feature story."

Spence nodded. "Anything else happen while I was gone?"

"We also had someone want to place an ad and then verbally assault Madison and me when I told her it didn't meet our publishing standards."

I picked up the ad Shasta had left to show him.

He read it and his face tightened. "That definitely doesn't meet standards," he agreed. "I can't believe the things people think are acceptable these days."

"Social media has really affected peoples' communication skills and their ability to be empathetic and kind." I was still holding the ad when the bell on the front door chimed and Annie Sparks came in wearing a huge smile. "Hey, Kate!"

"Hi, Annie!" Annie had become a good friend of mine since I'd moved back to Branson Falls. She was also unoffi-cially my mom's personal EMT every time my mom had a Catasophie: a combination of 'Sophie' and 'Catastrophe' and the word we all used to describe my mom's adventures. It happened more often than I wished it did.

Annie glanced at the ad I'd been holding. Recognition and then horror flashed across her face.

"Do you know her?" I asked.

Annie took the paper that declared the woman in the photo a SL,UT and shook her head, disgusted. "Yeah, Whit-ney's been doing sound baths for me for months. She's one of the nicest people I've ever met, and she's in the middle of a horrible relationship break-up."

I leaned against my desk. "I remembered her name from the photo and put two-and-two together when Clarissa mentioned Whitney at 111 Healing and Crystals last night."

Annie put the paper down on my desk. "Who brought this in?"

"I believe it was Whitney's sister-in-law, Shasta."

Annie blew out a long breath. "Of course it was. Shasta's a vile human. No wonder Whitney left town."

I paused, thinking that explained Shasta's comment about not getting sued because Whitney was gone. It also made me a little worried, and my stomach tightened. "Whitney left Branson?"

Annie nodded, folding her arms and leaning on the front counter. "Whitney's been gone for a week. No one really knows much, or at least they aren't talking if they do know. They're probably trying to respect her privacy considering everything that's happened."

"Why?" I asked. "What happened?"

"Whitney asked for a divorce. Almost everyone in her Mormon Ward sided with her husband, Cory Hatch, and Whitney was called out by Mrs. Olsen during Fast and Testimony Meeting at church."

My jaw dropped. "What?" Testimony meeting was always interesting, but usually consisted of small children going up to the pulpit with a parent who whispered in their ear what to say until they'd done it so many times that they'd memorized the script. It was usually something along the lines of, "I'd like to bear my testimony. I know the church is true. I love my mom and dad, and my family, and Heavenly Father. In the name of Jesus Christ, Amen." Though sometimes it would get entertaining if the kid went rogue and added on something about also loving their favorite toy or spilled a secret about their parents' bathroom habits. And every so often, an adult would also go up to the pulpit and make a scene. It sounded like that's what had happened with Mrs. Olsen.

Annie widened her eyes and gave me a look like she had all the tea. "Hold on, there's a video."

"What?!" I asked again, the shock making my voice louder. Spence even got up from his desk to come and watch.

Annie started thumbing through her downloads folder. "A few people in the Ward saw Mrs. Olsen stomping her way to the pulpit and had the forethought to realize whatever she was about to say might be film worthy. They pulled out their phones while it was happening," Annie said, finding the recording.

Annie scrolled to the right spot and I watched as none other than Mrs. Olsen, the most judgmental old woman on the planet and a thorn in my side since I'd moved back to Branson, stood in front of the pulpit in a brown skirt, white sweater, and bright orange scarf that made her look even more pale, grey, and almost-dead than usual. She had her arms out and was holding the pulpit with both hands like she was the preacher in "Brother Love's Travelling Salvation Show."

Mrs. Olsen looked out at the crowd as if she was ready to wield an angel's flaming sword. "Do you know what it means to get married in the temple? To agree to the vows you make inside that sacred space to your husband, and to the Lord? To tell your husband your new temple name and know that he'll raise you up in the resurrection? It means trust! It means commitment!" She paused for dramatic effect. "For eterni-tyyyy." She dragged the y out for more drama and paused again. "We don't get divorced because we made a promise to each other, to God, and to our eternal families. Anyone who would even consider divorce is bein' influenced by the adversary!"

It seemed like the pulpit shook a little when she referenced Satan. I wouldn't put it past her to rattle the stand. I'd witnessed her almost take a man's head clean off with a gallon of milk a couple of months ago. She might be evil, but she had good aim and a surprising amount of muscle dexterity.

She continued her monologue, "Divorce destroys families and makes it harder for men, and their wives, to achieve the highest levels of exaltation." She was talking about top tier Celestial there. "Women like Whitney Hatch have been tempted by Lucifer himself to even ask for an end to her marriage!" Mrs. Olsen pointed to someone sitting in a pew and the camera panned over the congregation, past Shasta and others, before settling on a woman who looked like the photo Shasta had brought in for her ad: Whitney. Whitney's mouth hung open and her eyes were wide with shock as Mrs. Olsen went on, "I'd admonish her, and anyone else fallin' prey to the wicked ways of the world, to let the Celestial Kingdom be their guide instead of fallin' for the temptations of this life and givin' in to the sin of divorce."

Mrs. Olsen kept her eyes slitted in anger as she stepped away from the pulpit and started to make her way back down the stairs and back to her pew.

Spence whistled and leaned against the wall, shaking his head. "I frequently get reminders about why I'm grateful I was never raised in a religion, and this is one of them."

My jaw had dropped way back at her *eternityyyyy* declaration. "Wow," I said to Annie, my eyes wide. "That's going to take me some time to process. Divorce isn't even technically a sin."

Annie was Mormon, but she frequently dyed her hair blue or pink, was open-minded, and definitely not as devout as most Branson residents. She tilted her head back and forth like she was undecided about divorce being a sin. "I mean, it's not written down as a sin per se, but it's highly discouraged unless there's no other option. We aren't supposed to get divorced because it affects our eternal salvation. Especially for women since we need a husband we've been sealed to in the temple if we want to get to the top tier of the Celestial Kingdom and not just be assigned as some guy's six-hundred-and-thirtieth-wife in the afterlife."

I wrinkled my nose, remembering the teachings from my Sunday School and LDS Seminary classes—doctrine the church now tried to downplay or not even teach because it prevented people from converting. "The polygamy in the afterlife doctrine was one of the things that made me realize the Mormon religion absolutely wasn't for me. That, and how women are treated in general." I'd always felt that polygamy was a convenient excuse for men to sleep with as many women as they wanted for time and all eternity, and women just had to accept it. In fact, it had always felt to me that women were expected to just accept a lot of things.

Annie nodded repeatedly. "I hear you. It feels like women in the church are put on a pedestal and caged at the same time. We're not given authority, and we're not supposed to talk about our Heavenly Mother—the deity we relate to. The church centers everything around family, and constantly stresses the importance of women staying members of the church and their responsibility to keep their families active, yet they also want women to keep quiet while they do it."

I put a finger up like I was making a mark. "That quiet part is another one of the reasons I left."

Annie nodded again and leaned forward, like she'd been needing to talk to someone about this for a long time. "And relationships can be lonely because we're taught that we're supposed to raise the kids and do all the invisible labor of running a family, while our husbands only have to worry about work.

"I know so many women who are unhappy and feel like they aren't in a partnership. People are complicated, with difficult pasts and origin stories that need to be navigated. There's a lot you don't know about a person when you've only been dating a few months before you rush into marriage. When it comes to relationships, we're taught that as long as we get married in the temple and live the gospel, we'll be happy. When a marriage doesn't work out, it kind of feels like we were lied to. I think that's how Whitney felt as well."

I nodded in understanding. "I get it, and have heard similar things from my female LDS friends. I feel bad for them, and for Whitney. Mrs. Olsen had some nerve getting up on that pulpit and criticizing others. Her speech was presumptuous on so many levels. What the hell does Mrs. Olsen know about what was happening in Whitney's personal life, or what prompted her to ask for the divorce?"

Annie rolled her eyes and put her phone back in her bag. "She doesn't, and that's the problem. Perfection is what we're all taught to strive for so that's the mask we all put on. No one ever really knows what's going on behind closed doors except the family that's living it. And men have so much power in the LDS religion and this culture. We're taught to defer to them for everything. I have a really hard time with a lot of church teachings because I think it creates a breeding ground for abuse and the acceptance of it. The church has tried to walk some of those things back, but thanks to the internet and social media, people can now share stories and talk about past teachings that are still influencing people, and it's shedding light on a lot."

I felt the exact same way, especially about the abuse and acceptance. "I completely agree. I think it's scary. People need to feel like they have others to turn to and that they can get support. But instead, they're taught to pretend everything is fine, and only go to church leaders for help. Especially in small towns. That's how people end up hurt, or become the main story in true crime documentaries—which Utah and Mormonism has a lot of."

Annie blew out a long sigh. "I think it's starting to change. I hope so, at least. Women's groups like the one at 111 Healing and Crystals make a difference. I think, and I hope, that if women realize they have support, they won't feel stuck in relationships that are unhealthy, regardless of what members of their Mormon Wards say they should do."

"I hope so, too," I said.

"That's actually kind of why I came in. I heard about the witch accusations from the full moon release and wanted to ask you to come with me to a sound bath at 111 Healing and Crystals. I've been going for months and find them really relaxing. I think you would, too. And I think you'd get along well with a lot of the women there."

I hadn't developed many friendships since I'd moved back to Branson, and thought it would be nice to meet some other women. "I'd really like that. Just text me and let me know when," I said, and I meant it. "I'm actually headed out there today, so I'll ask Clarissa about Whitney and her husband, Cory."

Annie pulled her lips back like she was trying to hold in the words she wanted to say, then settled on, "I'm sure Clarissa will have some thoughts." She gave one last glance at the rejected ad of Whitney and shook her head again before she turned to leave.

"Hey, can you send me that video of Mrs. Olsen?" I asked.

"Sure," she said, as she got to the door. "I'll text you."

My reporter senses had been prickling ever since Annie started the video. Between the ad from Whitney's sister-in-law, the divorce scandal, and now hearing that Whitney had left town, I wanted more information. And I wanted to know if Whitney was okay.

Chapter Four

I walked into 111 Healing and Crystals and a feeling of peacefulness immediately washed over me. I wasn't sure what I believed in, but I did believe in energy and that places, and people, could carry it and even influence how others felt.

Shelves of crystals in different colors sparkled in the sunlight. Candles, incense, chakra diagrams, and Celtic emblem stickers were scattered around the store, and there was an entire wall of tarot cards, and books related to tarot. Growing up, I was taught that tarot cards were basically the Devil in paper form. The tarot cards alone would make a lot of Mormons turn around and walk right out of the store. Mormons weren't supposed to take counsel from anyone but LDS church leadership.

Clarissa was at the front with a customer. She saw me, waved, and held up a finger indicating one minute. I waved back and walked around the store, snapping some photos and jotting down notes. I was reading the back of a book about connecting with your spirit guide when Clarissa found me.

"Hi," she said with a bright smile. She was wearing a

lavender sweater, grey leggings, and boots. "Thanks for coming in."

"No problem." I put the book back on the shelf. "I've already gotten some photos, but is there anything particular you'd like me to highlight?"

Her face brightened. "The salt cave is a favorite of mine."

I followed her to the back of the building. A door opened into a large room made completely of Himalayan salt. The walls were stacked with salt bricks, and an image of a lotus flower had been carved into the wall. Soft light glowed through the salt on the walls, illuminating the design. The ground was also salt that had been ground up to the consistency of sand on a beach.

"We have sound baths and mediations in here, but people can also book a session to just come in, sit, and meditate on their own. We use Halotherapy for this room."

"What's that?" I asked.

"A halogenerator grinds up pharmaceutical-grade salt into particles small enough to disperse into the room. You breathe in the salt. It's really helpful for a lot of health conditions, including respiratory issues."

"That's probably great at this time of year," I said, getting some photos.

She nodded. "We also have a yoga studio." She showed me a large room with light wood floors and mirrors, almost like a dance space. "And a crystal cave that I love sitting in."

She took me to a room where the walls were made of all white quartz crystals. Pillows lined the floor, and blankets were stacked on a shelf in the corner with headphones. "We do guided meditations in this space with a live practitioner a couple of times a week, but we also have recorded playlists for people who want to come in any time to relax and breathe."

This room felt different as well, but every space I'd been in so far exuded comfort and peace. I closed my eyes and took a deep breath before taking more photos.

"Do you want to sit for a minute?" Clarissa asked, gesturing to the floor. "I can answer any questions you might have."

"Sure," I grabbed a large, round, fluffy pillow and Clarissa did the same.

"How did you and Whitney decide to move from your basement to a space like this?" I asked.

She crossed her legs on the pillow and sat with a straight back. I tried to do the same and quickly realized my balance needed work.

"We had more and more clients coming to my house, and not enough time to help all of them. I also wanted a separation of home and work."

"That's understandable."

"Whitney worked out of her house at first, but didn't feel comfortable continuing to do that so she started working out of my basement too. Our clients kept increasing and we needed more space, so this was the perfect solution."

That caught my attention. "Why didn't she feel comfortable working in her house?"

Clarissa pulled her lips back like she was trying to decide what to say. "Her husband wasn't the most supportive."

I inclined my head. "I heard about Whitney's divorce."

Clarissa crossed her hands over one another in her lap, thinking. "Whitney didn't want her relationship to end. She believed what she'd been taught in church: that she just had to get married, live the gospel, and her relationship would be perfect. But it wasn't."

"Did she confide in you about what was going on with her husband, Cory?"

Clarissa's lips formed a soft smile that felt like it had a hidden meaning behind it. "We talked about a lot, and were there for each other through it all. Cory wasn't worthy of someone like Whitney."

My ears perked up. "Why not?"

"A lot of reasons. He definitely didn't support her, or her work helping people through our business here at 111."

I wondered if he didn't support her work, or if he didn't support this *kind* of work. "You said you'd both been offering healing services for a while before you opened this space. How long?"

"About three years."

"Was Cory Hatch always unsupportive?"

She took a deep breath and her eyes fell to the floor. "He didn't like anything that he couldn't control."

Ah, like a lot of men in general, but especially the religious men I had encountered in my life.

"He also didn't like that she was working outside the home. He believed in the counsel of church leaders, and that she was supposed to be concentrating on getting pregnant and starting a family."

"I didn't realize they don't have kids. How long have they been married?"

"Five years. Whitney is twenty-five and Cory is twenty-seven."

So, he'd gone on a mission and come home, then married her right after he returned. A two-year, or more, age gap between Mormon men and women wasn't uncommon. Men used to leave at nineteen, but now they left at eighteen—a recent change that many speculated was because it meant more of them were leaving for their missions straight from home and high school instead of getting the chance to go out into the world, start college, and live life—all things that were a threat to whether or not they decided to go on a mission at all. If they served a mission, they were more likely to remain a member of the church because they were more invested. High demand religions were high demand because that kept people engaged. When missionaries returned from the field, they'd start dating and the women they dated were often younger than they were. "Five years is a long time for them to be married and not have kids as members of the church," I said. "I bet they're asked about it constantly."

Clarissa closed her eyes and nodded slightly. "They are, and it drives Whitney crazy. Church members and leaders constantly tell her she should be having kids like she'd been commanded. It drives me nuts because it's no one's business. What about people having fertility issues? Imagine how awful they must feel when church members constantly ask when they're going to start their family—like they aren't enough of a family as a couple."

That frustrated me as well. "That's difficult."

Clarissa brushed some lint off the pillow she was sitting on. "Whitney isn't shy about speaking up about it, though. She tells people she's only twenty-five and has plenty of time to have kids. She wants to build her business first. She thinks it's fine if some women don't want a job outside the home, and want their sole focus to be motherhood. And it should also be fine that she does want a job."

"That's admirable of her, but I bet she gets a lot of push-back for that." It was one thing to not have kids because you couldn't; it was another thing entirely to deliberately choose education and career over getting pregnant.

Clarissa's jaw visibly tightened. "She did, and Cory has been the loudest."

"Is that why Whitney asked for the divorce?"

Anger flashed over Clarissa's face and her shoulders tensed. "One of many reasons. I'm glad she's getting away from that toxic situation."

That gave me an opening to ask about where she might be. "I heard she left town. How are you handling things here without her?"

"We have other practitioners as well, so we've been able to manage."

"How long has she been gone?"

"About a week. She needed to get away and had planned to take a trip somewhere at some point, but the testimony meeting situation was the last straw and sped up her plans."

"You're still in contact with her then?" I wanted to know that someone knew where she was and had spoken with her.

Clarissa gave a slight shrug. "I know she made it to where she was going, and she'll get in contact with me when she can."

That wasn't as reassuring as Clarissa probably meant it to be. "Does anyone know where she is?"

Clarissa looked confused. "Of course. She told me and her parents where she was going."

I pressed, "But you haven't heard from her?" Just because Whitney had said she was going somewhere didn't mean she'd actually made it there.

"No, but there's a reason for that. She didn't want to be found."

Interesting. Didn't want to be found by whom?

"You're not worried about Whitney at all then?"

Clarissa scoffed. "I would be if I thought she was in danger. I'm far more worried about her divorce, the fallout from that, and all of the people supporting Cory instead of Whit."

Clarissa's phone started to vibrate, and she looked at the caller. "I need to take this. I'll be right back."

I nodded, and stood up to follow her out of the crystal room and get a few more photos. My stomach felt heavy and I couldn't shake the feeling that this story was bigger than just a woman asking for a divorce and leaving town on a trip to get away from the rumors. What had happened for her to go to the extreme lengths of leaving her business and only telling one friend and her parents where she was?

Clarissa came back, holding her phone, her face pulled tight. "I have to go. Cory Hatch, Whitney's husband, just reported her missing."

I pulled into Cory and Whitney Hatch's neighborhood, a newer subdivision on small lots with cookie cutter houses. I parked on the street behind a police car. Clarissa parked in Cory's driveway, and was already on her way into Cory's house before I even closed my car door.

I followed her and she opened the front door to Cory's house for me as I approached. A tall man with short brown hair, bushy eyebrows, and a sharply angled nose, wearing jeans and yellow t-shirt was talking to Officer Bob. "I don't understand why you can't locate her. I haven't heard from her for a week and she turned all her tracking off on her phone so I can't find her. She's a missing person. You have the technology, so help me figure out where she is."

I grimaced. If he'd been tracking her like that on a daily basis, it was no wonder she'd turned all of her location services off. It was also probably one of the many reasons Clarissa had cited for Whitney wanting a divorce.

Bobby gave Cory an exasperated look that told me he'd already explained this. Repeatedly. "She's an adult, Cory. And you've got no proof she's in any sorta danger. We can't locate her without cause. And if her phone's been turned off, we can't track anythin'."

Cory ran a frustrated hand through his hair. "She could be in danger, but we'll never know because no one is looking for her."

"No one needs to," Clarissa said, injecting herself into the conversation. "She's fine."

Bobby turned to her, recognition flashing over his face. "And how do you know that, Ms. Hope?"

"Because she's my business partner and I've been in contact with her." Clarissa showed Bobby her phone with text messages Whitney had sent Clarissa once Whitney arrived at her intended destination. That seemed to be enough for Bobby, but I wasn't convinced and was on Cory's side for this discussion.

Bobby hooked his thumbs through his belt loops and turned back to Cory. "Based on the text messages, I'd say your wife is fine and just doesn't want to talk to you, Cory. If I were you, I'd leave it alone 'til you're both ready to have a conversation."

Cory's shoulders tightened like he was warming up for a fight. "You're the reason she's doing this," Cory accused, pointing at Clarissa. "You're a bad influence and always have been!"

Clarissa walked up to him, swagger in her step, and flashed a mocking smile. "If helping your wife get out of a horrible situation makes me the bad guy, so be it."

Cory's jaw tightened and he pointed at the door as he ground out, "Get out of my house."

Clarissa walked out, and Bobby followed her.

"Thank you for all of your help, Officer Burns. I appreciate it," Clarissa said.

Bobby sliced his head down once. "Let me know if you speak with Whitney and she does need help. Domestic situations are always complicated."

"They are," she agreed. "I'll keep you posted."

Bobby looked at me. "Nice to run into ya, Kate. Always a surprise to see when and where you'll show up."

"I'm kind of like a ghost that way," I said with a wink.

Bobby left and I turned to Clarissa. "Are you okay?"

"I'm fine," she said, shaking her hands and arms like she was trying to get the whole interaction to fall off of her. "Cory is infuriating and I'm glad the officer told him he wouldn't help Cory find Whit. She left to get away from all of this stress."

"Who called to tell you Cory was reporting her missing?" I asked as Clarissa started to walk away.

Clarissa gave a sly smile. "One of The Ladies is his

neighbor and posted about it on her socials. Every so often, their nosiness is good for something."

I hadn't had any experience with the good part, but would take Clarissa's word for it. She waved as she got in her car and I waved back.

Clearly there was no love lost between Clarissa and Cory. I wanted to talk to Cory and get his perspective, but he was pretty distraught right now. I did want to call Whitney myself, though, just to check on her and see if she picked up. I'd asked Clarissa for her number and she'd texted me back with Whitney's contact card.

I called and it went straight to voicemail. I left a message explaining who I was, then followed it with the same information via text, just in case she could get text messages but not calls wherever she was.

I got in my Jeep and breathed out a sigh. It had been a long day already and my stomach rumbled. I was about to pull away to find something for lunch when my phone buzzed with a text. I grabbed it, hoping Whitney had texted back. It wasn't Whitney, but it was someone else I'd been hoping to hear from.

Want to get lunch? I'm at your house.

That was perfect timing. I pointed my Jeep toward home.

I pulled up to my house with cream colored siding and royal blue trim. The boxwoods that were normally visible in my front yard were covered with a thick layer of snow. I missed my grass, shrubs, and petunias. A giant, black, F-450 truck that felt like it was almost as big as his bright yellow Hummer and lacking just as much covertness, was waiting on the street in front of my house. I gauged the height of the truck compared to the ground and wondered if he needed rock climbing equipment to get in and out.

Given what had happened with Hawke a couple of months ago on a gorgeous sun-kissed beach far away from Branson Falls, any interaction with Drake made me feel slightly guilty. I had to remind myself constantly that none of us were in a relationship, and I owed nothing to either one of them—and they owed me nothing in return as well. I wondered how long we would all feel that way. Because if I saw either one of them with another woman—which was a real possibility because none of us had agreed to be exclusive with each other yet—I knew I'd probably want to commit a crime.

"How long have you been waiting for me?" I asked as Drake shut the door to his truck and walked over to me.

"Since high school," he answered.

I blushed and rolled my eyes. "Really though. How long? Because I'm hardly ever home during the day."

He looked at the sky like he was trying to tell time by the position of the sun. "I'm not sure. I've just been working on my phone while I waited."

I scanned the street, neighborhood, and sky for spies and drones. "You know every single Lady in the vicinity has already posted about you sitting in front of my house—for the goddesses know how long—in their social media groups, and they've probably notified the podcasts as well. Let's go inside before they get even more information."

"Going inside is probably worse because then they can't

see us and it's left to their imaginations," Drake said. But he followed me in anyway.

A recent story about some bodies found on land being developed had put Branson Falls, and my love life, on the radar of some popular podcasts. There were bets about who I'd end up with and for a while right after I broke the story, the conversations around it had been nonstop and I felt like I was being stalked. My vacation with Hawke had been a nice way to get away from it all, so I totally understood why Whitney Hatch had left.

I'd thought The Ladies were bad, but it was nothing compared to podcast fanbases. The fervor had died down a bit, but still felt overwhelming at times. The fact was that even *I* didn't know who I'd end up with because I was still trying to get to know Drake and Hawke, and figure out what I wanted. Though, Hawke had made multiple compelling arguments on our trip—and those arguments had not come with clothes.

We took off our coats and hung them by the back door, then Drake followed me into my kitchen with white tile counters and lemon-yellow paint.

Drake was still grinning at my Lady and podcast comment. "Did you see the video someone made of us married and coming out of the temple?"

My blood pressure started to rise at the reminder. "Oh, I saw it. And made sure to leave a comment that the video was clearly A.I. because that will *never* happen."

Drake put a hand to his chest like he was wounded. "The wedding?"

"The temple. I've seen the hidden camera footage of what goes on there, and I seethed for days. In fact, I'm still not over it. I will never be part of the Mormon religion again and you know it, so if that's what you're longing for, let's make this easier on all of us and end whatever this exploration is between us now."

He didn't seem at all affected by what I thought was my short, but very powerful, monologue. "So, what you're saying is that a wedding is *still* a possibility?"

I gave a long-suffering sigh as I got some mugs out of the cabinet and started the coffee maker for me and made Drake some hot chocolate. "I saw a video of Mrs. Olsen preaching about weddings and divorces during her Ward's Testimony Meeting, so I don't think that's a good idea for us to consider either. According to her, I'd be taking you away from your entitled birthright as a Mormon man of eternal marriage, a harem of wives, and your own world to lord over."

He grinned and licked his lips. "I'll have to talk to Mrs. Olsen about ruining my chances," Drake said.

I crossed my arms over my chest. "You know, that kind of stuff is one of the many reasons people think Mormons are weird. And one of the reasons the church keeps trying to downplay it and a lot of new and younger members of the church aren't even taught it, or believe it's not real."

He inclined his head in concession. "I agree. It is weird. And the LDS church is trying to assimilate more with mainstream Christian culture, which means they're trying to fit in and make the teachings that seem strange, less prominent."

"It's lying."

"I mean..."

"By omission. You're a lawyer, Drake. You know this."

He tilted his head from side-to-side. "I could argue my way around it."

I knew he could, and it was another reason Drake as a boyfriend was a bit of a yellow flag.

I poured creamer and milk in my coffee, and handed Drake his hot chocolate. He sat at the table and leaned his back against the chair. "Mrs. Olsen shouldn't have used church doctrine to castigate Whitney and her decision to ask for a divorce. On the other hand, it's a tough situation."

I gaped at him. "You've got to be kidding me. How is it tough?"

"Relationships are difficult and each person has their own nuanced perspective."

I blinked as I tried to figure out how to respond. "I haven't had the chance to talk to Cory yet, but from the people I have talked to, Whitney wasn't happy and Cory was an ass. If the ad Whitney's sister-in-law brought into the *Tribune* and wanted to run about her is any indication, its clear Cory's family didn't like her. You don't know what was really going on between them behind closed doors."

Drake slanted his head to the side as he considered my thoughts. "That's true, but I know her husband, Cory. She left without any warning and he's been a worried mess since. He loves her."

I crossed my arms over my chest, studying him. "Again, you don't know what goes on behind closed doors. And it seems like Whitney gave plenty of warning if Mrs. Olsen had the time to call her out in front of three hundred people while they were all at church."

"Cory knew she'd asked for a divorce, but he didn't think she'd really go through with it, let alone up and leave. He thought they could work things out and had suggested marriage counseling. Then one day, she was just gone."

My reporter senses started tingling again. "What do you mean? She didn't leave a note? Divorce papers? Nothing?"

Drake shook his head. "No. She'd told Cory she wanted a divorce, and she'd told some friends around town so that's how people knew about it. They were staying in separate bedrooms, but still living in the same house, and he was asking her to work through it with him. Then one day a little over a week ago, she was just gone. She took some clothes and a few of her things, but left everything else. It's a strange situation, and I think Cory has the right to be worried."

I picked my coffee up and took a sip as I thought about it. Clarissa told me Whitney had been planning to leave on a trip and the divorce rumors propelled those plans forward, but I didn't realize that from Cory's perspective, she'd actually disappeared. That made Cory's reaction and reporting her as missing make more sense. It also explained why a lot of people in town were on Cory's side because it looked like he had been the one wronged. Knowing Clarissa's perspective as well, I wasn't sure I believed that, but could see how others might.

I could also see Cory's point to Officer Bob, that Whitney might be in danger but no one would know. The only person who seemed to be in contact with her was Clarissa, and even Clarissa hadn't talked to Whitney since she'd arrived at her destination—wherever that was. "No one thought to ask where she went?"

"She turned her phone's tracking app off so he couldn't see her location. She had a separate bank account that Cory didn't have access to, so there wasn't a way for him to follow her via credit or debit card, or find out where she'd gone."

That seemed unlikely in a day and age where everything

was tracked via GPS and even the apps on your phone monitored how you interacted with them. But if Cory didn't have access to her accounts and she'd turned off GPS tracking and the apps on her phone, I guess that would make it hard for him to find her. "Did he try calling her? Texting?"

"Yeah, but nothing went through. Cory thinks she blocked him."

I pushed my brows together. "There has to be more to the story. Do you know why she asked for the divorce?" I'd gotten Clarissa's opinion, but wanted to hear what others were saying.

"Cory said she told him she wasn't happy and he couldn't make her happy. He suspected she was cheating."

That was new information, and also explained Shasta's ad. "Did he have a reason to think that?"

Drake bit at his bottom lip. "I didn't ask for details."

The wheels were spinning in my head. "If they were active Mormons, cheating also seems unlikely."

Drake took a drink of his hot chocolate and closed his eyes to savor it for a minute. It was from a famous chocolate shop in Paris, so I couldn't blame him. "It happens. People become unhappy and think they can find something better with someone else."

"They also rarely get the chance to be with anyone else because they're encouraged to marry so young and they're not supposed to have sex until they're married, so it's not a surprise that a lot of marriages end up unhappy."

The corners of Drake's lips slid up. "You have strong opinions."

No shit. "You haven't heard anything yet," I warned and he grinned.

Something about it still felt off and I decided I'd look into it more. I wanted to talk to Cory, and some of Whitney's family members. Maybe Whitney had family who were also in contact with her, not just Clarissa, and maybe they'd heard from her more recently.

"The legislative session started. I got your message by the way."

I gave him a sweet smile. "Good. Don't disappoint me."

He gave me a look. "You know it's not that easy, Katie."

I gave him a look back as I held my coffee cup with both hands to warm up. "I also know you're not an asshole and I thought you supported a free press and lawmaker accountability."

"I do, but again. Nuance."

I stared at him and ran a tongue over my front teeth. "Are you trying to tell me that you'd sell out the media and the public's right to know for your political career?"

He rubbed a hand over the back of his neck. "I'm telling you that I'm going to fight back as much as I can."

I pressed my lips together, unsure how I felt about that, and the fact that we seemed to be on different pages about things that were important to me. I knew this wasn't the only issue, and wouldn't be the last.

He moved right past my questions and concerns. "With the legislature in session, I won't get to see you as much."

I decided to let the independent media rule go for now and see how Drake handled it. "You mean you won't have time to sit in front of my house?"

"Not for the rest of the month."

"Good to know you'll be back in March." I always wondered what idiot came up with the idea to make the session in February. It's a short month, and it's Valentine's Day. "Is there something else you needed?" Other than getting lunch, I wasn't sure why he'd stopped by.

"I haven't seen you much lately. Can I take you to dinner in a few days? It might be the only night I get off this month."

"Let me text my mom and see if Gandalf can stay with her, and I'll let you know."

"I'll be waiting on pins and needles."

His phone buzzed and as he looked at it, I could see his jaw clench. "Shoot. I have to go. I'll have to take a rain check on lunch, but text me about dinner as soon as you know."

"I will." I followed him out and watched him rock climb back up into his truck, then went back inside to make myself a grilled cheese.

Chapter Five

I was finishing my sandwich when I looked out the window and saw Phyllis, my neighbor and reality TV watching cohort, standing on her porch as a man with light brown hair, a set of broad shoulders that tapered down to a back made of muscle and an ass I was intimately acquainted with, cleared snow from her steps and walkway.

Hawke.

My mind immediately flashed back to our trip together.

We were in a beautiful white villa, nestled in a private cove on a white sand beach. The master suite had a king size bed, a chaise lounge, and was decorated in calming blues, greys, and whites. The room faced the beach and had glass folding doors that we'd kept open all night; the balmy breeze and relaxing ocean waves a reminder of the paradise we were in. A huge bathtub sat outside the room on the deck, and the ocean was only steps away.

I turned over in bed and Hawke had one arm behind his head, looking at the beach. He glanced at me and smiled as he stretched, the sheet covering him slipping dangerously low on his hips. Hawke followed the dip of my gaze and I dragged my attention back up to his face.

His green eyes darkened like they were heated from within. "This is a private beach, you know?"

I arched a brow. "Is it?"

He sliced his head down once, his tongue caressing his top lip. "You don't have to worry about anyone else if you want to take a bath outside, or swim naked."

I moved and slid out of the bed, my short, black lace robe hitting the backs of my thighs as I walked to the folding glass doors. I untied the belt holding the two sides of my robe together, and looked back over my shoulder at him. "What if I want to swim naked with you?" I dropped my robe and heard Hawke groan.

Fifteen seconds later, he had me in his arms and he was kissing me on sand.

I sighed, coming out of the memory.

After our secret vacation together, where I got all the answers I needed about whether we were sexually compatible, Hawke had helped me with a miracle investigation around Christmas time, and I was pretty sure he'd gifted me a coffee machine worth more than my car that he refused to admit to. I hadn't seen him for almost a month because he was away on some super classified work contract. I couldn't stop staring as he threw piles of snow off of Phyllis' path like they were puffs of cotton candy. Phyllis couldn't stop watching either.

People liked to think of Drake as the Boy Scout, but Hawke was just as much of one. He did it out of the goodness of his heart, not because it was simply what was expected of the men in town.

I grabbed my coat, scarf, and gloves, and went outside to better ogle him.

"Hey," I said, walking up to them both. Phyllis tore her eyes away from Hawke, but it was an effort. I related. As I glanced at some of the other houses in my neighborhood, I saw a few women standing by their windows. When Gretchen across the street saw me looking at her, she grabbed a blanket off a chair and pretended to be dusting her window with it. I couldn't blame her; Hawke was a sight to see.

"Hiya, Kate!" Phyllis gave me a smile. "Hawke got here and saw me tryin' to move all this snow and came right over."

"Of course he did," I said, with a grin. "He's kind of a superhero."

"Sure is," she agreed.

Hawke stopped working and looked straight at me. "Don't worry, I'm coming to take care of you next." He punctuated the sentence with a wink. He'd taken care of me before, multiple times in positions I didn't even know existed until that trip, and he wanted to give me the reminder—a reminder I didn't need because I thought of it often.

"Is that a promise?" I asked.

His lips spread wide and he licked them slowly. Another reminder as well. "Always, Kitty Kate." He lifted the shovel to keep clearing the sidewalk and I got distracted wondering what workouts formed an ass like his.

"Sheesh," Phyllis said, fanning herself. "It's a good thing it's so cold out or you two would start a fire!"

She had no idea.

I tore my gaze away from Hawke's...everything. "Are we watching the #HOTBS Reunion this week?" I asked her. #HOTBS stood for Homemakers of the Beehive State, the insanely popular Utah-based reality show that followed a handful of Utah women. Everyone had been talking about it for the past few months and it had already been renewed. I'd been invested, and Phyllis was just as intrigued. Annie usually came over to watch it with us as well.

"It's been on my calendar for weeks!"

"Good! I can't wait to drink some of your hot chocolate while they spill all the tea."

Phyllis slapped her hand on her leg. "Speakin' of that, I have some hot chocolate for Hawke and I bet it's ready now. Let me go grab it!"

She went in the house. Hawke stopped shoveling and turned to look at me. His gaze slowly trailed from my winter hat with a poof on it, to my scarf, double insulated winter coat, and down my jeans-covered legs to my boots. Somehow, he still managed to be turned on by all of that fabric because his eyes sparked.

"Winter clothes are the worst," I said, suddenly feeling too warm. "Let's go back to the beach."

"We weren't really wearing clothes there," he pointed out.

"Exactly."

"Phyllis came outside as Hawke was finishing the driveway, and handed us both hot chocolate cups with lids. "This should warm you up," she said.

Hawke took a sip and closed his eyes. "This is delicious. Thank you."

"Thank *you* for shovelin' for an old lady!"

Hawke shook his head like it wasn't a big deal. "You'd already done most of it when I got here. I just finished it off."

She laughed and laughed, slapping her hand on her thigh. "Everyone knows that ain't true, but you're a sweetheart. Take those cups over to Kate's with you and warm up!" She turned to me. "I'll see you for the #HOTBS reunion soon, Kate!"

"It's a deal," I said, taking my cup and walking across the lawn to my driveway, where Hawke's gigantic dark grey matte GMC Sierra 3500 truck sat. The truck brand was emblazoned across the front in bold letters, and framed by a black deer catcher that was so big it could have been used to catch bison...or Bigfoot. The rims of the truck were black, with grey lug nuts holding the tires in place. It looked edgy and kind of sexy—something I never thought I'd say about a truck. I knew it had already been photographed at my house. "If this thing is fitted with some secret government technology and can become invisible, that would really help our gossip and podcast situation."

One corner of Hawke's lips kicked up. "It can't become invisible, but it's great in the snow."

I scanned it from back to front. "What's with dudes and giant trucks? Did you have this monstrosity specially built?"

"All my vehicles are custom in one way or another, Kitty Kate."

Of course they were.

I glanced around and saw plenty of neighbors still standing at their windows, watching even closer than they had been before. "Want to come inside?"

His gaze heated. "Without question."

My heart started beating faster. I was certain this interaction was already on The Ladies social media, but as Hawke put his hand on my lower back and we moved toward my house, I couldn't bring myself to care.

I opened the back door and before I had the chance to start taking my hat, coat, and scarf off, Hawke had me pinned against the wall, his breath hot on my neck as he trailed kisses up to my jawline.

"I missed you," I said.

"Not as much as I missed you." He pulled my scarf off and unzipped my coat while continuing to kiss my neck.

"I'm really trying to be mad that you've been gone for a month." I said, barely registering my coat on the floor.

He moved his hands over my hips, and slid them under my shirt, his fingers warmed from the hot chocolate and sizzling against my skin as he said, "I checked in."

I leaned my head back against the wall as his fingers traced over the top of the lace of my bra, and then to the back where he unlatched it with one hand. "Sometimes," I breathed in response.

"I'm trying to do better with that." His other hand went down to my jeans and popped the button, then slowly slid the zipper down. "But trust me, there was never a time when I wasn't thinking about you, that beach, the waves crashing around us, and you naked and on top of me on the sand."

He pressed his lips against mine, and I melted into the kiss, opening my mouth and taking him in. His scent, his taste. Holy hell, I'd missed this, and him, and didn't even realize how much.

"I should probably get back to work," I said distantly.

"Give me five minutes first. I need to show you how much I missed you."

He took my hand and pulled me back to my bedroom.

It took thirty minutes because Hawke is a thorough kind of guy even when it comes to quickies.

"You know we're going to have to have a real conversation

about things at some point. Not just sex," I said, pulling my pants back on.

Hawke was laying across my bed, his abs a much better advertisement than the ones on the billboard and even more distracting. The sex was fantastic, but even on our trip, that's really all it had been. We'd both needed the outlet and had used the trip accordingly. It was bliss. It was also a fantasy because that wasn't real life. Sex was important, but it wasn't everything. I needed to know if we had a connection beyond that. Shared hopes and dreams. And someone who wasn't always flying off to somewhere secret for work where he often couldn't even call me, let alone tell me what he was up to. I needed to see him more than every month or two, and I needed to know if our definitions of a relationship were compatible.

"Maybe we should have the conversation while having sex," he suggested.

I angled my head in a knowing expression. "Then neither one of us would be having a productive conversation."

He grinned and licked his lips, lips that had just been *all* over my skin. "True. We should save the sex for dessert after the DTR."

I blinked. "I didn't realize you knew what DTR meant. I thought Define the Relationship was a Mormon thing." And it was usually done between one and three weeks of dating so you didn't waste time on the wrong person.

"I've lived in Utah for a while."

I stopped pulling my sweater on and stared at him. "How many people have you had to DTR with?"

He raised a brow. "How many are you currently having to DTR with?"

I winced. "Point taken."

He got up and started getting dressed as well. I leaned against my dresser to watch and it was an incredible show. "I actually came to ask you to go to dinner with me."

I'd just said yes to dinner with another potential DTR recipient. Guilt welled in my chest. "Sure. When?"

"Valentine's Day."

My eyes widened. It was still almost two weeks away and I'd been dreading trying to juggle both Hawke and Drake for a holiday that was all about love. "That's a big day."

He sliced his head down as he pulled his long-sleeved white shirt over his rock-hard stomach. "Yep. Will you go with me?"

I mean, he'd asked, and no one else had…yet. But I wasn't looking forward to having to explain that to Drake. Then again, it sounded like Drake wouldn't be getting Valentine's Day off anyway. "Okay," I answered slowly.

He laughed. "That was hesitant, but I'll take it."

We grabbed our coats and went out the door. He waited while I locked up and as I started to walk away, he pulled me back and pressed his chest into mine for one last kiss. "Just so you don't forget about me."

I smiled as we broke away from each other. "That would be impossible." He held my hand as he walked me to my Jeep. I paused before getting in because something Bobby had said made me curious. "If someone turns their phone off, are there still ways for the police to track them?"

"Officially, or unofficially?" Hawke asked.

I blinked. "Officially, like what the police have access to. But I'd like to hear the unofficial as well."

"Officially, police could still track them using old fashioned investigation techniques and police work—a lot like what you have access to. Unofficially," he leaned in to me, his tongue going over his lips in a way that made me want to drag him right back into my house, "governments have all kinds of tech most people know nothing of, but learning about that will cost you."

I bit the corner of my bottom lip. "I'll start saving up."

He grinned, grabbing his tongue between his teeth. "There are special deals for hot girlfriends."

I stared after him, unsure if the girlfriend part was a statement, question, or invitation. He didn't clarify. I watched as he got in his giant truck, which was more of a turn on than it should have been, and backed out of my driveway.

I had just put my Jeep in reverse as 'Forever in Blue Jeans' started playing on my phone. "You need to get to the grocery store," Spence said when I answered. "There's some sort of fight going on."

The last time there had been a fight at the grocery store, everyone had ended up covered in flour, and Mrs. Olsen had almost killed someone with her groceries. I hoped this would be just as intriguing. "I'm on my way."

The grocery stores in Branson Falls have community bulletin boards where people in town put up business cards, advertisements, and signs about local events. When I arrived, there was a crowd gathered around the board. As I got closer, I could see why. The board had been wallpapered over with familiar signs. Whitney Hatch's photo was enlarged on the front, with the word LIAR above her photo in caps, and her name below the photo with the words SL,UT Cheater.

People were pointing at the photos, murmuring gossip about Whitney.

"I knew she was cheatin' on Cory. Poor guy."

"I heard she's pregnant with someone else's baby!" That was a new one, especially since Clarissa said Whitney didn't want kids yet.

Teri Jones, a local craft store owner, came up to me. "The photos were put up an hour ago."

I nodded a hello and asked, "Do you know who did it?"

"Shasta Hatch"

I scanned row after row of the signs. "I had a suspicion. She tried to get us to run this as an ad in the *Tribune*."

Teri's eyes widened. "I heard they're all over town. Anywhere with a bulletin board, and they've even been taped to some light posts."

I rolled my eyes. "Shasta is persistent." And mean AF, I added in my head.

"She had help. Her friend was puttin' some up, too," Teri offered. "It's too bad they couldn't work things out," Teri lamented. "I feel so bad for Cory. Whitney wasn't very loyal to him."

"Do you know someone she was cheating on him with?" All I'd heard so far were accusations and slander. I wished she was here to defend herself.

"Not exactly, but I heard she was entertainin' a lot of men."

I pushed my brows together. "What does that mean?"

She leaned in like she was trying to whisper, but she neglected to lower her voice. "I'm not one for gossip," she said while gossiping, "but ask around, you'll find out more."

A voice broke through the noise of the crowd. "Break it up, break it up!" Rick Groot, manager of the store, came through with a ladder pushing bystanders out of the way. "We don't tolerate this kind of nonsense about members of our community. None of you better get any ideas about puttin' somethin' like this up again!" He started pulling the papers down, and putting them directly in a trash bag where they belonged.

I got back to the office and edited the Billboard Brawl article Spence had given me notes on. When that was done, I used my background check info to look up Whitney's family members. Her parents lived in a neighboring town, and she had one brother who lived out of state.

I dialed her parents. "Hi, this is Kate Saxee, editor of *The Branson Tribune* newspaper in Branson Falls. I know your daughter, Whitney, and was wondering if you've heard from her lately?"

The female voice on the other end sounded frustrated. "Not since she was humiliated at church. She left town to get away from everyone, and I don't blame her."

At least her mom was on her side. "Do you know where she went?"

"She didn't want anyone to know."

"Does your husband know where she is?"

She snorted. "I know more than he does."

"And you're certain she's safe?"

There was a pause. "Last I heard. Should I be concerned?"

"Her husband reported her missing, so I'm just doing some checking."

Her mom scoffed. "Cory is an idiot and will do anything to get attention and sympathy. Look at the way the whole town has rallied around him. He's just playing a part so he can keep playing victim."

"Thanks for your time and thoughts," I said before hanging up.

I called Whitney's brother next, but he hadn't heard from her. He lived out of state and they didn't have a close relationship.

I grabbed a pen on my desk and threaded it through my fingers as I thought about the calls and what I knew so far. I'd heard something similar about Cory playing a part from Clarissa. And I'd heard the exact opposite from people who knew Cory and felt that he really was the victim and Whitney was the villainess. Everyone had their own experiences and opinions about a person so it was hard to know who to believe, but it seemed the lines were pretty clearly drawn. People who were friends with Cory and in their Mormon Ward were on Cory's side, and people who were friends with Whitney all had the same bad opinions about Cory and were on Whitney's side.

"Heard you were busy this afternoon," Ella said, coming into the room and looking over the offerings on the treat table.

I leaned forward, putting my elbows on my desk. "What do you mean?"

She raised her brows. "What do you think I mean? A little afternoon delight with both your boyfriends."

I closed my eyes and tried not to scream. I knew someone had gotten photos. There were far too many witnesses.

She picked up a cookie from a local cookie shop. "No

one had a good viewpoint of your backyard so anythin' could've happened back there. The Ladies are tryin' to figure out if you even went in the house, or decided to do it in the snow."

"Excellent to know. I'll make sure to do all my crime in the backyard from now on. And plant some more trees to prevent nosy Ladies."

Ella put her hands on her hips in frustration. "That's not fair."

"It certainly is. It's my private property and The Ladies are peeping Toms!"

She latched onto that. "So, there *was* something to peep at!"

"No!"

She eyed me, trying to decide if I was lying, then continued before coming to a conclusion, "Drake was there first but he wasn't there long, so people are questionin' all the rumors about his love life and his skills since he didn't spend much time with you."

I pressed my lips together, trying to hold in the words I wanted to say that would have gotten me sent to the bishop's office to repent for profanity as a kid.

"Hawke was far more interestin'," Ella said, taking a bite of her cookie.

"Why is that?"

"Because there's more evidence."

My heart started to beat a little faster and I tried not to sound panicked as I asked, "What evidence?"

"There are before and after photos," Ella explained around her mouthful of food.

"Before and after photos of what?" This could be bad.

Beyond bad, if they'd somehow gotten pictures of us through a window, before we made our way to the bedroom.

"Before, of you and Hawke outside with Phyllis, and after, of you walkin' out of the house. You both looked like the cat that had just stolen the cream, and your hair was a mess."

Dammit!

"It's a new styling product that boosts volume."

"Sure, it is," Ella said with a smirk. "It's called Hawke-threw-me-around-the-bed-head."

I tried to keep my expression neutral, but she wasn't wrong.

"You didn't even try to keep it a secret," Ella said, her tone carrying a touch of criticism. "You should have gone to Hawke's house. He's harder to surveil."

I wasn't the least bit surprised that Ella and the other Ladies had tried. "I'll make sure he knows that, and he'll account for it, and probably do the same in my yard as well."

She tapped her hand on the desk behind her as she eyed me. "My money's on Hawke bein' the one you went away with. And based on today's evidence, most people think the same."

Good lord. "I didn't realize there was a betting pool."

"Oh, please," she said, waving her hand like I was ridiculous. "This has been a pinned discussion in the social media groups about you for months!"

I stretched my neck from side-to-side, trying to relax. It was futile. It was also late, and I'd had a long day and was ready to curl up on the couch and watch a movie. I gathered up my things, said good night to Ella, and left to pick up Gandalf.

Chapter Six

Five minutes ago, my phone had buzzed with a notification about the rule in the legislature banning independent media and making it even harder to talk to lawmakers. It wasn't introduced as legislation that would have required public hearings, and it wasn't debated publicly. It was simply adopted. I'd spent the next four minutes seething and mumbling swears and threats. I'd talked to Drake about this. He knew it was important to me. And he hadn't stopped it. I understood I wasn't the only one he represented, but there were times you had to take a stand, and he'd decided to stand with secrecy instead of advocating for transparency. I was too angry to call him myself, or even text, so I did the next best thing. I called his office.

"Hi, this is Kate Saxee, a constituent calling from Branson Falls, Utah. Can I leave a message for Drake?"

"Hi, Kate. Sure."

"Tell him to go fork himself."

The other line went silent for a good five seconds. "Oh, um, okay. I'll do that...just, let me see if there's some sort of way for me to add that to the list of concerns." She paused, clearly looking for something. "When you call, we have columns we mark constituents in for specific issues, and "forking yourself" isn't one of our predetermined columns."

"It's not?" I asked with a surprised tone. "I imagine that should be the first column on every politician's list."

Greycie gave a nervous laugh.

"Also, you can add another column, though I imagine this one is already there given his history. Tell him our date on Friday is off."

Another long pause. "Oh. *Oh*, you're *that* Kate Saxee! His girlfriend."

"I'm definitely that Kate Saxee, and definitely *not* his girlfriend. Especially after he didn't stop the legislature from passing the rule about the independent media ban and Capitol access restriction. Mark me down with a giant X in that column as well."

"I'll do that." She paused. "Would you like to maybe leave this message privately? I can patch you through to his voicemail."

"Nope. I have his cell phone number. I want to be on record for this."

Her tone was hesitant. "Okay, Kate. I'll make sure your name gets down. For all of it."

"Thanks, Greycie."

I hung up, grabbed a donut from the box on the table that Spence had brought in, and chewed it spitefully. I'd wanted to use the real word instead of 'fork' but knew that wouldn't get me very far and growing up in Utah meant I'd also become very proficient at pseudo-swears.

"That will probably get a reaction," Spence said, stepping

out of his office. He angled his head toward my phone, indicating he'd overheard the conversation I'd put on speaker.

I looked at him as I paced and chewed. "Good. I'm furious."

He put his hands in his pockets and looked at the carpet. "I am too. It's a bad day for the First Amendment."

I sat at my desk and tried to compose myself. I needed to do something to feel like I was taking a stand against this attack on my profession and freedom of the press. I got an idea, so I started the process, then I tried to take my mind off of it by working on stories for the *Tribune*, including the one on 111 Healing and Crystals. I added some of the photos I took, and highlighted all the different services they offered including the salt cave and quartz crystal cave. I only gave a slight mention of the police showing up during the full moon release ceremony, and explained that once the emergency responders knew there wasn't an emergency, everything was fine. I also edited some stories from the Community News. This week's big news story was that someone had tried a new dish called paella, and compared it to an instant rice mix. Clearly, they'd never tasted it in Spain.

I lifted my arms above my head and leaned back in my chair to stretch. I'd drained my coffee a couple of hours ago, and my stomach started to rumble. "Do you want anything from Fry Guy?" I asked Spence.

"Sure," he said, leaning around his desk so he could see me through the door. "A chicken sandwich would be great."

I nodded and grabbed my purse, then walked across the street to get our food. My phone started playing "Brother Love's Travelling Salvation Show" and I looked at it, then sent it straight to voicemail. I wasn't ready to talk to Drake yet.

I ordered at the counter before looking around the dining area to find a booth to wait at. As I scanned the restaurant, my eyes fell on none other than Cory Hatch, sitting at a booth by himself, picking at his food. He was wearing jeans and a red t-shirt with a comic book character on it. His hair was disheveled like he hadn't combed it in a while.

I walked over to him. "Hi Cory, I'm Kate Saxee with the *Tribune*. I was at your house the other day."

He glanced up at me, his eyes bloodshot. "I remember."

"Can I ask you some questions?"

He put his hands in his lap. "I guess."

I sat at his booth on the bench across from him. "Why do you think Whitney is missing?"

"Because she left without a trace and hasn't tried to reach me. I have no idea where she went, or if she's safe."

"But her friends and family say they've heard from her, that this was planned, and she's fine."

A muscle feathered at his jaw. "They say they know where she is, but why should anyone believe them? Maybe they did something to her."

I drew my brows together. "What motive would they have for that?"

"Not her family," he said, backpedaling a bit. "Clarissa is a schemer. She started the business with Whitney, but she wants it for herself. Getting Whitney out of the picture would help that."

Interesting. Clarissa hadn't seemed anything but concerned for Whitney. But maybe that was an act as well. "Why do you think that? Clarissa told me they were partners."

He rolled his shoulders like he was trying to release the tension there. "Whit had more clients and made more money. Clarissa wanted Whitney's name and clientele, but had no interest in sharing the business long term and she set it up that way. Then she used her friendship with Whit to try and manipulate Whitney's emotions and convince her to divorce me."

That was a lot of accusations and a completely different story than I'd been told by Clarissa. "I'm sorry to hear about your relationship. Break-ups are never easy."

He scrubbed a hand over his mouth and chin. "It's not just a break-up, it's a divorce. And it's not something that's done."

It had become more common in the last twenty years, but the older Mormon generations, like Mrs. Olsen, definitely didn't do it and had opinions about anyone who did. People would stay in abusive relationships before they'd get a divorce because of the eternal consequences.

"Why do you think she asked for it?" I wanted to know what Whitney had told him her reasons were.

"Aside from Clarissa brainwashing her?" He shrugged. "Who knows."

"Did you feel like you had a healthy relationship?"

His expression was pinched. "All relationships have issues. We were working through things."

Except for his opinions about Clarissa and her influence, he hadn't given me much more information than I already knew. He hadn't given a lot of detail with his answers, but I was a member of the press and a stranger to him, so that wasn't a surprise. "Have you seen the signs around town that indicate she's a cheater?"

His fists tightened, his fingernails pressing into his palms as he nodded. "The signs were out of line."

I was glad he was upset about that. "Your sister tried to run that same ad at the *Tribune*."

He sighed, his head falling backwards, and closed his eyes for a few seconds before looking at me again. "She shouldn't have done that. Shasta is protective of me."

"Why would she think Whitney was cheating?"

He flinched so quickly I almost missed it, then he lifted his shoulders in a shrug. "There have been rumors."

I'd heard some of those rumors at the grocery store, but needed to ask around and see if anyone would share additional details with me. "Do you believe them?"

His shoulders slumped and his chin dropped to his chest. "I don't know what to believe, but I love my wife and don't want a divorce."

Given how unkempt and worried he looked, I believed him.They called my number at the counter. "Thanks for your time, Cory," I said, getting up.

"Are you going to look for her?" he asked, and his face brightened with hope.

"I'm going to do my best to make sure she's okay."

"Why are you so interested?" Cory asked.

I paused before answering to gather my thoughts about something I'd marinated over a lot. "Last year, a teenager named Chelsea Bradford went missing and was then murdered. No one knew she was even gone, until she turned up dead in a Branson Falls lake. If more people had known she was missing, they could have done something about it sooner and maybe Chelsea would still be alive. I investigate stories for a living and if there's something I can do to make sure Whitney's okay, I want to do it."

His expression crumpled with emotion. "Thank you," he said, nodding with relief as I walked away.

"You're still concerned about Whitney even though her family and business partner say she's okay?" Spence asked, taking another bite of his chicken sandwich.

I pulled my bottom lip back with my teeth and thought about it. "I can't shake the feeling that something's off. Several people have made comments that Whitney was cheating, including her sister-in-law, and the only person who has heard from Whitney is Clarissa. She even admits that she hasn't talked to Whitney for over a week, since Whitney supposedly arrived at her destination."

"And no one will tell you where that destination was?"

I dipped a fry into my fry sauce. "No. The only people who seem to know are Clarissa and her parents. I'm actually not even sure if her parents know the location. They just know that she had plans to leave and she moved those plans up because of the divorce rumors and things being said about her."

"It's probably a good sign Cory seemed concerned," Spence said, grabbing his soda to wash down his food. I'd already filled him in on the conversation as we ate.

"Yeah, but Cory could also be acting. Look at every infamous case where a woman has gone missing and is later found dead and her husband was the one who killed her."

Spence moved his head back and forth like he was considering it. "That's a fair point. However, Cory's the one who reported Whitney missing."

"So do a lot of murder-y husbands. They know their partners will be missed eventually, and they think they can get away with it."

"But Clarissa said she knows where Whitney is and has talked to her."

"Not for over a week, and Cory implicated Clarissa and said she only wanted Whitney for her clients, and now she wants Whitney's half of the business. He said Clarissa brainwashed Whitney into believing he was a bad guy and she needed a divorce."

Spence wiped his hands on a napkin and cleaned up the wrappers from lunch. "Do you believe that?"

I pushed my brows together in thought. "I don't know. Clarissa seems like the portrait of a concerned friend and she has nothing good to say about Cory. There's a sound bath tonight at 111 that Annie invited me to. I'm going to go and see what more I can find out."

I threw my sandwich wrapper in the trash as a call came over the police scanner. I was at the other end of the room and couldn't hear it.

"What's going on?" I asked Spence.

"Someone reported a strange beam of light."

"Where?" I asked.

"Your mom's neighborhood."

I was out the door in seconds.

We'd had our fair share of strange sightings in Branson Falls. I'd even covered a UFO situation over the summer with the help of Hawke…and had gotten a little distracted in the process.

This wasn't a UFO, but it definitely qualified as strange.

I stood on my mom and dad's front lawn with half their neighborhood, and Officer Bob, staring at her firepit. The expressions on peoples' faces ranged from mortified, to perplexed, to livid. My dad had his palm against the side of his face and he was rubbing his temple with his fingertips.

There my mom's witches were, draped in the creations my mom had been working on in her craft room. The witches' regular everyday black costumes that they'd come with had been amplified. And the positions of the witches had been changed. One was standing next to the firepit that doubled as a cauldron, wearing a red lace corset with black boning. The skirt was made of several black feathered boas with silver and hot pink sequins glued so abundantly that it looked like the feathers had caught a case of sequin chicken pox. The witch had been given a long, stick-straight black wig that I had no idea how my mom had secured to a plastic inflatable, but she was ever inventive.

The second witch was leaning into the first witch's side, wearing nothing but an eight-inch-thick fuchsia fabric ribbon over her chest. The ribbon had been tied into a bow at the front that my mom had fashioned to look like a giant rose, and could probably compete with the dinner plate sized belt buckles the cowboys at the rodeo wore. Her red tulle skirt would have been completely see-through if it wasn't for all of the layers. Hot pink sequin hearts were sewn all over the ensemble with a border of even more silver sequins around the ribbon rose petals and the hem of the skirt. The witch's wig was shoulder length, wavy, and light brown.

The third witch, and probably the one responsible for most of my mom and dad's neighbors currently outside gawking, was sporting a long blonde wig of wind-blown curls that *some* people might recognize as Hawke-threw-me-around-the-bed-head. She was wearing a black lace corset with strategically placed hot pink sequins, and a skirt made entirely of silver and pink sequins that were hanging in rows like fringe. She was bent over the firepit cauldron, which was now full of sequin hearts, and a pole was sticking out of the cauldron like the hearts were meant to be stirred. While I think my mom had intended for the scene to look like the witches were crafting a Valentine's Day love spell, it looked a lot more like they were about to perform a pole dance and people were paying them in flair.

As a fan of Neil Diamond, I was also a fan of sequins, but even Neil would think this might be over-the-top. The light reflecting off the sequins was so bright that I thought it might start melting the snow. And the snow didn't help the situation because it was white, and reflected the light. Frankly, I was surprised they hadn't started a fire. She was lucky everything was currently covered in snow.

I couldn't fathom the yards and yards of fabric and lace that would have been required to make corsets, bras, and skirts for three six-foot-tall inflatable witches. The scene was a witch lust trainwreck. "Why are there so many sequins?" I asked, unable to tear my gaze away from the kaleidoscope of fabric, ribbons, and light.

My mom pushed her shoulders back and her chest jutted

out—not unlike her witches. "They sent me more than I thought they would and I wasn't going to let it go to waste!"

"Did you have to use all of it in one go?"

"I didn't!" she said, her tone defensive. "I still have almost a whole box."

Someone should take that away from her. I met my dad's eyes and knew we were thinking the same thing, and the task was appointed to him.

She tapped her index finger on her chin like she was getting an idea—always a scary sign. "I actually think Trixie, Diamond, and Velvet could use some sequin crowns!"

"Better not," I said flatly, trying to make sure the sarcasm came through. "Wouldn't want the scene to come across as gaudy."

My mom thought about it and nodded in agreement, my comment lost on her.

"Also, Trixie, Diamond, and Velvet? When did you name them?" Thank the goddesses my dad had been given some input into my name or I probably would have ended up as Sugar Saxee.

She scrunched up one side of her face like I'd asked the most ridiculous question in the world. "Months ago! Catch up, Kate!"

Bobby cleared his throat. "You're gonna have to reduce the sequins, Sophie."

"Why?" she asked, affronted.

"Because they're a hazard," he explained.

She put her hands on her hips and her chin jutted out sharply. "To who?" Her tone was meant to sound curious, but instead came out shrill and slightly scary.

"The whole neighborhood," my mom's neighbor yelled.

"It shouldn't be a surprise comin' from Korihor!" Korihor was the Mormon Antichrist and that particular barb had been yelled by my mom's biggest enemy, her neighbor Gladys Simpson. Gladys had been trying to get my mom's witches taken down since my mom put them up for Halloween. Because the witches made Gladys so mad, my mom had kept them up ever since and decorated them for different holidays. Passive aggressive was my mom's middle name.

The Korihor comment made my mom even more angry and she squeezed her fists like she might want to fight Gladys, or flip her off. I'd never seen my mom use that finger, even by accident, and was kind of hoping she would. Instead, she raised her hand, pointed at Gladys and said, "If you really think I'm Korihor, you probably shouldn't piss me off, Gladys!"

Gladys tensed her arms and curled her hands into fists like she wanted to punch my mom, but she was too far away to make contact.

My mom took that to mean she'd won this round and flashed Gladys an unfriendly smile that was as close to saying F you as she'd ever come. She turned back to Bobby. "Have I broken any laws?"

Bobby rubbed the base of the back of his neck like he was trying to prevent an inevitable headache. "Not yet, but you're close to a violation for indecency."

"For the sequins?" she asked, aghast.

"No, for the poses and outfits."

My mom took the outfit comment personally and glared at Bobby. "What in the world are you talking about? The witches are making a love potion!"

Did I know my mom or what?

Bobby's eyebrow shot up. "That's one way to put it."

She slitted her eyes and then pushed her shoulders back, determined. "Are you giving me a ticket?"

Bobby sighed and scratched his head. "Not yet, but maybe move them around and reduce the sequins."

She dug her heels in. "Then I'll be leaving them the way they are until I'm told I have no choice."

"That might be closer than you think," he said, inclining his head. "The sequins, and the outfits, could cause a driver to become distracted."

The phrase "could cause" indicated Bobby was offering up a hypothetical, but I was pretty sure distraction had already occurred from people driving, and walking. Anyone who passed my parents' house using any method of transportation from their feet to a scooter, or anything else with wheels, would be in danger of causing an incident.

My mom went to the front porch to talk to my dad, who had walked there under the guise of opening the door and liberating Gandalf from his house jail, but I felt like my dad was actually trying to retreat into that same jail. The neighbors started to disperse, and Gandalf ran out of the house to greet me. I bent down and gave him loves, then he ran over to Bobby and dropped a toy in front of him. Bobby grinned and threw it.

"Did you see the signs about Whitney Hatch that were plastered all over town?" I asked.

Bobby rolled his eyes. "Shasta Wentworth can be a menace when she wants to."

Menace was a nice way to put it. "Have you heard anything more about Whitney?"

He shook his head. "Just the same stuff everyone else

knows about the divorce, and her leavin' town, and rumors about her cheatin'."

"Do you believe the rumors?"

He gave an incredulous snort. "I don't believe anything unless there's proof."

I considered him for a minute. "Cory thinks Whitney's business partner, not-a-witch-Clarissa, was trying to take over the business and might have done something to Whitney."

Bobby threw the ball for Gandalf again. "Interestin'."

I tilted my head and put my hands in my pockets. "At what point do you get involved and start looking into it?" I knew his investigation resources were limited unless there was a clear and present danger, but mine weren't.

"When there's more evidence. Right now, Clarissa is the only one who's had any contact with her, and she says Whitney is fine."

That's what worried me. Clarissa was the only person with any information. So many situations that turned deadly could have been stopped if they'd been caught faster.

Bobby gave Gandalf a pat on the head, and I took some photos of the witches, but didn't think we'd be able to run them in the paper. The witches looked R-rated, regardless of the angle. My dad came to collect Gandalf. We had a short discussion about disposing of the rest of the sequins, and I went back to work.

I was stretched out on a yoga mat under a cozy blanket as the music flowed over me. I'd never been to a sound bath before and it almost felt like the music was penetrating my soul. I could understand why so many people came to this. It was a quiet space for my overactive mind, and incredibly relaxing.

When it ended, I sat up slowly, and stretched my arms. Annie was sitting next to me and did the same.

"I'm glad you came," she said.

"I am too. This is amazing." I folded the blanket that I'd been using.

Annie gestured to the people around her. "I've made great friends, and it really helps me get centered."

I recognized several women in class from the full moon release meditation.

"How long have you all been coming to 111?"

"About six months," Annie said. "I started attending before Whitney and Clarissa moved to this space."

Wendy Alpine, a local teacher said, "I met Clarissa first, and then started going to the events at her house a couple of years ago. I love this bigger space, though."

Jacey Frank nodded as well. "I've known Whitney since she started—back when she wasn't even making people pay for her meditations. She used to do them at church, but the bishopric considered it energy healing. They told her she couldn't do it there anymore because church leadership said members shouldn't participate in that. That was when she moved it to her house."

"I remember when LDS church leaders said energy work was unacceptable in General Conference, and remember a lot of women who felt angry and betrayed because they'd found community in that space."

Jacey's eyes widened like that was an understatement.

"Lots of women were angry, and a lot still are. Many have left the church since, for many reasons."

Annie looked at me, both of us remembering the conversation we'd had about how women in the church are treated.

I wanted to get a better read on what the women who frequented 111 thought about Whitney. "But Whitney's still a member, right?" She was at the testimony meeting where Mrs. Olsen decided to play the part of "fire and brimstone preacher" so I assumed she was still devout.

Jacey nodded matter-of-factly. "She is, but she's open-minded." That was code for she-doesn't-do-everything-she's-told. "The way she's been treated in town since it became public that she asked for a divorce is beyond awful. I hate that she's eternally sealed to Cory, and I hope she asks the church to cancel her sealing, too."

"Can she do that?" I asked, drawing my brows together in curiosity. That definitely wasn't what I'd been taught growing up.

Annie answered, "Years ago, you could get a legal divorce, but you couldn't get your temple sealings canceled unless you had special permission from the First Presidency. The only way they'd really allow a woman to get her sealing canceled was if she was getting married again to another man she wanted to be sealed to, because it was better to be sealed to someone than no one. Unlike men, who can be sealed to as many women as they want because LDS doctrine teaches that there will be polygamy in the afterlife, women were only allowed to be sealed to one man, until recently."

Jacey nodded as she shifted on her mat. "Now, when a woman sealed to two men dies, she'll have to choose which of her dead husbands she wants to be with because she can't be greedy and take two. Afterall, there will only be so many good men in top-tier Celestial."

It would be the ultimate love triangle.

Love triangles of the other side, in fact.

I thought about all the people seriously invested in who I was going to choose in my life here on earth, so imagine all the drama in Mormon heaven. Given the interest in Utah and Mormon culture, I was surprised it hadn't been greenlit as a reality show yet.

"That's true," a woman I'd been introduced to earlier as Brandy said. "My dad died when I was young and my mom met another LDS man she wanted to marry. She had to decide who she wanted to be sealed to: my dead dad, or the new man she was going to marry. It was even more complicated because she and my dad had kids, and her new husband also wanted to have kids, so if she got sealed to her new husband, what would happen to us kids who had been born under the covenant she made when she was sealed to my dead dad? And if she didn't get sealed to her new husband, would her kids with him be sealed to my dead dad?"

This felt like trying to figure out calculus and my brain wanted to explode. "That's complicated."

A perky twenty-something woman named Sandy who had recently moved to Branson Falls said, "But we don't have to worry about all of that! God will make sure it will all work out!" She was desperately trying to make everyone feel better by campaigning for ignorance through faith.

"The church has become more lenient and it's easier to get sealings canceled now," another woman named Julie defended.

I was glad of that. Mormon women should absolutely be

able to ask to no longer be eternally bound to someone they no longer wanted to be with.

I took advantage of the lull in the conversation to probe Clarissa and Whitney's relationship a little bit. "It's great Clarissa and Whitney were able to open a business together. A lot of times business and money can ruin friendships."

Stephanie Gress and Monica Pack both exchanged glances.

"They're still friends, right?" I asked.

Wendy pulled some lint off the blanket she'd been using as she answered, "As far as we know. But Whitney hasn't been around for a while."

"I've heard that. How well do you all know Whitney's husband, Cory?"

Jacey's chin jutted out sharply. "Well enough to know I don't want to know him more."

Wendy gave her a playful slap on the arm. "Be nice. He's had some issues and Whitney was patient, but she needed to get out of that situation."

My ears perked up. "What were the issues?"

Wendy tucked one shoulder up by her ear like she was uncomfortable. "He was controlling, like a lot of men, especially in this culture and religion where men are told it's part of their role to lead the family."

Anytime I heard the word control in reference to a relationship, alarm bells went off in my mind. "Controlling how?"

Jacey pressed her lips together like she was trying to decide if she should say what she wanted. "He criticized her, and manipulated her for not being enough. And when I say that, I mean not being enough of what he wanted and what he thought she should be. Her own opinions about her life didn't matter to him. He turned everything around to make himself the victim and Whitney could never do things right. He wasn't supportive of anything Whitney did, especially with her business, and he wanted her to stop working and start having kids."

"But it's not like he had a way to support them," Wendy said, shifting to cross her legs. "He'd been in school for years and Whitney started her business to help them have some extra cash. She started doing well, offering classes for sale online and doing private events. Now she's the breadwinner, which was helpful when they needed the money."

My eyes went wide. "That's a rare thing for this area."

Annie nodded slowly. "The church has become a bit more lenient about women who work, but women are still encouraged to not have a job outside the home, raise their kids, and support their husbands. And a lot of people, especially men, still expect that from their relationships."

I pressed my lips into such a tight line that they probably turned white. I hated that women were encouraged to stay dependent. "Based on what I've heard from several people, that expectation is one of the things that caused problems between Cory and Whitney."

Jacey and Wendy both nodded.

Stephanie piped up. "I don't think it's all Cory's fault. And I don't agree with how Whitney has treated him."

"What has she done?" I asked.

Stephanie looked at me like I was naïve. "I'm sure you saw the posters, Kate."

I lifted a shoulder. "I did, but there's no proof Whitney cheated on him."

Stephanie gave a knowing smile and got up. Monica followed. "We'll see."

Me, Annie, Wendy, and Jacey all watched them walk away. "That was weird," Wendy finally said.

Clarissa came over and sat next to us. "That seemed like a lively conversation," she said.

"People have opinions about Whit," Jacey explained.

Clarissa rolled her eyes and sighed. "It's sad. They don't know what they're talking about."

I decided to test the waters to see how Clarissa would respond to what Cory had said about her, "Cory Hatch told me you were a bad influence on Whitney."

She laughed out loud. "Of course he did. Because I got divorced from my abusive husband and when Whitney told me how miserable she was, I encouraged her to do the same."

Ah, that made more sense.

She shook her head and continued, "He's playing the part of dutiful, concerned husband. He's not. If he was concerned, he would have treated Whitney better."

"Where are the cheating rumors coming from?" I asked

Clarissa raised her hands in an I don't know gesture. "People need a reason for things they don't understand so they can make those things make sense. Most people in town think Cory is a nice guy because that's how he presents himself. He's also local and from a good family, and given his pedigree, he was on track to be called into church leadership. But it's harder to get called to a leadership position if you're divorced, or if you're having any family life or marriage problems. Blaming Whitney makes things easier."

That would explain Shasta's posters. "Do you think his family is spreading the rumors?"

"It wouldn't surprise me one bit," Clarissa said. Wendy, Jacey, and Annie all nodded in agreement.

We were the only ones left in the space at that point. We all got up and started toward the door when Clarissa stopped us. "I'm keeping this quiet," she said, her voice hushed, "but I'm having a private event next week—just a fun thing for Valentine's Day. I booked a traveling male revue to come do a show."

My lips stretched into a wide smile. Male strippers in Branson Falls were not something I had on my bingo card, ever, but I kind of loved it.

"I've been careful about who I invite, but you're all open-minded so I'd love you to come if you want to."

The other women giggled and fanned themselves, their faces lined with excitement and intrigue. "Count me in," Annie immediately answered.

"Me too," I almost answered over Annie and we both laughed.

Wendy and Jacey looked at each other, and then back to Clarissa. "We'll be there!" they both said in unison.

"I'll text you the details," Clarissa said with a wink.

Branson Falls certainly wasn't what it used to be, and that was okay. I was beyond supportive of progress, change, and adaptation while still keeping the heart of the city—the thing that made it special here.

I said goodbye to everyone and made my way to the car. Annie was parked next to me. "You're coming over for the #HOTBS Reunion, right?"

She flashed a wide grin. "I wouldn't miss it."

I got in my Jeep and waited for it to warm up. Clarissa seemed genuinely concerned for Whitney, and so did Wendy and Jacey. Stephanie and Monica were defensive of Cory, but I wasn't sure how much of that was from personal knowledge, and how much was the conditioning they'd been raised with —to protect men. I needed to ask Clarissa about Cory's accusations that she was trying to steal the business, but I wanted to do that when there weren't so many people around. As someone who was constantly the victim of rumors, I didn't need to help add to rumors about someone else, especially if it could hurt her financially.

When I got home, I was accosted by my furry boy. My dad had brought him over so I wouldn't have to stop at their house. Gandalf was the best boyfriend. He loved to cuddle, gave me lots of kisses, and never left me for months at a time, or voted for things I was deeply opposed to.

We played fetch for ten minutes before I got up to get Gandalf some of the treats I'd promised him. My phone buzzed. It was a text from Drake.

DRAKE

I know you're upset. I understand, and I want to talk about it. We're still going on our date. I'll pick you up at six tomorrow night.

Part of me wanted to put my doctorate-level profanity training to good use. He didn't get to dictate my choices. This was a team sport, not one where he was the King and everyone just did what he said. The other part of me felt like I should probably be an adult and have a conversation. I wasn't sure which part would win, but decided I'd sleep on it and find out tomorrow.

Chapter Seven

I spent the morning working, then went to Beans and Things in late afternoon and ordered a salted caramel mocha. Once again, I didn't pay for it. "Whoever is paying for my drinks is running up quite a tab," I said to Kelcie, my favorite barista because she always gave me extra whipped cream.

She handed me my drink with a smile. "They always pay it."

"I was really hoping to catch you off guard and have you say 'he' or 'she' so I'd be able to narrow my suspects down." I was fairly certain it was Hawke or Drake, but it could have been a friend or someone else as well.

Kelcie gave me a wink. "They pay us all to be careful about that."

I took a sip from my coffee and it was like drinking magic. "That might just confirm my suspicions." It had to be Hawke.

"I don't know. I was actually pretty surprised when they asked us to do it."

I narrowed my eyes. If she was surprised, that would

suggest Drake because he was less likely to want to spend money on my sinful coffee habit.

I turned around and saw Shasta Wentworth at the community billboard in the corner, pinning up another photo of Whitney, the SL,UT cheater. I went up to her. "What do you think that's accomplishing?"

She recognized me and pinned me with a solid glare. She slammed a tack into the paper and board like the force would help prove her point. It was so childish.

"It's lettin' everyone know what a whore Cory's wife is."

I angled my head wondering if she knew she was vile. "Do you think that's helping Cory or making him feel better?"

She grabbed another paper and tack and put that one up too. "Cory's not gonna defend himself, so someone has to."

I thought it was strange that she felt responsible for his emotions, and wondered how much enmeshment had happened in their home growing up. Based on what he'd told me, Cory didn't seem to appreciate Shasta's efforts. "I talked to Cory and he said he's still in love with Whitney and doesn't want this played out publicly. He said you stepped over a line with the pictures."

Shasta rolled her eyes. "My brother is overreacting, and panicked. He's also whipped. He's been in love with her since he saw her because he thought she was way out of his league and he'd never get someone like her. Beauty doesn't make up for being a liar. One day he'll be glad she's gone."

That was ominous, and made me wonder what Shasta knew. "Do you know where she is?"

Her expression twisted like she'd stepped in something unpleasant. "No, and I hope she never comes back."

Shasta walked out, and I yanked the papers down, crumpled them up, and threw them in the trash.

Kelcie gave me a round of applause. "If someone wasn't already buying you a drink, I'd buy you one for that."

"I'll remember that just in case the person buying my coffee every day isn't the one I end up with."

Kelcie grinned. "You never know what will happen. Maybe you'll end up with one guy and then change your mind? Or maybe you'll choose yourself."

Someone else had said the exact same thing to me recently and I hadn't forgotten it. "I think if I choose myself, the right person will end up standing next to me."

Kelcie pointed at me with both fingers in celebration, like I'd just made the buzzer-winning goal in the state soccer tournament. "That's a life lesson right there."

She wasn't wrong.

I went back to the office.

I had an hour or so to work until I needed to leave early to get ready for my date with Drake. I'd decided to go, but I had a bone to pick with him, and some statements to make. He hadn't given me any hints about where we were going. He'd only said to dress up. Drake wouldn't take me anywhere scandalous so dressing up meant something different to him than it had last fall when I'd helped Hawke on an investigation. Hawke had given me a dress that was so low cut and see-through I might as well have been naked, and Hawke made it even more revealing when he pushed me against the wall, kissed the hell out of me, and tore the dress.

Speaking of Hawke, I'd finished my work for the day and had some time to do a little research. I'd been looking into Hawke since I met him, trying to figure out more about his past, a past he kept hidden as much as possible. He was a master of curating any information available about him publicly. I couldn't even find birth records, or family members, and wondered if Ryker Hawkins was his real name. He'd told me some things, like when I'd guessed about his government contracts, but never a lot of details. As a reporter and potentially his girlfriend, there was no way that I wasn't going to try and find out more.

I knew Drake and Hawke had some sort of history. There was no love lost between those two, and they both disliked each other, but neither one of them would go into detail about why. Drake had mentioned something about the two of them being involved with the same organization for a time, and that caused the division between them. I thought it might be the break I needed. I'd been looking into organizations Drake had been linked to and trying to cross reference them with Hawke ever since. The problem was that Drake was a philanthropist and involved with so many organizations, I'd needed a spreadsheet. I pulled it up and went to the next non-profit in the list. Friends and Family Law Consultants.

Drake was a lawyer so it made sense he'd work with that organization. I looked them up and checked their current and past board members. Drake was still on the board, and had served for several years. Then I did a search for mentions of them in the media and any clues that Hawke might have assisted the organization in some way. I didn't see Hawke's name, but as I was searching, I came across someone else familiar: Clarissa Hope. She had a quote on their website that said, "Family Law Consultants have been instrumental in helping my business. They will always have my support."

That was interesting. Technically, it was Clarissa and Whitney's business…wasn't it? Then I remembered Cory saying Clarissa wanted the business for herself and had set it up that way.

I pulled up Utah's business records database and did a search for 111 Healing and Crystals. It was listed as an LLC with Clarissa's name attached, but not Whitney's. That was also a surprise, and supported Cory's statement. When I looked through the Articles for the company that would disclose the business and company ownership percentages, Whitney wasn't listed at all. Clarissa had told me they owned 111 Healing and Crystals together. Had she been lying to me? Was Cory telling the truth about Clarissa wanting Whitney out of the picture?

An alarm went off on my phone. I'd spent more time combing through the papers than I thought and I was going to be late for my vengeance date if I didn't hurry. I'd considered how I wanted to show up and what I wanted to say to Drake, and had decided on somewhere between "profanity Kate" and "reasonable adult Kate." I started grabbing things and shoving them in my bag.

"Why the rush?" Spence asked.

"Ella was standing by the treat table, looking over what she wanted to try next. "Yeah, where's the fire?"

"I have a date," I said to them both.

Ella's eyes sparkled and her lips spread into a wide smile. "With Hawke?"

I put my coat on and grabbed my keys. "No, Drake." I looked to Spence. "And I have some things to say to him."

Interest sparked in Spence's eyes. "I can't wait to hear about it."

Ella shook her head as I passed her. "You're the luckiest woman I know. You're gonna have to choose one of 'em at some point."

"Not yet, I won't," I said, but knew she was probably right.

My hair was curled in loose waves with a deep side part, and the other side tucked behind my ear. My eyes were smoky and my lipstick a shimmery pale pink. Drake knocked and I grabbed my coat and buttoned it, smoothing it over my hidden outfit. When I opened the door, I deliberately looked him up and down, taking in his grey pants, sky blue dress shirt that highlighted his cobalt eyes, and his black sports coat. His dark hair was combed back and if I hadn't been so frustrated with him, I would have been turned on. I met his eyes. "Well, well, well. If it isn't my own personal Judas."

A muscle worked in his jaw. "You're colorful tonight."

I flashed a devious smile. "Oh, you haven't seen anything yet."

He raised his eyebrows. "Let's talk on the way to dinner."

Snow had started falling and he held out his arm for me to take. It was solid muscle as he helped me down the stairs at my house.

He opened the door to his gigantic truck, which had steps because that was the only way to get in without a catapult, and we settled in for the drive. He had the heater set to swelter, so I shrugged off my coat, revealing my dress. It was a strapless A-line that pushed my cleavage up to my chin. It tapered to a narrow waist, and hit my legs mid-calf where the skirt was full enough to swish. It was black, but the best thing about it was the additions I'd asked my mom to help with when I'd dropped Gandalf off this morning. Black and white patches with the phrases "First Amendment," "Free Press," and "Free Speech" were sewn all over the dress. When Drake had insisted on us being adults and going on our date despite my anger and his bad political choices, it had been easy to decide what to wear.

Drake glanced over at me and almost drove into a snowbank. I wasn't sure if the reaction was because of my cleavage, my tempting and immodest—by Mormon standards—dress, or the patches.

"I like the dress."

"Do you?" I asked, turning my head. "I felt it was perfect given the situation."

He stretched his neck like he was trying to release tension, and draped his hand over the steering wheel. "I know you're disappointed and I want to talk about it."

"I'm willing to hear you out."

"Politics is all about influence. I try to use mine strategically."

"So, you helped disenfranchise the press—strategically."

He took a deep breath through his nose. He was usually better at hiding his emotions. "I tried to use that influence to stop the rule. I spoke out against it to my colleagues and said it would hurt accountability. I tried to fight it, but in the end, they adopted it without even giving it a vote. I was vocal about my disagreement, and will probably pay a price for that."

I took that all in, thinking about how it made me feel. I

was glad to hear that he hadn't been part of passing the rule, and that he'd tried to stop it. But I wasn't sure how I felt about him being part of a system that would do this. "I appreciate that you spoke out against the rule and tried to convince others not to accept it. But you're part of the system and even saying you'll pay a price for disagreeing makes it seem like you care more about yourself than the people you represent. Not only that, but it makes it difficult to know what you personally believe, and what you're supporting or disagreeing with to help your career."

"I understand that. I want you to know I do support independent media and transparency. I was working to try and come up with a compromise, but compromise wasn't what the majority wanted. I would say I'm more moderate in my elected position, and I'm that way in my personal life too."

I listened to his explanation and still wasn't sure where he stood. "I worry that what you say and what you do are two different things. You're a lawyer and a politician with impressive situational ethics."

"Ouch."

"Am I wrong?"

He considered it. "No, you're not. But I think we all tolerate and allow different things depending on what our beliefs justify. I did my best with this situation, and I'll keep advocating for accountability and the issues that matter to me."

"Issues that matter publicly, or personally?"

"I'll try to do both."

"And what happens when those two things don't align?"

"Then I'll have to make a decision."

"That's where my concern comes in. You can't say for

sure." I took a breath. I was a principled person and this was a yellow flag for me. "I can handle us having different opinions, but some things are dealbreakers."

"Is this one of them?" Drake asked.

I considered it. "No. I think we're on the same page, but you're less vocal than I am. I just worry about what this would look like for a relationship long-term."

"I think we would figure it out, don't you?"

"I don't know. I guess we'll have to see."

It gave me something to think about.

We'd driven about forty-five minutes away and pulled up to a stunning, white granite, historic house.

"Where are we?" I asked, as Drake took my hand to help me out of his truck. I was bundled back up in my coat.

Drake flashed a grin. "A surprise. We haven't had a romantic date in a while and I wanted to spend some quality time with you." He gave me his arm again and I took it.

We walked up the steps between two pillars and Drake opened a large, black door for me. Inside the opulently decorated foyer, we were greeted by a host. "Dylan Drake, party of two," Drake said, threading his fingers through mine. A spark ran through me at his touch and judging by how he smiled, he felt it, too.

The host led us through the hallway and out to the back where six beautiful, giant, round glass globes trimmed with cedar wood were placed around the yard. A table lit with candles and covered in rose petals was in the middle of one of the globes. The host opened the globe door where blankets and pillows lined the bench seats. A heater glowed from above. As the snow fell around us, it was like a scene from a painting.

We settled in, exchanging coats for blankets over our laps. Between the heater, the blankets, and Drake's testosterone, the temperature was toasty. Our server brought wine for me, and soda for Drake. I couldn't help wondering if that's what our life together would be like. Dylan Drake and his sinner wife. Maybe it was one of the reasons he liked the thought of us.

"I'll pay for my wine," I said, seriously. I knew he was supposed to avoid the appearance of evil and here I was, drinking it with him right next to me.

He looked horrified. "No, you won't."

"I don't want you to get in trouble."

"With who?"

I pointed to the giant, alabaster white, one-hundred-million-dollar temple—one of hundreds around the world—clearly visible on the hill behind us.

His gaze tracked to where I was pointing. "I'm pretty sure no one from the temple will be checking my receipts."

"I'm just looking out for you. You never know who's watching." I took my index finger and pointed up repeatedly.

He laughed. "I appreciate the sentiment, but I don't care what anyone thinks about my personal choices, and I can handle them."

I suspected he actually did care. A great deal, given the discussion we'd had on the way here. And would care even more when he got pressure from his family, friends, clients, and voters. But I didn't want to ruin the rest of the night so I let it go for now.

The server brought our food; steak and garlic mashed potatoes for Drake, chicken with a side of browned butter ravioli for me. As we started to eat, I remembered my research from earlier today that I wanted to ask him about.

"You're on the board of a non-profit called The Family Law Consultants. Clarissa Hope, Whitney Hatch's business partner, used the organization for something business related. Do you know what?"

He drew his brows together. "I'm on the board, but I'm not one of the attorneys who assist clients. I don't know what she was using FLC for, but even if I did, I wouldn't be able to tell you what she needed."

I flitted my hand in front of me. "Yeah, yeah, attorney client privilege, I get it. Her quote said the organization was instrumental in helping her. Does FLC do a lot of work with women specifically?"

Drake considered that before answering, "They work on a lot of different cases, but for women specifically, I would say they assist on abuse cases and helping women and kids to get out of those situations."

I nodded, remembering what Clarissa had said about her ex-husband. "That makes sense then. Clarissa said she divorced her ex-husband because of abuse. Maybe the organization helped her while she was going through the divorce and trying to keep her business." She said she ran it out of her basement for years before they moved to the barn. She could have still been married then.

"It's possible. We help a lot of people."

The server came in to refill our drinks. "How are things at the legislature so far this year? Aside from the media ban mess, I've already seen some other epically stupid bills being proposed."

He took a drink of his soda. "We always have a few of those."

My brows shot into my hairline. "More than a few."

He inclined his head in agreement. The snow falling outside the glass caught my eye. When I turned back, Drake was watching me with unwavering focus.

"You look stunning."

I felt my cheeks flush.

"Thank you," I said, picking up my wine glass to take a drink. "So do you."

His eyes dipped to my elevated chest, and slowly trailed back up. "I've been thinking about you. A lot."

I put my glass down and leaned toward him, resting my arms on the table—which only enhanced my boob situation. "What have you been thinking?"

He bit his bottom lip and pulled it back. "That I'd like to see what's under your dress."

I widened my eyes and gave him a coquettish smile. "That's not very pious of you, Dylan Drake."

He didn't take his gaze from mine. "I don't give a shit."

He put his hand on the side of my cheek and moved his head toward me, his eyes searching mine for permission. I leaned into him in answer and he pressed his lips to mine. His tongue glided over my lips, tangling with my own, and my veins were suddenly on fire with liquid heat. I breathed him in as I explored his mouth. He smelled like the mountains after a storm and I couldn't get enough. I sucked his bottom lip into my mouth and he groaned. His arm snaked around my waist, pulling me closer as his other hand trailed down my neck. I reached around his hard stomach, and threw my leg over his lap. Sparks of energy went through me like shivers as his hand reached my chest. His fingers lightly traced the top of my sleeveless dress as bright lights began flashing outside our dinner globe.

"What the…," Drake muttered a string of swear words that he wasn't even supposed to know, let alone use, but it was kind of hot to hear them.

We both turned to look, and found an entire group of people standing in front of our little dinner globe. A small bus painted all black was right behind them with the words Dead and Gone Ghost Tour. We could hear the guide through the glass as she explained that this historic-home-turned-restaurant was one of the most prominent bootlegging locations in Utah during prohibition. More photos flashed, and I started laughing at the absurdity. There we were, eating dinner, when a ghost tour suddenly rolled up. The tour guide didn't even try to find another location to tell the story. They had their spot, and they were holding their ground.

Drake couldn't hold his own laughter in. "I picked this place because it was supposed to be intimate and romantic. I didn't realize we were going to have an audience or I would have booked somewhere more private."

I leaned in next to him, unable to stop laughing, and he wrapped his arm around me.

"I don't know," I said, taking a sip from my glass of wine. "This is probably going to be one of the most memorable dates I've ever had."

He grinned. "Well, at least there's that. They definitely got a show before we knew they were there."

"Maybe if we keep going, they'll get uncomfortable and leave," I suggested.

Drake's eyes heated. "We'd probably have to start removing some clothes."

I glanced down at my dress. "I don't have much to remove," I said suggestively.

He gave a predatory grin. "I'm willing to give it a try."

I shook my head, pointing to the temple again. "Better not. You'd get in even more trouble for that, personally and professionally."

He pushed his lips together and nodded like he was thinking.

More lights flashed as photos were taken, and we waited until Dead and Gone was gone again to order dessert.

When Drake pulled into my driveway, my stairs and sidewalk had been cleared.

"Who cleared your walkway?" Drake asked.

I looked at the clear concrete and had a pretty good idea. "I don't know? Maybe it was my dad when he dropped Gandalf off a couple of hours ago. He knew I'd be home late."

A muscle feathered at Drake's jaw. He clearly didn't believe that. If I was being honest, neither did I. Considering that the levels of surveillance on my house were higher than that of a convicted felon, I had a feeling Hawke knew exactly where I'd gone tonight, who I'd gone with, and had come over to remind me he was still here—as if I could forget either one of these men.

"I'd like to take you out for Valentine's Day, but with the current legislative docket, I won't be able to get home in time."

"That was really poor planning on the legislature's part."

"Don't get me started. Marriages almost end because of it every year."

"Nah," I said with a grin. "You're all Mormon and don't believe in divorce."

He gave an amused snort. "Women seem to believe in it strongly on Valentine's Day."

I angled my head in understanding. "I mean, I don't blame them. The way I see it, couples get two days during the whole year where they get to celebrate their relationship: their anniversary, and Valentine's Day."

Drake frowned as he walked me up the freshly shoveled steps. "Well, that makes me feel even worse about missing it. I'll have to make it up to you."

After already being caught by paparazzi once tonight, and cognizant of all the potential Lady spies, Drake gave me a light kiss goodnight on my porch, much more chaste than the one the ghost tour had caught on camera.

"I look forward to that," I said. I didn't tell him I already had Valentine's Day plans.

Chapter Eight

I was drinking coffee at my desk, and had just finished sorting
through my emails. I picked up my phone and texted Hawke.
He replied right away, which was nice because it didn't always
happen—especially when he was gone for a month.

KATE

Thanks for shoveling the snow at my house.

HAWKE

You're welcome. How did you know it
was me?

KATE

It was either you, my dad, or the Mormons in
the Ward my neighborhood is assigned to. I
checked my cameras and the video jumped
an hour and suddenly my driveway was clear.
I knew my dad and the Mormons didn't have
the ability to hack into my security cameras.

HAWKE

I wouldn't put it past the Mormons. They have
enough money to do anything.

KATE

> LOL! Thanks again. It was nice to not have to do it myself.

HAWKE

> I considered staying, but knew you were out with Drake and thought three might be company.

Of course he knew. He'd probably seen Drake arrive on my cameras. That would have been awkward. Especially if I'd invited Drake inside for some reason…milk, and kissing he wouldn't have to confess to his bishop about.

KATE

> He had to get back to work. The legislature is in session so February is hectic.

HAWKE

> So I have you all to myself this month?

KATE

> If you're around.

HAWKE

> I will be.

I finished editing some articles that had come in from our correspondents. I didn't have a lot on my plate and given the conversation with Cory, and then Drake, and the information about Whitney not being listed on the 111 business paperwork, I wanted to talk to Clarissa.

I drove down the dirt road to the 111 barn and pulled into a parking space after I finally found one. It was busy today.

I walked in the store and found a lot of women dressed in active wear browsing around. They were probably here for a yoga class—or using active wear to avoid wearing their Mormon garments like LDS church leaders had accused them of in a recent General Conference. There was only one employee working and there was a line at the checkout, so I hung back and looked at some of the crystals and their various healing properties while I waited. A group of women behind me were talking in hushed tones.

"No one has heard from Whit. I don't know what's going on," a high, soft voice said.

"Did Clarissa say anything about where Whitney went?" A lower-pitched voice this time.

"Just that she needed to get away, but she'll be back soon," the same high, soft voice replied.

One woman gave a deep sigh. "I don't know if she should come back considering she was cheating with the husbands of clients."

My brows raised.

"There's no proof of that," another voice said.

"Not yet," the sighing voice replied in a knowing tone. "Just wait."

The women walked away.

I'd heard the cheating accusations, but not the cheating with clients. I'd add that to my list to ask Clarissa.

It took another ten minutes, but the line diminished. A woman in her twenties with full, high cheeks and a warm smile greeted me. She was wearing a name tag that said Starr. "Sorry for the delay," she said, genuinely apologetic. "We have a lunch time salt cave meditation and it gets busy. How can I help you?"

I smiled back. "No problem. I was hoping to talk to Clarissa. Is she around?"

Starr shook her head. "Not right now. Do you want to leave her a message?"

"Sure. Can you tell her Kate Saxee from *The Branson Tribune* stopped by and has some questions for her?"

Starr wrote the message down. "I'll do that."

I paused, thinking about the conversation I'd overheard from the women, and Whitney and Clarissa's relationship. "Thank you. Have you worked here long?"

Starr grabbed some papers off the desk in front of her and threw them in the trash. "Since Whitney and Clarissa opened this new space."

"Do you know them well?"

She lifted her brows slightly. "I think so. They're fun to work with and gave me a job when I really needed it. I appreciate them."

"Do you all work closely together?"

"Yes and no. We do different things." She started rearranging some display baskets in front of her with bags that read Mystery Crystals on the front. "I take care of the store side and customer service. Whitney manages the classes, schedules, and teaches a lot of classes as well. Clarissa takes care of the business side. It's a great place to work, and I get to go to classes for free—a definite bonus!"

"That's great you're all friends. I'm sure it's hard having Whitney gone right now."

Starr's shoulders slumped, but she answered brightly, "It is. But she should be back soon."

I noted the juxtaposition between what her body was saying, and what she was saying out loud. "Do you know where she went?"

She lifted her shoulders and shook her head with quick

movements. "I know she went away for a few weeks. But I don't blame her. This town can be hard on women." She blinked repeatedly like she was trying not to cry.

"I'm sorry, I didn't mean to bring up something difficult."

Starr waved it off. "It's totally fine. I was internalizing. I'll be happy when Whit is back, though. It will take stress off of everyone. Even Clarissa seems worried and she's pretty hard to rattle."

That was an interesting nugget. "Why do you say that Clarissa seems worried?"

"She's always on her phone, talking to people in hushed tones and I hear Whitney's name a lot."

Another piece of good information.

A customer walked up to the counter so I thanked Starr for her help and turned to leave the shop. That's when I ran smack dab into Satan's apprentice, and second ranking member of The Ladies, Amber Kane. She was wearing yoga pants and a halter tank top. Her short, currently-colored light brown hair, was spiky and styled like the wind had done it, and her red, talon-like nails were armed for a fight. If she'd come here to help herself relax, it hadn't worked. We were both always startled to see each other, which was funny given we lived in the same town and she was part of the group that surveilled me daily. "Hi, Amber. Are you here to try and calm down?" I couldn't help myself.

She looked me up and down, taking in my jeans and black designer sweater that fell off my shoulder and had deliberate holes in it. "You'd think that with all the money your boyfriends have, and the sexual favors you're offerin', they could pay you enough so that you could buy some decent clothes."

Insinuating I was a prostitute, hussy, or whore was one of The Ladies' fun, go-to insults so I didn't take it too personally. We all knew it was a lie, and since high school had ended a long time ago—for me, at least—I was past letting them hurt my feelings. Amber and her mentor, Satan, or as others around town knew her, Jackie Wall, were both interested in a relationship with Drake, and were beyond jealous that he wasn't interested in them.

I gave her a too-sweet smile. "Unlike you, I don't choose my romantic partners based on their bank account balance or annual salary. I make my own money and always will. I got this at Nordstrom. I'm not sure if you know of the store, but it's the best we can do for designer clothes in Utah. You might want to look into it."

Angry heat rose on her cheeks and started spreading. Steam was going to come out of her ears any minute. The banger she came up with next was another word in her insult arsenal that meant the same thing as all the others she'd called me. "At least I'm not a slut."

I let my mouth fall open and spread my fingers out in a fan across my breastbone. "You're not? I didn't get the news release about your status change."

Her lip curled in a sneer. "No wonder you're so interested in Whitney. You're both evil sinners who give themselves to men."

She'd probably seen all the photos of Hawke and Drake at my house. I gave her a smile that was anything but sweet. "I don't need to give myself to anyone. They're the ones throwing themselves at me while you watch and wish you had my life."

I winked and left her standing in the middle of the room, then walked out the door and went to grab lunch.

When I got back from 111, Ella was leaned back in my chair, her legs up on my desk while she sipped on a dirty soda. Her grin stretched from ear-to-ear. I eyed her with suspicion.

"What's going on?" I asked.

She wiggled her eyebrows. "You haven't been on socials, have you?"

I put my purse down on my desk and took off my coat, throwing it over my arm until Ella moved from my chair. "No. I try to avoid them."

She gave a tsk tsk noise. "Probably shouldn't when you're makin' out with Drake in a glass globe wearin' an ode to the First Amendment!"

I closed my eyes, took a deep breath through my nose, and then blew it out of my mouth. As soon as I saw those flashes, I knew it was only a matter of time. "Who posted the photo?"

"Who didn't!" Ella exclaimed, putting her feet down on the ground and tapping them with excitement.

"It's true," Spence said, his lips sliding into an amused smile as he came out of his office. "At least ten people have texted it to me."

I slitted my eyes. "Nice of you to send it on to me."

He leaned against the wall, crossing his legs at the ankles. "You were there, so I figured you already knew."

Funny guy.

"Wearing that dress on a date with a state representative in a state that just banned independent media and restricted access for established reporters was absolutely epic," Spence said with a wide grin. "I'm proud to have you as a friend. It's only a matter of time before you become a meme."

"Because that's been my goal all along." I gave him a wink.

Ella walked over to the treat table to grab a cookie that contained an entire day's worth of calories. "Someone on the ghost tour recognized you both because they watch the Murderoonies. They posted their pics, and lots of people reposted. Now everyone thinks you're with Drake."

I rolled my eyes and leaned against my desk. "Yesterday they all thought I was with Hawke. And the day before that, it was probably Drake. I'm living it and can't even keep up with it."

"Well, you're gonna have to figure it out soon because people wanna know who you're gonna be with."

"I haven't even known them for a year."

"That's an eternity in Utah time," Ella said, standing up. "You should be married or at least engaged by now."

I shook my head and decided I needed a treat as well. "That's not a timeline I follow," I said, opening a box of donuts from Frosted Paradise. "And my life isn't a reality show." I picked a white frosted donut with chopped peanuts, and tried not to think about the gossip being spread about my love life. But I couldn't help smiling at the fact that Representative Dylan Drake had been caught making out with a woman wearing the First Amendment.

I walked in the house and found a black metallic box, tied with a hot pink ribbon and note that said:

Kitty Kate

A gift from Hawke. I opened the box and found a white robe, the lush kind you get in expensive hotels. The fabric was soft and it looked perfect for wrapping up in. But I wasn't sure why it had been left in my living room.

I called him. "I got your gift."

"Did you open it?"

"Yeah…is it a hint to take a bath?"

He laughed. "Only if it's with me."

I thought of Hawke, sitting in a giant bathtub with me on our trip, his thick forearms resting on the sides, and the tattoo of a mountain storm that snaked over his biceps and shoulder. That thought led to thoughts of what else had happened in that tub, and how much water had been left on the floor of the house we were staying in. It got me hot and bothered just thinking of it. "That could be arranged, but we'd probably need to go to your house because you're far too large for my tub."

"Thank you," he said, and I could absolutely hear the male pride in his tone.

"Thank you for the robe. Is there a reason you gave me a gift early?"

"There is. It's a piece of your Valentine's Day present. You'll be getting more as Valentine's Day gets closer."

"That sounds exciting."

"Just wait until the big reveal."

I bit down on a smile as my mind raced, imagining what Hawke had up his sleeve.

Chapter Nine

My phone rang. I looked at the caller and saw Annie's number. Annie was obviously my friend, but also the local EMT who was usually the medical professional on scene for my mom's adventures. Which meant she was either calling about the upcoming male revue show we'd been invited to by Clarissa, or she was calling about my mom. The fact that she was calling instead of texting was an immediate cause of concern.

"Hello," I answered, my tone hesitant.

"Hi, Kate. Are you busy?" Her tone sounded normal, but a little hushed.

"No," I answered slowly. "What has my mom done now?" I hadn't heard anything come across the scanner, but you never know with Sophie Saxee. She might be on a covert chaos causing mission instead of her usual overt plans.

Annie gave a laugh that felt like she was trying to act non-concerned and failing. "You should come to the Fourth Ward church house. Like, immediately."

I wrinkled my brow. "Okayyyy. Is there a reason my mom

is at a church?" She wasn't an active member of the Mormon church but in a town where over ninety-five percent of people are Mormon, it's hard to avoid church-related events and social activities.

"Yes. And there was an incident." I heard some yelling in the background and Annie's tone turned more urgent. "Just come down."

"On my way," I said.

My mom was dressed up in a curly blonde wig with a floppy garden hat. She had on a bright pastel floral dress in white and yellow that looked like a costume straight out of pioneer times. She was wearing oversized glasses, and carrying a basket full of treats. The kids were crowded around her like Gandalf and his little friend, Pocket, circle when a human near them has food.

I knew this costume. She'd worn it when I was a kid. My mom had been an actress in her youth and had continued acting in community theater as she got older. She liked to create characters, and one of her more well-known personas was Mrs. Friendly. The LDS Church puts out a magazine for kids every month called *The Friend*. Mrs. Friendly would come and talk about the articles in the magazine and act her way through them. It was a favorite of the kids in Mormon primary…mostly because she always brought treats. I thought she'd retired Mrs. Friendly years ago, but that didn't seem to be the case.

A group of parents were arguing near her.

Annie walked over to me, her shoulders tense. "Thanks for

coming," she said, scratching the side of her lip nervously. "I thought you might be able to help."

I gave her a bewildered look. "I'm not sure if I can, but I'll try. What's happening?"

Sheila Groll stomped up to me, her cheeks red with rage and hissed, "Your morally decrepit mother was teaching them the song about the drug dragon!"

My mom's face screwed up into an angry expression and she speed walked to Shelia's side. "That song is NOT about drugs. It's a sweet song about a boy who believed in dragons and then got older and stopped believing. I can't understand why you would say such a silly thing, Sheila."

Sheila fisted her hands at her side. "I should have known someone who believed in keeping witches on their lawn year-round, and celebrated a Satanic holiday like Halloween, would do something like this."

"Halloween actually takes its roots from the Celtic festival of Samhain and Paganism," I pointed out—not for the first time. It drove me nuts when the only religion people were an expert in was their own. "And the song writers have said repeatedly in interviews that the dragon song is not about drugs."

Sheila shot daggers at me with her eyes. "For a long time, I thought you were the only sinner in the family, Kate. But between her horrible witches and the drug indoctrination of children, now I see where you get it from."

My mom's response was immediate. Her back arched, her spine straightened so she was even taller than her usual five-foot-two inches, and her expression went from livid to expressionless, which I knew was actually scarier than anger because it meant she'd transitioned to barely-controlled fury.

Have you ever seen a cobra right before it strikes? Because that's what she looked like.

"How *DARE* you, Sheila Groll!" Her tone was low and came out a little demonic, which probably didn't support her overall case for being a good example. "Attacking me, and my daughter, and trying to turn me into a devil in the eyes of these little children. I was teaching them a sweet song and you're the one who declared it was about marijuana! How do you even know about that drug and the song, Sheila? No one else did. So, I'd say that makes you the sinner, not me!"

"*Everyone* knows it's about marijuana!" Sheila said, throwing up her arms. "I can't believe you would bring such wicked ideas to kids!"

"I learned it in primary!" my mom countered.

"*Well,*" Sheila answered with a heaping amount of judgment, "You must have had a *much* more liberal primary teacher than I did. I won't have my grandkids brainwashed like this, and I'm going to petition the church to no longer allow you to act as Mrs. Friendly!"

Sheila stomped off and my mom's expression was warring between anger and worry that she really had done something wrong.

"If it makes you feel any better, I always loved that song," I said, putting my arm around her.

"Me too," Annie said.

"And neither one of us became drug addicts," I pointed out.

My mom laughed and hugged me back. "Maybe it's time to retire Mrs. Friendly. I have better things to do with my time."

A friend came over to talk to her and I stepped to the side with Annie. "Thanks for calling me."

She rubbed a hand over the back of her neck in a soothing

gesture. "Thanks for coming down. I was a little worried Sheila and your mom would come to blows."

Sheila had once criticized my mom's cookie frosting, so she was high on my mom's list of enemies. "It's been building for a while. They aren't each other's biggest fans."

"Are you still coming to the," she paused, trying to figure out what to call it, "event this weekend?"

I laughed at her attempt to be stealthy. "I'm a fan of hot, naked men, so I wouldn't miss it."

Annie grinned. "Oh, I know. I've seen the photos."

I shook my head and gave an amused snort, thinking about how ridiculous it was that the ghost tour had shown up right as Drake decided to make a move. "I think everyone has."

"I'm just jealous you got to go to a beach. The snow is nice at first, but by January, I'm over it and ready for sand, sunshine, and the ocean."

I froze. Like, every muscle in my extremities had stopped receiving messages from my brain. I blinked to see if my face still worked. "Wait. What beach?"

She drew her brows together. "The beach you were on with Hawke."

A chorus of swear words that started with F flew through my head.

Her lips turned down in a frown. "I was sad it was blurry. I wanted a better look at Hawke's tattoo."

Holy shit. Holy shit. Holy shit. Please tell me we weren't naked.

"I'm surprised you weren't naked. I would have been."

Phew. I blew out a breath. We weren't naked in those photos, but there were plenty of times we were. I needed to get to my phone and see what had been released. "I have to go," I said, my tone more urgent than I wished it was. "Tell my mom I'll talk to her later, and I'll see you this weekend."

I'd been trying to spend less time on my phone, so I'd shut off all my personal social media notifications, and had started turning my phone color to greyscale at certain times of the day because black and white videos weren't nearly as entertaining as color ones and I didn't spend as much time watching funny dogs. I'd also set times for my phone to be on Do Not Disturb, like this morning while I was meditating. Only numbers I'd given permission to could get through, and Annie's was one of those. Not knowing when scandalous photos of me dropped was an unintentional side effect I hadn't considered when I'd implemented this dumbass plan.

I got to the car, flipped my phone back to color, and immediately found the photos of me and Hawke on a beautiful Puerto Rico beach with golden sand, and gorgeous turquoise water. In some of the photos we were sitting next to each other. In others we were curled around each other and kissing. And then there were the ones where we were in the water with my arms around his neck, and though you couldn't see it, my legs were wrapped around his rock-hard waist and his hands were on my ass. I breathed a sigh of relief that the photographer hadn't caught us having sex, and was also dumbfounded about how they hadn't. Maybe they'd decided not to release those photos. Or maybe Hawke had already killed the person who took them.

I called Hawke and when he answered, I tried not to shriek. "How did this happen?"

He sighed. "I'm not happy about it either. I pride myself on security and had vetted that location and used it before."

I tapped my finger on my leg, trying to rein in my anxiety.

"I mean, I thought we were in the clear. We've kept it a secret for over two months."

"The photos came from a drone. Interest in our love triangle picked up again on the podcasts and chat forums when you and Drake were photographed the other night. The person who had the footage of us realized who we were and posted it."

I closed my eyes and leaned my head back against my seat. "I guess there's nothing to be done about it now." The cat was so far out of the bag that it was in another country.

"I'll get them removed and make sure there aren't more photos," he said that like he meant the naked ones, "but it will take a little time."

I sighed, trying to process it all, and something Hawke had said earlier came back to me. "Hold on, did you say you'd used that location before?"

The line went silent.

Anger started to bubble in my veins and with lethal calm I asked, "Do you take all of your sexual conquests there?"

"Only the special ones."

I couldn't tell if he was trying to be funny or just telling the truth. Either way, I didn't feel great about it. I'd thought I mattered to him and that the first place we went away together, let alone had sex, would be special. I took a deep breath, trying hard to be an adult. We both had pasts and that was fine. It was fine. Everything was fine. I felt like the meme with the dog and everything on fire while he sits in a chair. "Okay. I can't tell if you're joking right now so I'm going to pretend that you had that spot picked out for us and it mattered. I'm hanging up now."

I sat in my Jeep with my head on the steering wheel and

my eyes closed. If anyone walked by, they'd probably think I was having some sort of medical event. Maybe I was. My phone buzzed with a text message. I'd wondered how long it would take Hawke to do damage control.

I picked up the phone.

It wasn't Hawke.

The text was from Drake.

It wasn't even a phone call. Just one text.

Five words.

DRAKE

I know about Puerto Rico.

Shit.

Chapter Ten

I knew Drake was beyond busy with the legislature and there was no way he'd be able to come home so we could talk about this in person. I felt like I owed it to him to have a face-to-face conversation. So, I drove to Salt Lake City to the state Capitol where we could talk.

The last thing I wanted was for him to find out about Hawke and Puerto Rico this way. To be honest, I didn't want him to find out at all. I wouldn't want to know if Drake had been having marathon sex on a beach for days with another woman. I didn't know what was going to happen with Hawke and Drake in the future, but I didn't want to hurt the relationship as we were still exploring it. Talking to him was the right thing to do.

I walked in, my media badge in hand, and was promptly denied access by Capitol police.

"You can't come in," the officer said.

I held up my badge. "I'm media."

"You have to be escorted now."

I clenched my teeth. They hadn't wasted any time implementing the new rule. "I've been a reporter for years and have always had media access."

"You have to go through a special process now."

I straightened my spine and pulled back my shoulders, ready to launch into a policy critique when I heard a male voice behind me and turned, recognizing Senator Tanner. I hadn't seen him since I was investigating Chelsea Bradford's disappearance and murder last summer. "It's okay, John," he said coming forward. "She's one of Drake's."

My eyes went wide and I stared at him, hard. "One of Drake's what?"

Senator Tanner ignored my question and waved his hand like he was telling a dog to sit. "I'll take her to Drake's office."

I was getting more irritated by the second. "I don't need an escort."

He gave me a knowing look that bordered on condescending, then took my hand and wrapped it around his arm. "Help an old man get down the hall, Katie."

We started walking. "I'm happy to walk with you, Senator Tanner, and I appreciate your help, but I can get to Drake's office by myself."

"Not without someone from the capitol with you. You're a member of the press."

"I'm credentialed."

Senator Tanner shook his head. "Things are different now."

I could feel my heart pounding hard in my chest and it was just getting louder. "The change in law was wrong and I've talked to Drake about the lack of transparency, but we're still supposed to be given access."

"Not in certain areas," he said, and dropped me by Drake's

door. "It was good seein' ya, Katie! Make sure Drake walks ya out!"

I was seething. This was a massive miscarriage of justice and as a member of the press, I was livid. I took some deep breaths because I came to talk to Drake, who was probably pissed as hell at me, and I didn't want to take my own anger out on him.

When I felt like I'd gotten myself under control, I opened the door to his office and walked inside. A pretty woman with strawberry blonde hair was sitting at the desk. I recognized her from her nametag. "Hi, Greycie. Can I speak to Drake?"

She looked at my press badge and her eyes widened with recognition. "Of course, Kate. It's nice to meet you in person. Let me see if he's available."

She got up and opened the door leading into the next room, then shut it. She was inside for about thirty seconds before Drake walked out wearing black dress shoes, blue slacks, and a white shirt with the sleeves rolled up to his elbows showcasing his muscular forearms. A silver tie hung from his neck and every dark hair on his head was perfectly placed.

"Kate," he said, a smile on his face that was not a smile at all. "Why don't you come into my office."

I nodded and followed him. He closed the door behind me.

A grey couch was in the corner of the room and he gestured to it.

I sat, and Drake leaned against the front of his desk, his arms folded across his chest and his legs crossed at the ankles.

I looked at him. He looked back at me. We were both waiting for each other to go first but based on the vein bulging in his neck, I gathered that he probably wasn't speaking because he was afraid of what he'd say.

This was my mess to clean up. I put my hands in my lap and met his eyes. "So, I got your text."

He sliced his head down once.

"I wanted to talk to you about it, and felt like it should be a conversation in person."

"Noble of you."

I pressed my lips together and took a breath through my nose. "I didn't mean for you to find out this way."

His forehead wrinkled and his eyes widened. "Find out that you took a sex-filled vacation with Hawke? Or that you're choosing him?"

Okay, so it *was* sex-filled, but that hadn't been in the photos. "First, the photos didn't show us having sex."

He rolled his eyes. Hard.

This was going well. I sat up straighter, still looking him in the eye. "And I haven't chosen anyone. I told you both when we discussed this arrangement that I'd been burned by my ex and I wasn't ready to jump into a relationship. That I needed time to get to know you and figure out how we would work together as a couple. You both agreed. We didn't put ground rules around what that would look like."

His shoulders tightened. "You lied by omission."

Funny we were having the omission discussion again.

"I guess, technically?" I lifted my arms with my palms up and shrugged. "This is a strange situation we're in Drake. I'm learning to navigate it at the same time you are. Do you want me to tell you everything I'm doing with Hawke, and when? Do you want me to tell him when I'm with you and what we've done? Where are the lines?"

He angled his head. "That's a good question."

I leaned forward. "Do we need to answer it?"

A muscle pulsed in Drake's jaw. "I heard you were with Hawke the other day after I left your house."

I licked my lips and wished I'd brought some water with me. "I'm with him sometimes. Just like I'm with you."

"Any reason he was at your house for so long?"

I considered how to answer that because he still hadn't answered the question of how much he wanted to know. "He'd been gone for several weeks for work and we were catching up."

Drake's tongue ran over the inside of his cheek. "Catching up."

"I caught up with you the other day, too."

The tip of his tongue traced his top lip and he shook his head. "Not that kind of catching up, I think."

He was right and I didn't know how to respond to that, so I didn't.

He stared at me, his arms still crossed and his index finger tapping on his biceps. "The problem here is that I'm at a huge disadvantage. Hawke has taken you on a damn trip to an island. And more."

I knew what was bothering him and I couldn't blame him for it, but also, it was naïve. "I'm not bound by the same rules as you, Drake. Did you think I wouldn't have sex?"

Based on the way the vein at his temple popped, that's exactly what he'd thought.

"We've kissed, and that's it," he ground the last part out.

And that's all we'd probably ever do because Drake was Mormon. "Do you want more than that?"

He stared and waited several long seconds before answering, "Maybe I do."

I tilted my head to the side, trying to understand. "You're kind of bound by your beliefs in regards to that." Growing up as a Mormon in Utah, I'd been taught that the only sin worse than sex outside of marriage and other sexual sins, was murder. Drake still believed that.

I watched his expression change as he seemed to make some sort of decision. He unwrapped his arms from his chest and put his palms on the edge of the desk, next to his narrow hips. "When do I get the opportunity to take you on vacation?"

I furrowed my brow. "I mean, is that even allowed?"

"Dating?"

"Going off with a woman alone when you're both unmarried. I was raised Mormon, Drake. In high school, we weren't even allowed to go on single dates because of the threat that we wouldn't be able to keep our hands off each other."

His eyes sparked. "That's absolutely still a threat, and one that I'll embrace."

My heart started speeding up at what he was suggesting. "A trip like that would make you lose your temple recommend."

"There are degrees."

My eyes widened. "To sinning?"

He tapped his foot against the stone floor and seemed to be thinking.

I didn't want to be the reason he got kicked out of the church. He wouldn't, because he was a man and an influential one at that, but still, I didn't want the guilt of being blamed for his transgressions. As a woman, I'd been blamed like that by the LDS church my whole life and told my actions, words, and the clothes I wore were responsible for men's actions. That wasn't true, and I wasn't about to be held up as a bad example for people who still believed that way. "Look, the bottom line is that I care about you." I threaded my fingers together and paused before meeting his eyes. "I don't know what that means, and I'm not ready to define it yet, or make a choice between you and Hawke, but if you don't want to keep doing this, I understand."

I had been pushed into relationships before and had learned the hard way that I needed to figure out what I wanted if I expected a relationship to work long-term. If Drake wasn't comfortable waiting for me to do that, I wouldn't fault him for it. I could also admit that I'd have a hard time if the situation was reversed. Maybe things wouldn't work out with Hawke either, and maybe I'd lose them both. I had no idea what would happen, but I knew if I was true to myself, I wouldn't have regrets.

Drake met my eyes, his face an unreadable mask. "I need some time to think."

I nodded and stood, grabbing my purse. "That's understandable. I'll give you some space."

Drake walked me out of the Capitol building and we said goodbye. My stomach felt hollow, and I wondered if we'd just said goodbye for the last time as a potential couple. I was sad because it felt like we'd never really had a chance.

I checked my phone when I got in my car and had a message from Spence. Someone on social media said Whitney had been spotted at a ski resort. I would be passing the resort on my way home and could be there with a twenty-minute detour. I needed something to take my mind off the conversation I'd just had with Drake, and steered my Jeep toward the mountains.

I went to the front desk and pasted on a big smile with bright eyes. "Hi, I'm looking for a friend named Whitney Hatch."

The hotel worker did something on his computer. "We can't release personal information to anyone."

I pushed my bottom lip out, lines forming between my brows in disappointment. "Oh, okay. I was supposed to be with her, and I can't get ahold of her. Do you mind if I leave her a note, just in case she's staying here? And if she is, you could give it to her?"

I was trying to get more information or some confirmation that Whitney was there, and he knew it. "You're welcome to do whatever you'd like, ma'am."

I tried not to take the 'ma'am' personally. I grabbed my notebook and pen from my purse and scribbled out a note introducing myself, telling her I was concerned, and asking her to call me and let me know she was okay.

I pulled up a photo of her and showed it to the hotel worker. "This is Whitney. Does she look familiar at all?"

He took my phone. "There are a lot of pretty blonde ladies here, ma'am."

I nodded in concession. "That's the truth. Please give this to her if she happens to come back."

It was a dead end for now, but maybe it would turn into something later.

Chapter Eleven

I turned over in my bed the next morning, Gandalf cuddled next to me in an adorable little ball, half under the pillow. It had been a long day yesterday and I'd come home and crashed. It was a weekend and Spence was on call, so I'd slept in this morning. I couldn't stop thinking about Drake and our conversation. I had no idea when we'd talk again. Probably after February when the legislature adjourned. The thought made my stomach clench and I was sad.

To be fair, he wasn't wrong. Hawke did have an advantage because sex mattered to me and making sure I was sexually compatible with the man I was with also mattered. There had been a lot of gossip about Drake's prowess with women over the years, but he'd denied it and I wasn't sure if he'd ever really been with a woman before, let alone as many as he was rumored to be with. But I didn't think he'd be with one now. Not when his job, and his future as a politician, and his eternal life—if he was a true believer, depended on it.

Drake could probably get away with whatever he wanted —men usually did. The bigger question was: could I participate in his downfall. And that was a question I didn't have an answer for.

I got out of bed and did yoga, then moved on to weights and cardio. When I was done, I took a long shower, then made breakfast for myself and Gandalf. I turned on the fireplace in the living room while I drank my coffee and read a romantasy novel about a woman with two soul mates—I could relate. I played tug of war with Gandalf, made another cup of coffee from my ridiculously complicated coffee machine, and worked on a puzzle while I re-listened to one of my favorite podcasts, *Witch* on BBC. It was nice to take the day, be with myself, and just relax. I rarely took time to decompress and needed to do more of it.

At five, I got ready for the night's festivities. I didn't get a chance to wear sexy clothes often in Branson Falls, so I'd carefully selected my outfit. I was wearing black leather skintight pants, and a light blue metallic backless top that was being held together by a jeweled string that attached to both sides of the fabric across my shoulder blades. The neckline draped in a U-shape cowl neck, showing my cleavage. My heels were black, high, and had silver studs on them. My hair was curled in beachy waves, and my lipstick was hot pink. When I was finished, I took Gandalf to my mom and dad's.

My mom opened the door and seemed a bit frazzled, but paused her frenzy to look me up and down. "Well, at least that's more than you were wearing in the photos I saw of you and Hawke yesterday."

And she hadn't even seen the missing back of the shirt because I was wearing a coat. I arched a brow, my eyes sparkling. "Just be glad the more revealing photos weren't leaked."

She shook her head like she was pretending to be disappointed, but I knew if she'd been given the opportunity to go away with someone who looked like Hawke when she was my age, she would not have said no.

A bark came from inside the house and Gandalf ran through the door to inspect the noise, confront any potential intruders, find his toys, and secure the treats my mom had probably left out for him. "Pocket came over to play with Gandalf."

I smiled. "That's adorable. I love that they each have a buddy."

She shifted from one foot to the other, antsy. "Is there anything else you need?"

I gave her a confused look. "No. Are you okay? Do you need to pee?"

She snorted and shook her head several times before wiping her hand on her shoulder towel. "What a silly question. What time will you be back to pick Gandalf up?"

I paused, analyzing her expression and trying to figure out what was going on. "I'm not sure. Probably before eleven."

"Okay then!" she clapped her hands together and grabbed the edge of the door to shut it even though I was still there. "We'll see you later tonight!"

I wasn't sure what was going on, but it felt like she was trying to get me to leave. "Bye," I said uncertainly as I stepped off the porch and walked to my Jeep.

She gave an overly enthusiastic wave and closed the door. It was weird, but in the realm of strange behavior for Sophie Saxee, it was about a three out of ten so I wasn't too concerned.

I pointed my Jeep toward "111 Healing and Crystals and

Hot Mostly Naked Men," and hoped to arrive early enough to talk to Clarissa.

I got there before anyone else. Clarissa smiled when she saw me, and motioned for me to follow her into her office. She was also dressed to impress with a short, gold, spaghetti strap bandage dress and gold heels.

"I heard you were trying to find me the other day?"

I sat across from her. "I was. I have more questions for you. Is Whitney at a ski resort?"

Clarissa pressed her lips together. "I'd rather not say."

"Someone recognized her there yesterday."

Clarissa's eyes widened before she could school her reaction.

"I stopped to leave a note for her to call me just in case the tip was real. Have you heard from her yet?"

She took a breath and put her palms on her desk. "No."

"But you aren't worried?" I asked.

She lifted a shoulder. "No," she said, completely unconcerned.

It was so strange. She had to know something she wasn't telling me. "I was looking up public records information on Whitney and glanced at 111's business registration info."

Clarissa's breath hitched in her chest and lines of worry quickly formed and then eased as she caught herself.

"Why isn't Whitney listed as one of your business partners?"

Clarissa sighed and leaned back in her chair. "It's compli-cated. We each had our own businesses going into this together, so we kept our companies and 111 pays Whitney a salary for now. Whitney knew she was likely filing for divorce, and didn't want Cory to be able to take half of the business, so we did it this way on purpose. Once everything is settled with her marriage, we plan to make changes."

Okay, that made sense. I'd heard of people having to sell their businesses because one of the partners was going through a divorce and their spouse was entitled to half of their portion of the company. It could get messy, fast. "That was smart thinking on your part."

"I know some good lawyers," she said, and I wondered if she was referencing Family Law Consultants.

Still, that's a lot of faith to put in a friend. "Whitney trusts you that much?"

She lifted her shoulders like it wasn't even a question. "I think we both trust each other implicitly."

"Were you worried about her divorce affecting your business with the community?"

She winced. "I'm not going to lie. Yes. I've seen other businesses have to close because people in town refuse to support someone who asked their husband for a divorce. Luckily, 111 has a pretty open-minded clientele, and it hasn't affected us too much yet. It wouldn't have mattered if it had hurt the business, though. I still would have encouraged Whitney to leave him."

I tilted my head in interest. "Why do you think Cory is such a bad husband?"

She pressed her lips together. "It's not my story to tell, but I hope Whitney will share it eventually."

I hoped so too, and hoped she'd be found, or come home

soon, to tell it. "Does she have a timetable for when she's supposed to be back?"

"I haven't heard from her, but she's slated to come home next week."

I was getting a bit frustrated with all the non-answers and decided to push. I put my hands in my lap and sat straighter. "I've tried calling, and can't reach her," I said. "Her number goes straight to voicemail. I understand why some people are worried. I know I'm a member of the press and you don't know me well. I also understand that you're her best friend, and she asked you not to tell anyone where she is. Given the way she's been treated, I don't blame you, but I'm just trying to find out if she's okay. No one can reach her, including you, and you're the only one who knows where she is. Can you give me something?"

Clarissa closed her eyes and put her hand to her temple for several seconds before looking at me. "She's at a no-tech retreat. A lot of places are doing retreats like that now to help people decompress. She felt like it would be a good space for her to have some time to think. I know she arrived at the retreat and haven't heard from her since, but I didn't expect to. That's why I'm not worried."

I blew out a breath. "That makes a lot more sense. Thank you for telling me."

She nodded. "Please don't share the information with anyone. Whitney really didn't want anyone to know."

"I won't." I crossed my legs and shifted in my chair. "I was here the other day looking for you, and overheard some women talking. They said Whitney had been cheating with the husbands of her clients."

Clarissa pressed her lips together. "There was an accusation."

"Is that why you encouraged Whitney to leave Branson?"

Clarissa scratched the corner of her mouth like she was thinking. "She was already planning on taking the trip, like I told you before. But I did tell her she might want to leave early. I thought it could help her to get away and give things time to cool off."

I inclined my head in agreement. "That's not a bad idea. Do you think things will have cooled off by the time she comes back?"

She frowned. "I don't know. I feel like it might be getting worse."

I did too.

A tinkling bell on the front door rang, indicating someone had walked in. Clarissa looked at her watch. "People are going to start arriving so I better go out there. But let me know if you have any other questions I can answer, Kate. I really do appreciate that you're so concerned about Whitney. She means a lot to me."

"Thanks for being willing to answer my questions," I said, following her out the door.

She went to say hello to the people who had walked in, and I took some notes on my phone.

The information about the no-tech retreat was helpful, but it didn't prove she was okay. Cory thought she might be in danger and Clarissa was the only one who knew where she was and even Clarissa couldn't reach Whitney to guarantee that she was fine. If this was one of my closest friends, I'd be concerned. I wasn't sure who to believe, Clarissa, or Whitney's worried husband. They both claimed to care for her, and they both had motive for making Whitney disappear. Clarissa, because of the business and what Whitney's reputation could do to it, not only with the divorce, but also the cheating accusations. And Cory because of the divorce, which I now knew was also related to the business and Whitney's refusal to leave it and do what he wanted her to. There was more to this story, and I had to be patient if I wanted to figure it out. Clarissa wasn't the type to trust easily. Or maybe she had been at one time and life, and her ex, had made her into who she was today.

We walked into the yoga room decorated with hearts, shiny metallic balloons, and glittery ribbons that hung from the ceiling. My mom would love it. The room had light colored hardwood floors, and the front was currently reserved as a dance space. There were doors on the sides of the dance area. Chairs were set up in rows in the middle, and a table with snacks and drinks was set up at the back.

Annie walked in, her hair freshly colored in blonde with streaks of teal, and wearing sexy black leggings and a shimmery green spaghetti strap tank top. "You look great!" I said, and meant it. I'd never seen her in something like this. "Just don't let your bishop see you in that."

"He doesn't see me much at all anymore, to be honest. We don't go often anymore."

"I didn't realize that."

She lifted a shoulder. "We're figuring it out, but my shelf cracked a while ago."

The shelf was referred to by Mormons because any time a

member had a question or doubted the church, they were told to put their questions and doubts on the shelf because all would be answered later—once they died, or the Second Coming occurred. Some people had very full shelves, and at some point, there was usually something that would make it crack and then break. My shelf had been overflowing and destroyed by age ten. But in such a small Utah community, I would have been ostracized if I'd left the church at that age, so I'd waited until college.

Jacey and Wendy both walked in, their expressions excited and nervous all at once. Other women also arrived, some confidently striding into the room, others walking slowly, eyes darting around like they were about to do crime. In a place like Branson Falls, this level of defiance and sexual exploration kind of was a criminal act, but I was proud of every woman here for defining what she wanted instead of letting beliefs set for her by others do it for them.

"Do you want to get food?" Annie asked.

"Definitely," I answered.

We walked to the table at the back, filled our plates with treats, and grabbed a drink. I'd just taken a bite of a petit four when two disco balls walked into the room and I almost choked. It was like the room had gone supernova. I'd never seen so many sequins, and again, I was a Neil Diamond fan.

"Aren't those sequins the same ones the inflatable witches on your mom and dad's lawn are wearing?" Annie asked.

I nodded as I took a drink of water and tried to wash down the shock and awe campaign that had just been performed on my eyeballs. When I could talk again, I answered. "She bought the sequins in bulk and will probably be using them for the rest of time, though after this, I'm not sure how she has any left."

She was wearing a shirt covered with black lace, the hems of the arms trimmed in lace scallops. Silver sequins covered so much of the shirt that I could barely see it. Her pants were wide legged and looked like they'd come straight from the set of a 1970s TV show. Every inch of them was covered in hot pink sequins. Every. Single. Inch. She'd added sequin bows to her black high heels, and she was wearing a long, straight black wig.

Her cohort, Ella, was wearing a similar outfit, only hers was a jumpsuit completely covered in silver sequins. At Mormon Girls Camp, we used to make tin foil dinners and Ella looked a lot like the personification of the meal. She was wearing big hoop earrings, and a yellow wig that looked exactly like my mom's Mrs. Friendly hair. I wasn't sure if that meant Mrs. Friendly had come a long way, or finally fallen. She was wearing pink flats and judging by how much glitter she was leaving in her wake, she'd hot glued it on right before she left home.

My mom saw me and froze. Her gaze darted around the room, clearly looking for a place to hide. I recognized the reaction from when I was young and got caught for watching an R-rated movie.

I waved at her. "Too late to run, Mom. I've already seen you."

She schooled her expression into a surprised smile as she walked toward me and I could practically see her mind churning to quickly come up with a plausible explanation. "Kate! I didn't know you were coming here tonight! I read your article about the store and was *so* intrigued! I was just coming to look at the crystals!"

I put a finger to my lips as I listened to her impromptu explanation. "Except the store closed two hours ago."

She scrunched up her face and gave up the lie faster than I expected her to. "Oh, *fine!*" she said, throwing her arms up in the air. "I heard about the show and have always wanted to go to one and see if they really wear the little bowties."

I burst out laughing and Annie full-on lost it and almost spit out the dirty soda she'd been drinking. "That was *not* something I *ever* expected to hear from you."

"I like to keep you on your toes," she preened, wiggling her shoulders.

Keeping me on my toes was something she excelled at. "How did you find out about the show?"

She looked down and rearranged some of the sequins on her shirt. Clearly, my dad hadn't performed his civic duty and removed the box of shiny circles from my mom's craft room. "I overheard you and Annie talking about it at the church the other day and asked around."

There weren't many people she could "ask around" about this.

Ella was looking up at the ceiling, walls, and anywhere but me. Bingo. "So, you asked *Ella*, and the two of you found out the details about the show and decided to come."

Ella looked straight at me. "Do you know how hard it is to find male strippers in Utah? I certainly wasn't gonna miss a buncha hot naked men right here in Branson!"

I raised my hands in defense. "I wouldn't dream of asking you to."

"Well," she said, her arms crossed over her chest in offense, "you certainly didn't tell me about it."

"Or me!" my mom chimed in, crossing her arms as well. The two of them looked like sparkly twin furies.

"Because I was under the impression this was an invite-only event. And also, it didn't even occur to me that the two of you might want to get air-fondled by some guys in their twenties."

My mom gasped and shook her head adamantly. "It's a performance, Kate!"

She was right about that.

"You knew I was going to be here, but acted surprised when I saw you. Did you think I wouldn't notice you?"

She wrinkled her nose. "That's why we wore disguises."

My eyes bulged as I lifted my hand up and down in front of them. "If you were going for stealth with these nuclear outfits, you missed the mark."

Ella reached a hand up to her hair. "We also wore wigs! No one's ever seen me as a blonde."

I put a hand to my mouth to try and cover my smile. "I don't think either one of you has a future as a spy." I looked my mom over with the same level of scrutiny she'd given me when I'd dropped Gandalf off earlier. "The pants are new. I thought you would have chosen a dress."

She squinted at me and scrunched up her face. "A dress isn't very functional for a situation like this. I need to be able to move."

I blinked. "Do you think you'll be fighting someone?"

"No, but I don't want to flash people if I get thrown around a bit!"

I eyed her. "You know far more about how these *perfor-mances* work than I would expect someone like you to know."

The corners of her lips curled up slowly in a satisfied smile that seemed to hold more secrets than I was comfortable with.

Ella interrupted my thoughts, "Did ya get my texts about you and Hawke on the beach?"

I looked at her with no small amount of annoyance. "I did. And my mom's *right* here."

My mom backed Ella up. "I'm pretty upset I don't know details as well."

No.

Absolutely not.

"It was a private beach and no one was supposed to know any details. What you saw is all you'll get."

My mom frowned and Ella made a hmphh noise. "I'm goin' to get some refreshments before this starts. Wanna come, Sophie?"

My mom nodded. "Yes, hydration is important for something like this."

Annie and I watched them walk away. "I think they have a different set of expectations for tonight than I do," Annie said.

They stopped, my mom putting her hands on her hips and gyrating in a circular motion. Ella mimicked her, practicing. I couldn't do anything but shake my head. "Me too."

Music started to play and Clarissa walked in the room and told everyone to take their seats.

The chairs were arranged in rows, but they were spread out so everyone had a good view of the stage. We had seats on the front row, and my mom and Ella had secured their seats there as well so they "wouldn't miss a thing."

A new song started and doors on both sides of the room

opened as five men came out, dressed like firefighters. They started dancing immediately and moved in time to the song. The women were screaming, standing, and dancing as the men, with zero body fat, slowly removed their heavy coats, then shrugged out of their suspenders, and ripped their pants off in synchronicity revealing shiny black G-strings.

"Take it off!" Ella yelled, throwing dollar bills at them in a frenzy.

Annie leaned over so I could hear her above the music. "She came prepared."

"I think she thought this was a stripper situation like my mom's Valentine's Day witch display, not a male revue."

The men turned around, nothing but skin covering their asses, and my mom almost fell off her chair. She righted herself, never taking her eyes off their butts.

Annie laughed and the music died down as the guys left the stage. Five more came out as the next song started.

This one was a cowboy scene. They started with tight jeans being held up by big belt buckles. They had plaid shirts, brown cowboy boots, and cowboy hats. The shirts came off first, then the belts. Two of the dancers pulled Ella and my mom up on stage, dancing around them, and then sitting them in a chair for a lap dance. Ella was having the time of her life, and my mom's face could not have been redder, but she was enjoying it. As the dancer in front of my mom picked up her chair, I had to admit that she'd been right about wearing pants. The song finished, and Ella and my mom stumbled back to their chairs like they'd just had a religious experience.

The room darkened and smoke machines whirled as fog filled the room, creating a feeling of spooky mystery. Five men wearing black suits and face masks appeared through the smoke. Male revues were centered on telling stories. This must be the sexy billionaire masquerade scene. Seductive, slow music started playing, and the men started moving to it, telling a story as they slowly removed their suit jackets, then untied their ties. Suddenly the lighting shifted and everything went black. A spotlight focused on another man walking in from one of the side doors, and out on the stage. He was wearing a white shirt, flat black tie, and black slacks. His shoulders were wide and tapered down to narrow hips. He had hair that was dark, shoulder-length, and a little messy. Like the other men, he was wearing a full masquerade face mask, decorated in black and white. He resembled one of the sexy villains from a fantasy novel.

He went from woman to woman, teasing and getting bolder with each interaction. Ella looked like she might lunge and try to climb him. My mom looked like she might faint, and Annie's eyes sparkled with appreciation. And then he turned his attention directly on me. He came over, stopped in front of my chair, and held out his hand.

"What are you waiting for?" Annie said, encouraging me to accept his offer.

"Get out there or I will!" Ella yelled.

I took his hand and he grabbed the chair I'd been sitting in with his other hand, dragging it with us to the middle of the stage. He guided me to the chair and stepped back, slowly unbuttoning his suit jacket and discarding it on the floor. He came toward me, a tower of muscle. He held out his hand again, asking for permission. I reached toward him and he ran his fingers up my arm to my bare shoulder, and back down again. Heat burned through me at the touch. He put my hand on his belt buckle and helped me pull, the buckle coming undone and hanging open.

As the music ramped up, he put one hand on the back of my chair, and used the other to almost caress my neck, like he was going to pull me closer and kiss me. He didn't touch me, but it sure as hell felt like he did. Instead, he swung his leg over my lap and straddled me, his other hand going to the back of the chair while his hips moved in circles above me, thrusting and gyrating. He shifted off my lap and his head trailed down, so close to mine that if it wasn't for the mask, his lips would surely be on my skin. He kept moving slowly, over my neck, between my breasts, to my belly button, and lower.

He ran his hands down one of my thighs before getting to my ankle, and shifting so his head was between my legs, each one resting on one of his shoulders. He didn't take his gaze away from mine as he powerfully pulled the chair I was sitting in toward him. He reached around my waist, put his hands on my ass, and lifted until we were both on the chair, and my hips were moving in tandem with his. The song hit a crescendo and he leaned back, ripping his shirt open, his straight black tie coming apart with his shirt. He took my hands and put them on his stomach, running them down his abs, then took the tie, and pressed it against my lips before he wrapped it around my wrists, pulling my arms above and then behind my head. He leaned down, his mouth next to my ear and breath hot on my neck, and in a rough, muffled voice whispered, "Find me later and I'll show you the rest."

I could hear the other women yelling with excitement, but my focus was completely on the man in front of me as he stood, taking my hand to help me out of the chair, and then dragged it back to the space next to Annie. He ran his fingers down my shoulder again before he pulled back slowly, as I took in every inch of his chest, his open shirt and abs, and his unlatched belt. He faded into the dark near one of the doors on the side of the room, and I felt like I needed an ice bath to recover.

The rest of the show was just as fun as the first part with scenes that included construction workers with tool belts, police officers with handcuffs, and some vampires with fangs. The show ended with the answer to my mom's question: yes, they really do wear the little bowties. But for me, nothing could beat that lap dance. It had just become a core memory, and I had a feeling not much would ever top it.

The show ended and all the women in the room were laughing and excited. I had a feeling that every one of them were about to go straight home, find their partners, and recreate some scenes.

"Well, I've never seen anythin' like that," Ella said, fanning herself as the men walked off stage. We were all flushed to varying degrees.

"I'd like to see it again!" my mom said. "Those Velcro pants gave me some ideas!"

I wasn't sure I wanted to hear what those ideas were.

The men came back out and women lined up to take photos. I looked at them all, trying to figure out which one of them had been wearing the mask. There were two with hair that could have been his, but that didn't really mean anything since they used different props and wigs to change their looks throughout the show. It could have been any of them, really. The offer had been tempting. There was a real possibility I was no longer dating Drake and I hadn't heard from Hawke since he dropped the news that I wasn't the only one he'd taken to that beach house. So, maybe I'd be searching for a new sex buddy soon, and this guy seemed like he definitely wouldn't be a disappointment.

My phone buzzed as I watched a woman on stage sit on a shirtless guy's thigh for a photo. I glanced down and saw the text was from Spence.

SPENCE

Have you seen this?

A photo popped up on my screen of Whitney Hatch, wearing nothing but strategically placed silk. The outline of her chest was clearly visible, and the fabric fell from there to wrap between her legs. Her head was tilted back, her eyes closed, and her expression euphoric. A link was attached to the photo. I clicked on it, and was sent to a Fanzy page. It was Whitney's.

My jaw dropped. I started to hear other phones buzz and ring around me, then the gasps that followed.

And all hell broke loose.

Chapter Twelve

Whitney's Fanzy account had spread like wildfire. The whole town was talking about it all night. The first thing I did the next morning was go to Cory's house.

He opened the door, looking even worse than the last time I saw him. His hair was matted like he hadn't showered in a week, and his beard hadn't been shaved in days. He was wearing wrinkled jeans and a t-shirt that needed a washing machine. "When was the last time you slept?" I asked as he motioned me inside the house.

He raised his shoulders slightly. "No idea."

"I'm so sorry about Whitney. I'd heard the rumors about her cheating, but I thought they stemmed from jealousy."

He looked down, his fingers fidgeting. "Yeah, me too."

"Did you have any idea about this?"

He ran his hands through his hair. "I thought something was going on. She was acting weird and that's one of the reasons I was worried when she left without a trace. No one will listen to me, though."

That had to be hard. His wife had an entire secret life he

knew nothing about. "Do you think she asked for a divorce to be with one of the guys she met on Fanzy?"

"I don't know. I just want to know where she is." He ran his palms down his thighs. "People are crazy! What if she didn't leave on vacation? What if she was taken?"

I didn't want to break Clarissa's trust and tell him where she was, but I also wanted to try and reassure him. "Clarissa said she knew where Whitney was and that Whitney should be coming back next week."

"What if Clarissa is involved?" he asked. "You're still looking for her, right?"

I shifted my head to the side. "Yeah, but it's mostly been dead-ends."

He grabbed my hands, his expression frantic. "You have to find her."

"I'll try," I said. He seemed more concerned with where she was than the fact she had a Fanzy page and a secret life. He was sleep deprived and exhausted though, so he probably wasn't functioning on all cylinders.

Someone knocked on the door and Cory answered it. Three men walked in, patting Cory on the back, and one gave him a hug. Cory introduced them as his friends. They came to bring him breakfast and see how he was doing. I was glad he had support.

I left so he could spend time with them. "Thanks for talking to me, Cory. I'll be in touch."

"Please keep me updated," he said, his tone pleading.

"I will."

As I walked away, I couldn't help thinking that Cory seemed nothing like the abusive husband Clarissa had described him as. It made me wonder what Clarissa might be hiding.

"Hot dang!" Ella exclaimed and clapped her hands together as I walked into the office. "This is the juiciest gossip since we found out you got naked on the beach in Puerto Rico with Hawke! Maybe juicier because Whitney's naked for money!"

I ignored the naked in Puerto Rico comments. "I was just at Cory's. He didn't know about the Fanzy page, and he's not doing great."

"Who do you think released the images and told people about it?" Spence asked.

"I've been wondering that myself."

The bell on the office door chimed and Shasta Hatch walked in wearing a smile made of spite. "Are you happy now, Kate?" she asked, folding her arms across her chest and taking a wide stance with her nose in the air. "You have *proof* that my sign was true."

I shouldn't have been surprised the bargain soda had come here to gloat. "No, I don't. She had a Fanzy page. Lots of people do. That doesn't mean she was cheating, and doesn't make it any less irresponsible to publish something so defamatory about another person."

Shasta pointed at me. "*You're* part of the problem. Whitney is ruinin' lives, and people like you are still defendin' her." She shook her head in disgust. "I hope she gets what's comin' to her."

I cocked my head to the side. "What's coming to her?"

Shasta raised her arms like she didn't know, but really did. "Probably excommunication from the church for starters. Losin' her husband and chance at top-tier Celestial, too. Her reputation is destroyed. Lots of consequences for somethin' like this. I just want you to remember whose side you were on."

I pushed my brows up. "Is that supposed to be a threat?"

Spence walked up next to me. "Threats aren't something we take lightly, Ms. Wentworth. We get the police involved with threats."

I'd be more afraid of Hawke than the police if I were her, but still.

"Not a threat, just information." Her voice had a sing-song mocking tone to it. Shasta picked up a piece of candy from the candy jar and sauntered out of the office.

Spence turned to me, his expression lined with concern. "I'm going to report her."

I lifted a shoulder. "On the list of things I'm worried about, she's low. I'll talk to Hawke, though."

Spence nodded and gave a relieved sigh.

I picked up my coffee thermos and took a drink. "Given how Shasta just acted, I wouldn't put it past her to have been the one who released the photos and sent the link."

"Is there any way to track where the messages originated?"

"Not really, at least, not without a warrant and time. There were a lot of screenshots, and anyone who followed her account could have accessed it and taken screenshots they shared, or downloaded photos."

I'd gone through the account the night before. There were a lot of sexy photos, and some X-rated ones, and she had hundreds of thousands of followers.

"How does Fanzy work?" Ella asked, like she hadn't been

on the site before. But I knew she'd looked at porn because she'd mentioned using a VPN for a similar site in the past, so I doubted she was ignorant of Fanzy. I gave her a look indicating I knew that she knew. She caught the look and put a hand to her chest, acting shocked. I rolled my eyes.

Spence must have forgotten about her habits. "Privacy is paramount," he said, "so you can't search for someone by name. You have to have a link. A lot of people put their links in their other social profiles so they'll get views, but it doesn't sound like Whitney did that. She had to be getting followers from somewhere though, because she has a lot of them."

I tapped a pen on my desk. "She had a ton of followers and was probably raking in the cash. I wonder where she got her followers from?"

"Wait!" Ella said, holding up her hands like everything needed to stop. "You can get paid on the site?"

Spence leaned against his door jam. "A lot. People pay to follow the creators, and they pay more for specific content. They can even request content. I know people making six figures a month."

Ella almost toppled over. "For showin' their boobs and naughty bits?"

"Some of them are doing more than that," I explained. "With videos, and requests. Some even go live and the more money they make, the more they perform. It doesn't have to be porn either. I've heard of people who dress up like their favorite romance novel hero or heroine, and read excerpts from books. But to be fair, the content that did best was sex. How did you think it worked when you were on similar sites?"

She glared at me like I'd broken an unspoken contract by

bringing it up. "I thought people just liked takin' naked pics and postin' 'em for people to see. It's like today's version of the old sculptures with naked hot people."

I pressed my lips together. "I'm not sure I'd compare Fanzy sites to ancient Greek and Roman sculptures."

Ella had already moved past that thought. "Why didn't anyone tell me about the cash! I could be makin' a fortune!"

I snorted. "You're already rich."

She tapped the side of her chin like she was thinking. "You can never be too rich. What if I want a super yacht?"

"To sail around The Great Salt Lake and collect brine shrimp and flies?" I asked, flatly.

She ignored me. "Think of the boat men I could hire!"

I was sure a Captain and their crew would be thrilled at her description of them.

I woke up my computer. "I'm going to do some digging and see if I can figure out where people were finding Whitney's link. If either one of you hear anything, let me know." This was all unfolding quickly and I was sure some of the information would fall through the cracks.

Spence nodded, and Ella grabbed a drink while contemplating the topic of her Fanzy page and the super yacht she was going to purchase with her earnings. I didn't want to know what she had up her sleeve.

I did a search for Whitney's Fanzy page link, which was really unhelpful now because it was everywhere. I couldn't pinpoint where she'd been advertising it before it was blasted out to everyone on earth. Some Fanzy account pages would post their content to online forums to get traction, but now Whitney's photos and videos were saturating the search results, so that was a dead-end as well. Someone had to know something, though. I just needed to keep an ear out.

I left to grab lunch for the office and it seemed like everyone in town was talking about Whitney and her downfall. No one had anything good to say. I listened to the conversation of women standing in line in front of me. They'd all heard of someone Whitney had cheated with, and I knew this was just the start of the stories. Now the question would become which stories were true, and which ones were made up or exaggerated to fit the narrative.

I was about to place my order when I heard yelling coming from outside. A large group carrying signs was marching down the street, and they were headed straight for the Branson Falls City building.

I picked up my phone and dialed Spence. "Did we get a notice about a protest today?"

Spence paused. "No."

"Well, there's one happening. I'm heading over there."

I hung up and left to follow the crowd.

The impromptu protest was clearly last minute, and in direct response to Whitney's Fanzy page. Handmade signs about the dangers of pornography dotted the snow-covered landscape, and the woman leading the way was a woman who'd never met a perm and hair color combination she didn't like: Jackie Wall. She was wearing white boots, beige pants, a tan colored coat, and a slouchy pink beany cap on her head.

She had a whole herd of The Ladies behind her. The Ladies, who were no stranger to protests, had used their crafting skills gained from years of Young Women's and Relief Society activities, to make their signs. They looked like they'd gotten a deal on poster board shapes because they were all oblong or round. As they stomped by me, the oblong posters stood higher than the round posters, and the perspective made it look like they were carrying around a bunch of penises with opinions. The irony of that was not lost on me, and I made sure to get photos. I probably couldn't run them in the paper, but I'd at least have them for my own enjoyment.

Jackie was currently leading everyone in a chant of, "Porn Ruins Lives!" I walked around taking photos and videos as Jackie changed the chant to, "Church, Not Porn!"

Annie walked up next to me. "It's funny because the majority of people in Branson who are looking at the porn are probably church members."

The fire station was located behind the Branson Falls city building. Annie was an EMT, so she must be on duty.

"I believe it," I answered, watching the group of mostly women yelling and thrusting their signs in a way they probably didn't realize was obscene. I turned to her. "You know Whitney better than me. Do you think she was cheating?"

Annie's lips turned down and she shook her head. "No, but I didn't know she had a Fanzy page either, so maybe I don't know her like I thought I did."

I chewed on my bottom lip, thinking. "It's crazy. If all of the rumors are true, Whitney was the busiest woman on the planet. Who has time for cheating, a Fanzy page, and running a business full-time? And there's no way she could have kept it all hidden."

"I agree," Annie said. "It makes me wonder who knew about it."

"Clarissa?"

Annie pressed her lips together as we watched a protester skid back and forth on the ice, holding her sign. "That's my guess."

"Do you think Clarissa sent Whitney away because she knew the information would eventually leak and she didn't want it to affect their business?" Clarissa had said she was worried the divorce would do that, but maybe she knew about the Fanzy page and that's why she'd really encouraged Whitney to leave.

Annie raised her shoulders. "Anything is possible at this point. The women at 111 don't know what to think."

"Does anyone know who leaked Whitney's Fanzy page?" I asked as The Ladies changed formation like a protest Colorguard.

"I haven't heard anything, but I've been at work since the show last night."

Jackie's yelling changed to, "Stop Strippers!"

I looked at Annie and she looked at me in confirmation that we'd both heard what we thought we had.

Jackie, who had now somehow acquired a bull horn, said, "Porn isn't our only problem! We have women right here in Branson Falls watching male strippers!" She pointed directly at me, and I wondered how she knew I'd been there. Ella, probably, but Ella also wouldn't have wanted to out herself.

"Women like that shouldn't be role models!" She pointed again. "We have to stop this attack on marriages, families, and morals!" Jackie started another chant of "Marriage, Family, Morals!"

I rolled my eyes thinking how hypocritical it was for people like Jackie to say they had the right to live, think, and believe whatever they wanted, and also that everyone else needed to live, think, and believe exactly like them.

"I'm going to stop by 111 again today and see if I can talk to Clarissa."

Annie nodded as we watched the protest Colorguard change position again. "That's a good idea. Maybe she's been able to talk to Whitney."

That was an excellent point.

I got more photos and listened a little longer. Annie leaned over and said, "Did you notice Jackie looks like a human penis?"

I burst out laughing. The all-beige ensemble finished off with the pink beanie cap definitely resembled one. "I wonder if she did it to match the posters?"

We both laughed before Annie left to go back to work. I asked a couple of people questions about why they were at the protest and why this was important to them. Then I went back across the street to order cheesy breadsticks with extra cheese for the office

I filled Spence and Ella in on the unplanned protest.

"It's interesting they were also protesting the male revue that was supposed to be a secret, *Ella*." I said her name as an accusation.

Her gaze went skyward as she said, "I heard some of The Ladies *might* have found out about the male revue, and *might* have some opinions."

I slitted my eyes. "How would they have found out about that?"

She pushed her lips down, her chin out, and shrugged with her hands in the air like she couldn't be more innocent and guilty at the same time. "Someone *might* have posted some photos of the hot men so everyone who wasn't there could enjoy the show, too."

I shook my head slowly. "You've ruined it for all of us. Now the dancers will never be able to come back."

"Oh phooey," she said, waving my comment away. "It means they'll have a bigger audience next time."

"Not if The Ladies run them out of town!"

Ella scoffed on her way to the archive room. "They just need some time to untwist their underwear. They'll probably try to host their own show." Mormon male strippers sounded like a hilarious SNL skit. I'd watch it, but not for the same reasons I'd watched the guys last night.

I finished lunch, and then left to talk to Clarissa.

Chapter Thirteen

111 was even busier than it had been last night, a shock considering there weren't any mostly naked men running around.

The room was teeming with people, mostly women. Annie had said the 111 community didn't know what to think about the scandal. I was sure most were there because they wanted to make sense of Whitney and her Fanzy page, and wanted to talk to other people who understood.

Clarissa was standing in the books section talking to a group of women. I waved back, and waited for her to come over. I browsed the store, going from table-to-table and listening to conversations the whole time. Every woman I heard seemed to be in shock. Some talked about how this was so out of character for Whitney. Others said Whitney was two-faced and had been friends with the women at 111 during the day while she was cheating with their husbands at night. It wasn't clear if they thought their husbands looking at Whitney's Fanzy page was cheating, or if someone had actually caught Whitney having a relationship with men other than Cory.

Stephanie Gress and Monica Parks were standing in the corner whispering. I went over to them.

"Are you here to get the story about Whitney?" Monica asked.

I cocked my head to the side, interested. "If you know a story, I'd love to hear it."

"She's been on Fanzy for months," Monica said. "She's just been biding her time, waiting for the right moment to ask for a divorce and leave."

"How do you know she's been on there?"

Stephanie and Monica exchanged glances before Stephanie answered, "Friends have been sharing scandalous photos of her. We just didn't know where the photos were coming from until a woman caught her husband on the Fanzy page."

My forehead wrinkled. "Is that how her Fanzy page was released?" An angry wife would do it, but at the same time, the wife probably wouldn't want people to know it was her, or that her husband was involved. She'd be afraid people would judge her.

Monica hedged. "I don't know who released it, but I'm glad it's finally out there and we can talk about it in the open instead of just having whispered conversations behind closed doors."

"Do you know who shared the link?"

They looked at each other and then shook their heads. Almost like they were having a silent conversation before answering me.

"No, but a lot of men in the community have been

subscribing to her Fanzy page; we just didn't know about it," Monica explained. "A lot of their wives are members of 111 and feel betrayed."

I couldn't fault them for that. "That's understandable. Do you think that's why Whitney left? She knew about the photos going around, and was worried people would find out about the page?"

"I wouldn't put it past her," Stephanie said, folding her arms. "She's a coward."

That seemed harsh.

Monica brushed a piece of hair behind her ear and smoothed it like she was trying to soothe herself. "I hope Whitney comes back because she owes a lot of people an explanation."

Stephanie and Monica walked away with their heads close to each other, talking in hushed tones. It would definitely be difficult to find out your spouse was interested in looking at other women, but it would be even harder to find out the woman was someone you knew, or even a friend.

Clarissa came over to me, her eyelids heavy. She looked exhausted.

"How are you doing?" I asked her.

She wrapped her arms around her torso like she was giving herself a hug. "I've had better days, but I'm holding it together."

"Have you heard from Whitney?" I asked.

"No," she said, closing her eyes. She still doesn't have access to her phone. "I wasn't expecting this."

I tilted my head to the side. "So, you didn't know about Whitney's secret life?"

She let out a long sigh. "It seems there was a lot I didn't know."

I noticed that wasn't a denial. "Who do you think released the information about her Fanzy page?"

Clarissa shrugged. "It could have been anyone with access to her page, or even a family member of someone who'd been looking at the photos."

Those were the same conclusions I'd come to. "Do you think this is going to negatively impact your business?"

She looked around at all the people and the line at the register with customers waiting to buy their products. "It certainly hasn't so far. I was surprised by that."

I was too, but thought things might die down once the gossip did.

"Do you still expect Whitney to come back in the next few days?"

Clarissa moved some crystals on the table in front of us. "As far as I know. I'm sure plenty of people have warned her about what's happening here. I know I left her a message and texted her, so she'll have a lot to deal with when she turns her phone back on."

"I'm sure." I hoped she would get one of my messages and call me back. "One other thing. The Ladies held a porn protest at the Branson city building a couple of hours ago, and they were also protesting the male revue. Apparently when you said it was secret, some people didn't listen." And by *some*, I meant Ella.

She lifted her eyes to the ceiling and took another steadying breath. "I know, I heard."

"Have you had anyone complaining about it?"

Clarissa shook her head. "No, if anything, I think it's

brought in more business. I've had women asking how they can get an invitation to the next one."

That also surprised me. Especially given the protest about it, but maybe Ella was right.

Starr was the employee at the register and called to Clarissa. "Excuse me, Kate," Clarissa said, and walked away.

I'd expected Clarissa to be more stunned, but maybe she was still in shock. Then again, her business certainly wasn't hurting from all the exposure. Maybe she was the one who released the link to Whitney's page. I had no idea, but I couldn't shake Cory's accusation that Clarissa had done something to Whitney.

I talked to a few more groups of women who were all upset about Whitney's page. As I was about to leave, Jacey Frank, who had been sitting next to me at the first sound bath I went to, came up and pulled me aside.

She scanned the room to make sure we were somewhere somewhat private. "You know I'm friends with Whitney, right?"

"You mentioned that at the sound bath."

She wrung her hands together and looked worried. "I haven't heard from her since a few days before she disappeared. She stopped texting me."

"How often was she texting you before that?"

"Daily."

"Did you know about her Fanzy page?"

She chewed on her bottom lip. "No, and that's really strange because we talked a lot and she told me she'd been having problems with Cory. I'm worried something happened to her. If she's safe, I can't imagine she wouldn't be back here defending herself."

That was a good point. "Maybe that's why she left. She knew the link and photos were going to be released and she didn't want to be here for it."

"That's not like her," Jacey said, shaking her head with concern. "She's not the type to hide." Jacey shifted her weight and looked around the room again, then leaned in to me. "Something was definitely off before she left. I was here late one night after a sound bath because I'd fallen asleep. When I woke up, I saw Clarissa and Whitney. Whitney's eyes were red like she'd been crying, and Clarissa looked upset. I think they were fighting."

My ears perked up. "I thought they were best friends?"

"They're close, but any relationship or friendship can have issues."

"Thanks for letting me know," I told Jacey. "That helps."

She gave me a kind smile. "Thanks for looking for her. I hope she's okay."

I hung around 111 a little longer, seeing if I could glean any other information from people there. Clarissa was the only one who'd had any contact with Whitney, or knew where she was. She also seemed to be the one Whitney trusted most, but maybe it was all an act and Cory was right. Maybe Clarissa really had done something to Whitney because she was worried about the business being affected by Whitney's actions. I needed to figure out the next best steps, and how to find Whitney.

Hawke was waiting outside my house when I got home that night. I saw him exit his truck as I let Gandalf out of my Jeep.

He went running over to Hawke, doing spins and jumps...it was how most women also treated Hawke, so he was used to it.

I grabbed my bag and my coffee. It had been a long day and coffee had been my main food group.

Hawke squatted down to pet Gandalf and rub his little head before glancing up at me. "I heard you had an interesting night last night."

I cocked my head to the side. "I'm guessing you got the link to Whitney's Fanzy page as well?"

"I did, but I was referring to the mostly naked men at the male revue you attended."

I froze. "How did you know about that?"

He gave me a look. "There's not much I don't know about, Kitty Kate."

I took a deep breath, ready to defend myself. "When you found out I was there, did you make sure 111 was secure like you made sure the Puerto Rico house was secure for all of your liaisons?" The gatekeeper between my brain and my vocal cords was clearly napping because that came right out of my mouth before I could stop it.

He gave me a look and stood, catching his tongue between his bottom lip and top teeth. "We both have pasts, Kitty Kate. I won't apologize for that and don't expect you to, either. But I've never taken another woman there. I have used the spot as a secure location for clients, though, and was upset someone was able to get photos. My security sweeps are thorough and it exposed holes in my intelligence. I won't be using the location again."

"Oh," I said, my stomach dropping. I felt ashamed for

thinking the worst of him. "I'm sorry for jumping to conclusions."

"I came over to explain last night, but you were a little busy."

I studied him, trying to gauge his reaction. "You're not upset?"

"Why would I be?"

I guess he hadn't heard about the guy who had basically had sex with me in a chair with our clothes still on. "Most men in Utah aren't super supportive of women they're interested in seeing a bunch of hot men dance mostly naked."

"And getting manhandled by the men in front of an audience," he added.

So, he had heard. "That, too."

He shook his head. "No. I think it's important for everyone to have a healthy relationship with their sexuality. Especially women, and especially in a place like this with so much purity culture. Women get reprimanded for the same things that are expected of men, and it's another avenue men use to control women. It's wrong. Besides, the more you're thinking of sex, the more often we're having it, and I support that one thousand percent."

I stared at him for several moments, suspicious. I'd never heard opinions like that from a man in Utah and felt like it might be a trick. Maybe Hawke was different because he wasn't from here and wasn't LDS. "I don't know many men who think like you."

"I'm one of a kind."

"That's the truth." I took a drink of my coffee. "Speaking of things you can do that no one else can—"

"Give you six orgasms in a night?"

My cheeks heated, along with other parts. "I actually need your help with something."

"Does it involve me giving you a lap dance?"

My stomach tightened at the thought. "It can later."

He ran his tongue over his lips as they stretched into a smile.

"Can you help me look into Whitney's finances? I want to know how much she was making from her Fanzy page, but I don't have access to that kind of data. You do."

He grinned, coming toward me. "Let me see what I can find out." He grabbed my hand, and pulled me into him as his arms wrapped around me. "Now, why don't you show me some of the things you learned last night."

Chapter Fourteen

I woke up with my face pressed against a rock, and my arms and legs tangled around the same piece of stone that smelled like salt, the ocean, and orgasms. I started to move away from Hawke, but he pulled me back to him. "You're like a body pillow if the body pillow was made of cement."

He laughed, his abs rippling with the movement, and I couldn't help but trace them with my fingertips.

"I pulled into your garage so people wouldn't see my truck and think I stayed over."

I shook my head, my hair trailing over Hawke's chest. "I don't think that matters. People will just think you moved in."

"I'm fine with that."

"If we're moving in anywhere, it's your house. It's basically a compound, Gandalf would have his own wing, and I could live in your shower." It was huge, with a rain shower head in the middle, and additional shower heads all around it on the sides. It also had convenient benches for leverage and I was ensorcelled by the whole thing.

"You're welcome to use my shower any time, preferably with me in it."

His fingers started slowly brushing up and down my back.

I moaned. "I could get used to this."

"I could get used to hearing that noise as well."

His other hand started doing interesting things near my thigh and it wasn't long before we completely lost track of time.

Eventually, we both got out of bed and neither one of us was happy about it. I wrapped up to take Gandalf out for his morning snow inspection and "happy chocolate ice cream" making, as my mom liked to think of it. Hawke followed me out the back door with a cup of coffee.

"That coffee maker is excellent," he said, his mug steaming. "Better than the coffee shop, even."

I angled my head, looking at him. "Yes, it was a *very* nice Christmas gift that was left on my doorstep by a mutual *friend*," I said, implying it was a gift from him that he'd never owned up to.

He grinned and took a sip of his coffee before he said, "That must be a good friend." Hawke was a master at not confirming or denying things.

I watched as Gandalf bounced through the snow like he thought he was a bunny. "Hey, can you help me with one more thing?"

"I already offered that again on the way out the door, but you said you didn't have time."

I rolled my eyes and heat crept into my cheeks. "Since you're looking into Whitney's finances and Fanzy anyway, can you also check and see if she's been accessing money in any way? Taking cash from the ATM, buying gas, spending money on her credit card? If she's staying somewhere, she probably paid for a hotel. If she's fine and just at a retreat like Clarissa said, there has to be a money trail somehow. And her finances would help us pinpoint her location."

"I'll add it to my list." He came over, put one hand on the back of my head, and pressed his mouth onto mine, tracing my top lip with his tongue. I responded by pulling his bottom lip into my mouth with my teeth. He growled, and I wrapped my arms around his neck, continuing our dance until Gandalf, now done with his morning routine, jumped up on my leg and gave a little yelp to let me know it was *way* past breakfast time. I broke away from Hawke, licking my lips and he did the same with a smile. "I'll see you soon, Kitty Kate."

He got in his truck and pulled out of the garage. Phyllis was outside and waved. I had no doubt that she wasn't the only one to see him leave, or note that he seemed very comfortable at my house and had probably been there awhile —like all night.

I went back in the house, got myself and Gandalf breakfast, and then pulled up Whitney's Fanzy account. I started searching through it and saw the last post was made yesterday, and she had several posts the day before, and many before that. Despite being at a "no tech" retreat like Clarissa claimed, Whitney had been posting the entire time she was gone. It was odd, but it could be explained. There were services and apps you could use to schedule posts, and that was probably what she'd done to keep her followers engaged while she was away.

I looked around her page. It was mostly beautifully shot photos of Whitney in various states of nakedness, and poses. There were also some videos that looked like they'd been done at home, but were still titillating. I scrolled through the most recent chats. People were talking about her page, welcoming new members who had found the page thanks to the link drop, and discussing what they'd like to see Whitney dressed and undressed in next.

I leaned back against the couch and wondered why Whitney had chosen to join Fanzy. It was a strange decision for someone who was a devout Mormon. When I'd grown up, one of things drilled into me in LDS Young Women's lessons was that nothing was more important than guarding our purity. Because if we weren't pure, a man wouldn't want us, and we wouldn't be able to reach the highest levels of the Celestial Kingdom without one. I was surprised she'd risk her eternal salvation with something like this. Then again, nothing is more motivating than greed, and if she was making a lot of money, the Fanzy page wasn't a surprise.

Her disappearance still bothered me though. Clarissa insisted Whitney was fine, but Clarissa was literally the only one who had been in contact with her, and she couldn't show me any recent proof of that contact. I was taking Clarissa at her word while hearing from Cory and Jacey that they thought Clarissa was involved with Whitney's disappearance, or vacation, depending on who you asked.

I thought Clarissa's reaction to Whitney's Fanzy account was also strange. Clarissa seemed far more interested in the number of sales she was getting at the store than she was in her best friend's boobs and who-ha being broadcast to the world.

Cory was also suspect because he didn't want the divorce and several people had said he was controlling. He was also the one most concerned about Whitney and where she was.

Then there was Shasta, who hated Whitney with her whole being. And the women who had caught their husbands with Whitney's photos, or caught them watching Whitney on Fanzy. All of those people had something against Whitney, and a motive to have her to disappear. I just wanted one of them to show me some proof of life.

A knock sounded at my front door. Gandalf, my Notifier in Chief, barked to let me know the porch had been breached and we were under attack by unseen forces.

I opened the door to a wall of muscle, dark hair, and blue eyes on the other side. Drake. I hadn't seen or heard from him since our discussion at the Capitol. He'd said he needed some time and I didn't think I'd see him until after the legislative session ended. "Hi," I said softly. His face was neutral and I couldn't tell what he was thinking.

"Hi," he said back. "Can we talk?"

"Yeah." I invited him in, and Gandalf did one hundred spins, and got almost as many pets back from Drake, who smiled and called him the best boy. Drake wasn't wrong.

Gandalf ran down the hall to grab a toy.

I gestured to the beige couch for him to sit. "Do you want anything to drink?"

He shook his head so I sat next to him, but left some cushion space between us.

His jaw was set in a determined line but I couldn't read him beyond that.

"I wasn't expecting to see you." I picked up my coffee from the black coffee table and took a sip, mostly to calm my nervousness and the butterflies that seemed to have migrated to my stomach.

He glanced at me, his eyes catching on my lips as I licked a little stray liquid off of them. "I was home for the weekend and didn't want to leave things undone."

Gandalf brought the toy back to show Drake, and Drake threw it. Then Gandalf brought it back again, sat on the floor, and started chewing on it. He clearly knew this was an important conversation.

Drake turned to me so we were facing each other, and gave me all of his attention. "I've thought a lot about our situation, and Puerto Rico. I was hurt because it seems like you're moving faster with Hawke and I'm not getting a chance."

I wanted to reach over and touch his arm or leg to comfort him, but I still didn't know where this was going and wasn't sure if he'd want me too. "That's not how I want you to feel, I just think the two of us have limitations that I don't have with Hawke."

He nodded, his jaw set and expression decisive. "I agree. And I want us to be on equal footing."

We'd already talked about the sex issue and his membership in the church. "I might not agree with them, but I don't want to disrespect your beliefs, or you."

He angled his head in acknowledgment and sat straighter. "I know, and I don't think you're doing that. This is about what I'm comfortable with, and I don't want to have any regrets. Intimacy is important to me, too, and I think we need to explore that."

I stared at him, trying to dissect what he was saying. Intimacy meant a lot of things and sex was about connection as much as it was about the physical act. "What does that look like for you?"

He threaded his fingers together in his lap, and held my gaze. "Let's find out. I want to move forward to a place where we're both comfortable, and see what happens from there."

This would be a slower pace than I was moving with Hawke, but I was fine with that, especially if it meant he still wanted to give us a shot to figure out if we could work as a couple. "Okay, I can do that."

He let go of a breath and ran his palms down his thighs. "I want to have those discussions. To know what makes you excited, and what you want from sex in a relationship."

I arched a brow. "I mean, in the spirit of honesty, I went to a male revue show a couple of nights ago and came away with some ideas." I was fully expecting him to be just as mad about the erotic dancers as he'd been about Puerto Rico, but figured he'd hear about it eventually anyway since The Ladies had put it on their crusade list, and I might as well get it out of the way now.

Instead, his lips spread into a wicked grin. "I'd like to hear about those."

I almost dropped my coffee. "Wait, you're not upset I went to see mostly naked men dance?"

He snorted and lightly shook his head. "You're already dating another guy. Seeing some performers dance is far tamer than that. Plus, I think a lot of relationships would be better if women were more in touch with their sexuality, and could talk to their partner about it. That's why I wanted to discuss it with you, learn what you want, and explore that a bit."

My mouth gaped. "Who are *you*? Mormon dudes don't think like that."

He looked straight at me and held my eyes. "I do."

I shook my head, unable to wrap my brain around it. "They think women who explore their sexuality are sluts, and they call women that."

Drake's jaw clenched at the word. "I've always thought it's interesting because that word is just someone judging women for doing what men are expected to do, and even praised for. The rumors about me are a prime example of that. I'm patted on the back when other men think I've had some conquest, but a woman like Whitney Hatch is burned at the public stake."

I stared at him. I had no words. He was echoing everything I thought about this same issue and it was not something I ever believed we'd align on.

Two vertical lines formed between his brows. "You seem shocked."

I snorted. "Because I am. I feel like I might not know you as well as I thought I did."

He nodded decisively. "Why don't we start to change that. We've already talked about the fact that my February is packed, but I'll try to see you when I have time, and after that, I'd like to see you more. More dates, more talking, more… everything."

I licked my lips and the corners turned up. "I'd like that."

Gandalf decided the serious conversation was over and

jumped on Drake, giving excited sneezes. We got down on the ground and played with Gandalf, and talked for a few minutes. Then Drake said he had to leave to get to a meeting at church. He walked out the door and I was left wanting a lot more of him.

"This reunion is nuts!" Phyllis said, handing me and Annie our hot chocolate refills. It was so thick that it was like drinking actual melted chocolate. I'd have to do three hours of cardio to make up for it, but it was absolutely worth it.

"That baking contest among the women with the men judging them, was cringe. I'm glad the reunion host brought it up," I said, grabbing a handful of popcorn from the bowl on the table. "Next time, the men should bake and let the women judge them for something for a change."

Annie grabbed a chocolate frosted mint brownie. "I agree."

"My husband never baked a day in his life," Phyllis said, her eyes going to a photo of them on the wall. "He just expected me to do it all, raise the kids, and take care of things. All he had to do was work, and after work, he did whatever he wanted while I continued to work non-stop as CEO of the house."

"How did you feel about that?" I asked, curious about the generational difference in perspectives.

She considered it. "I didn't see a problem with it at the time because it was normal. But now, it makes me angry. I had goals and plans outside of the house, but they weren't my 'role' so I didn't get support or encouragement to pursue them. Reflecting on it now in my old age, I think he made my life harder and didn't let me live the way I wanted to. I loved my husband, but to be honest, I was kinda glad when he died. I finally had freedom; it just took seventy-six wasted years to get it."

My heart broke for her. "That makes me sad."

"Me too," Phyllis said. "I wish I'd demanded it while he was still alive." She pointed at Annie, and then me. "Don't you make the same mistake, girls."

Annie laughed. "I had that discussion with Rich before we got married because nothing kills a relationship faster than unsaid and unmet expectations."

I pointed my brownie at her. "That's really good. I'm going to write that down."

She grinned. "Definitely important for someone in your situation."

"What's going on with Hawke and Drake, anyway?" Phyllis asked. "I see both of 'em at your house all the time. In fact, they were both there today." She gave me a side-eye and I knew she was wondering about Hawke staying the night.

"We're figuring things out. I'm not ready to commit to either one of them until I know them better. I jumped into a relationship with my ex too fast and he was awful. I don't want to make that mistake again. So, I'm dating them both, and they both know it. They might be dating other women, too." I paused. "I don't *think* they are, but I also haven't asked." I didn't really want to, if I was honest.

Annie popped a potato chip in her mouth. "Everyone makes such a big deal out of that and says you need to choose, but you're dating and you're not exclusive with either one of them. It's really no different than going on a dating app. I have friends talking to twenty guys at a time and going on four or five dates with different men daily."

Phyllis put a hand to her chest and almost fell out of her chair. "Oh, my. How do they find the time for that?"

Annie shrugged with her hot chocolate in one hand. "They manage."

The reunion continued and the big bombshell they'd been advertising for weeks dropped. Kaeleigh Wright, super Mormon and super popular influencer, had cheated on her husband.

"I can't believe she cheated on him." Annie's mouth was on the floor. "She's been denying it all season."

Phyllis scratched her head. "It's hard to deny it when there's proof."

"I don't know," I said, my reporter brain going through all the possible scenarios. "The proof is kind of sketchy. It came from a few other anonymous accounts and we don't know who was actually behind it. You never know who could be involved, or what their motives are."

Phyllis's eyes lit up. "I hope the guy she was with comes forward to confirm and shows up next season."

"Speaking of cheating scandals," Annie said, "have you heard anything else about Whitney?"

I shook my head. "Not yet, but I'm looking into her Fanzy account, and have Hawke helping me try to access her finances so I can hopefully find out where she's spending money and where she is." A thought came to me as I was explaining. "Do you think anyone else in town has a Fanzy account? Maybe Whitney was working with other women on it."

Annie tilted her head to the side, considering. "I wouldn't

say no, but I haven't heard anything about anyone else. I imagine if there were any other local accounts, we'd know about them by now."

She was probably right. "Let me know if you do hear anything."

The show came back on, and we turned our attention from the scandals in our hometown to the scandals on-screen.

Chapter Fifteen

My day had started with moderating comments on one of the *Tribune*'s social media posts about Whitney. One man had posted that men wouldn't be so obsessed with sex if women didn't wear such revealing clothes. Someone else asked for clarification on what the revealing clothes were, and other guys started listing things like yoga pants, sports bras, tank tops, crop tops, shorts, skirts, bra straps—you know, women's clothes. Then one guy took it a step farther and said crossbody bags. He'd written a whole dissertation in his comment on the post about why crossbody bags should be banned because the strap cuts a woman's chest in half and draws attention to her boobs and that's distracting.

That had been a clarion call for a response to women everywhere, and they immediately arrived to clap back.

The crossbody bag comment had led to a slew of women posting that they were not responsible for men's thoughts, and that simply existing with boobs was not temptation. Men responded back saying that's what they'd been taught. Women told them to do better and one woman astutely asked if the original commenter was also going to ban women from wearing seatbelts for doing the same thing as crossbody bags to boobs.

The comments also turned to Mormonism, including some people who pointed out that the LDS church was not known for promoting healthy sexuality among members. Another woman said the men wanted their wives to be pure, but they were turned on by women who looked and acted like porn stars.

The women on the post weren't backing down, and I was trying to mediate the discussion as best as I could. From a journalistic standpoint, I was letting both sides speak up. But from a personal standpoint, I agreed with the majority of the women posting.

I took a break to get coffee from Beans and Things and there was a guy in front of me in line wearing jeans and a white sweater. He was blonde, with brown eyes and an average build. I recognized him as one of the men from Cory's house a couple of days ago—the day Whitney's Fanzy account link had been released.

He ordered a peppermint hot chocolate, and I ordered a browned butter caramel coffee. Of the two of us, it was clear that I was both the winner, and the sinner.

As we waited for our drinks at the end of the counter, I said, "You're Cory Hatch's friend, right?"

He nodded.

"I'm Kate Saxee, the editor of the *Tribune*."

He held out his hand to shake mine and smiled. "I'm Harry Bracker."

I met his hand with my own and smiled back. "I saw you at Cory Hatch's house the other day. How is he doing?"

Harry frowned and looked down at the ground. "Not great. He's definitely not the guy I knew on my mission."

"Were you missionary companions?" I asked.

"No, but we served in the same area. He was so outgoing then, and the most successful missionary we had. We knew he'd end up with a hot wife because he was so successful on his mission."

Anger and irritation rose in my chest at the memory of people saying those things—like women were nothing but rewards and possessions for men. "Ah, yes. I've heard those stories. The lore is that the more faithful a missionary is, and the more people they convert to the LDS church, the hotter their wife is supposed to be." The idea had made me livid as a teen in the Young Women's program. Women in the church were being dangled as a prize for men who were faithful, and it was all based on how we looked.

"Yep, and Cory got *seriously* rewarded, but it didn't turn out so well for him," Harry said, lowering his chin. "Whitney was attractive and all the guys wanted her. Everyone said Cory won the wife lottery because he'd had the most baptisms in the mission field. But that's the problem with having a wife who looks like Whitney. Women like her want attention, and Whitney wasn't afraid to ask for it, and ask people to pay for it."

That was judgy. I had to fight back a scowl.

Harry continued, "Cory used to be so confident and controlled. We thought he'd have a family by now, and be called as an LDS bishop by twenty-eight."

I hadn't seen that confident side of Cory at all. I'd only known him since Whitney left him and he seemed nothing but defeated, which was understandable given the circumstances. "What do you think changed?"

"He got depressed when he lost his job. He worked in sales and marketing, and did really well for himself, but the company downsized and he couldn't find another position. Eventually it sent him into a spiral because he wasn't able to provide and do the things he was supposed to do as a man in the church. They had some savings, and Whitney had her business on the side to help keep them afloat. But Whitney shouldn't have been working. She wanted a career and that had been a source of contention between them. Now she had an excuse to keep working because they needed the money, and Cory became even more ashamed."

I'd wondered if extra money was why she'd started the Fanzy account. To make extra money. But it seemed like she was really committed to her business with 111, so that didn't totally track.

"He finally seemed to be pulling himself out of it," Harry said, grabbing his hot chocolate from the counter. "He'd found some contract work on the side, and he was getting better and felt like a man again. That's when Whitney asked for the divorce."

My lips turned down and I felt bad for everyone involved. "That's really difficult."

Harry nodded. "I hope he can get some answers about where she is, and get back to himself soon."

I thanked Harry for talking to me and took my coffee back to the office. Clarissa had indicated that Cory was an abusive asshole. Maybe that had stopped while he was depressed, but it sounded like once Cory had work again, he'd started changing back into the man he was before. I wondered if

Whitney had asked for the divorce because Cory was once again pushing her to give up her business.

Hawke was at my desk when I walked in. Ella was sitting across from him with her elbow on the desk, chin in her hand, and watching him like a teenage girl with a crush. "Hey," I said, smiling at the surprise. "I wasn't expecting to see you here."

I took my scarf and coat off, and Hawke's eyes heated more with each thing I removed. "Need some help?"

I heard Ella gulp.

I gave Hawke a look. "I think I'm fine for now."

Ella slapped her hand on her thigh. "Goll dangit! I thought I was gonna get a real life repeat of you two rollin' around on the beach."

I scrunched up my face. "The *Tribune* floor isn't sand, and not anywhere near as sanitary."

Hawke grinned. "I could make it work."

"I bet you could," Ella said, nodding as she looked him up and down. "The other night, we were watchin' some hotties who looked a lot like you dance around and do sexual gymnastics. I bet you'd be *great* at it."

He wiggled his eyebrows and his eyes lit with a twinkle of mischief. "I bet I would, too."

I stopped what I was doing and watched him closely. He caught my eye.

Ella's brows shot up. "You have some experience?"

Hawke ran his tongue over his lip. "I have experience with a lot of things."

He looked straight at me and I had the sudden suspicion that maybe Hawke had been one of the dancers at the show. Specifically, the dancer who had targeted me in the crowd, and brought me to the floor, gave me a very sexy lap dance, and then told me to find him when the show was done. He dropped his eyes from mine like he might be giving too much away and I had to fight to keep my mouth from falling open. The dancer had been wearing a shirt the whole time, granted he'd lost some buttons when he'd ripped it open, but it had stayed on his arms. If the shirt had come off, I would have been able to identify Hawke from his tattoos. I replayed the sexy scene over in my head. I thought it was a dancer with the revue, but there was no reason why it couldn't have been Hawke. That kind of thing probably came as a required course with his other secret government training classes—just in case.

"Let's see it!" Ella demanded, leaning forward in anticipation. "Show me what you can do with a chair."

I laughed and since I suspected Hawke had come here for a different reason than his desire to turn the *Tribune* into the headquarters for sexy, I changed the subject. "Were you able to find out some information about Whitney?"

Ella didn't look happy about missing out on Hawke using my chair as a sex toy, but Whitney info she could share was the second-best option in her list of scenarios. She'd have something to tell The Ladies.

"I was. Whitney had an LLC called Love and Light Holdings. All of her business-related expenses went through the accounts associated with it. The business account is where she was paid from 111 Healing and Crystals, and the account where she was paid from private clients who used her for sound baths. Companies that hired her to do sound baths, mediations, and other wellness-related events also paid her in that account. It's a successful business."

I couldn't hide my surprise. "She was still doing all of those private events even while being in business with Clarissa and owning 111 Healing and Crystals?"

He angled his head. "Looks like it. Her accounts are active and she routinely gets deposits from reputable clients going back several years. I checked the companies who have paid her, and the people."

Huh. That could be a conflict of interest. "Doesn't that put her in competition with Clarissa and 111?"

He put his elbows on the arms of my chair and then threaded his fingers together to rest on his hard stomach. "They're doing the same things, so yeah. But I don't know what her agreement with Clarissa was. Maybe they were both still moonlighting with their private clients on the side."

"What about Fanzy?" I asked. "Did you see any deposits from them?"

Hawke sliced his head to the side once. "Nope. Nothing from Fanzy, or any company related to Fanzy. So, she wasn't using this account, or business, for her Fanzy income. She could have registered in a state that doesn't require a social security number to open a business. And she could always go through shell companies if she had advice and knew how to set them up."

I leaned against the edge of my desk, thinking. "What about her personal accounts?"

"She only had two joint bank accounts with Cory. A checking and savings. There was nothing suspicious there either, as far as deposits or transactions. She has her own cards on those accounts and I'd be able to see if she'd used them. She hasn't. There have been no charges to her personal accounts with Cory, or to her business accounts, since almost three weeks ago."

That made my heart rate pick up speed. "That's concerning."

"There are explanations. Someone else could have made the reservations for her and paid for the trip. Or she could be paying with cash."

Cash was harder to track than bitcoin. It felt like a dead end, but all information was good information.

"How do we know those clients were all for her sound baths?"

He eyed me. "Are you asking if people could have been paying her for Fanzy through her business account?"

"Yes."

"It's a slim possibility, but not likely. If they were paying her on the side and knew her personally, then it could happen. But if they knew her from Fanzy, that money would be going through Fanzy for legal purposes, and so Fanzy could take their cut."

"Can you access Whitney's Fanzy account and find the name of the business associated with the account?"

"I'm already trying. Fanzy is very careful about privacy and has a lot of security protections for the accounts. It's taking me a bit longer than usual."

Meaning he was being even more illegal than usual. "Thank the goddesses for your situational ethics."

He flashed a wicked grin. "They've gotten me pretty far."

My phone buzzed with a text from my mom.

MOM

URGENT! COME TO MY HOUSE!*!&#@

I wasn't sure if the punctuation marks were intentional and meant to represent a swear, or if she was so flustered that they'd just appeared. Either way, I probably needed to go.

"My mom has a situation."

Hawke grinned. "Those are my favorite kinds. I'll come with you."

My mom's expression was almost as fiery as her temper while she surveyed her witch display. Her arms were crossed over her chest, but I could still clearly see the pink t-shirt she was wearing with the words "Agent of Satan" written in pretty white script across it. She shook her head, one eye squinted in a determined expression that had terrified me as child. It meant she was thinking about something batshit crazy, and in this case, it had to do with whatever had happened to her front yard love spell.

Someone had turned my mom's witches into the erotic dance club that everyone already thought they were part of. The intent of the display was just far more clear now, and there was no room for misinterpretation. The pole the witches had been using to stir their love spell in the cauldron had been secured so it was vertical. One of the witches was wrapped around it like she was doing a pole dance. The other had a leg lifted high in the air. And the one that had been the most controversial and bent over, was still bent over, but now she was holding handcuffs. Fake one hundred-dollar bills and coins were scattered all over the ground, and in the cauldron.

The sign my mom kept outside to irritate her neighbors, Sophie's Satanic Sunday Sermons, had a piece of paper placed over it so it now read: Sophie's Sexy Sunday Sermons.

Bobby surveyed the scene with a fist in front of his mouth. The corners of his lips were twitching and he was trying desperately not to laugh.

Hawke, however, didn't try to hide his amusement. Neither did my dad.

My mom, who had worked her way into a tizzy before I arrived, was now on her way to full-on rampage. "I demand you investigate this…this…this…" she was struggling to find the right descriptor, "holiday *blasphemy*!" There it was. "They've vandalized my ode to love!"

Hawke and Bobby both had to turn away, but I could see their shoulders shaking. My dad snorted with laughter, and my mom whipped her head around so fast that it seemed inhuman. "You better not be laughing, Damon Saxee!"

He put his hand over his mouth and mumbled, "I wouldn't think of it."

She turned back to Bobby, her hands on her hips. "What are you going to do about this destruction of my personal property and art?"

Bobby scrubbed a hand over his mouth, trying to wipe the amusement away and failing. "What would you like me to do?" he asked.

She threw her arms in the air and growled, "I want you to find out who did it!" she said, her tone menacing.

"Do you know when it happened?" Bobby asked.

My mom pulled out a paper with color coded notes. "I left

to take some cookies to the Dint family at two-fourteen today. When I got home at three-twenty-seven the witches had been raided! It was an assault!"

'Assault' seemed like a strong word.

"It happened in broad daylight," Bobby pointed out, scanning the area. "Someone had to have seen somethin'. Have you talked to your neighbors?"

She pursed her lips. "Yes. And very *conveniently*, none of them saw anything."

Of course they didn't, because they'd all complained about the display and didn't want it up anyway. "I'm not sure they'd tell you anything considering your shirt," I observed.

She glared at me. "Since they already think I'm evil, I decided I might as well embrace my villain era."

Villain era? Apparently, she'd also turned into a Swiftie.

Hawke looked around until his gaze stopped on something and a smile crossed his lips. "I think I can take this one on if that's okay with you, Bobby?"

Bobby put his hand out like he was giving Hawke the right-of-way. "Feel free."

"Hawke!" my mom said, "How do I get some fancy surveillance cameras like Kate has? Clearly, my witches need more security."

"I can help you with that, too," Hawke said, giving her a wink.

My mom's eyes slid to me and her tone lowered enough to be menacing. "Hawke sure is helpful, Kate. I'd hate for him to not be around someday because *someone* made a poor relationship decision."

"Mom!"

She lifted her arms in the air. "Just sayin'!"

I gave Hawke an apologetic look. We threw the ball for Gandalf before my parents took him inside and we got back in my Jeep. I'd had enough time to think about it and my curiosity couldn't be contained any longer. "Were you dancing at the male revue the other night?"

He gave me a look that betrayed nothing. "If I was going to dance for you, I'd do it somewhere more private."

"That wasn't a yes or no."

"Someday you're going to stop being so obsessed with absolutes."

I shook my head and drove us back to the *Tribune*. "I'm a reporter so I wouldn't count on that if I were you."

Hawke left before Ella could accost him again and demand a sexy performance with office furniture. I spent the rest of the day unable to get the mystery, or maybe not-so-mystery, man and his dance skills out of my head.

When I got home that night, there was another black metallic box with a pink ribbon tied around it. This one was smaller. When I opened it, there was a bottle of French wine with two wine glasses. Both of the glasses were etched with pictures of Gandalf. It was adorable.

KATE

The picture of Gandalf on the wine glasses is the cutest thing I've ever seen.

HAWKE

I couldn't resist.

KATE

Is Gandalf part of my Valentine's Day present?

HAWKE

No, but the wine is.

I looked at the wine, and thought of the robe in the box in my bedroom. I wondered what the two gifts could mean. Maybe we were going to a spa retreat. Or maybe getting a massage and dinner. Valentine's Day wasn't far off and I couldn't wait to find out!

Chapter Sixteen

I was editing articles at my desk the next day when my phone rang and I answered it.

"Hi Kate, my name is Jess Wing. I heard you're looking into Whitney Hatch, her Fanzy page, and possible disappearance."

"I am. Do you know anything about it?" I grabbed a pad of paper on my desk and started taking notes.

"I think so. I'm a photographer and I specialize in boudoir photography. A group of women in the Branson Falls area asked me to take photos about a year ago and Whitney was one of them. I've seen her Fanzy page, and she used some of my photos on the page."

My eyes went wide. "Did you know she was going to use the photos for that?"

"No. I don't usually pry and ask what the photos are for, but if I'd known they were going to be used for commercial purposes, I would have charged differently. She also didn't give me credit for the photos."

Maybe she didn't know she was supposed to do that, but

still, it seemed sketchy. "Do you remember any of the other women you took photos of?"

"I don't remember names except for her friend who set the whole thing up, Clarissa."

"How were the photos you took distributed to the women?"

"I sent them each a digital link to their private photos. They chose the ones they wanted for the book. I edited the photos, printed the copies, and made a sleek album for each of them with the photos they chose. They also got a thumb drive with the edited photos, and all of their unedited digital copies so they would have a physical backup. The album and thumb drive was packaged into square boxes with each woman's name on the box. I dropped the boxes off at Clarissa's house to distribute to all of the women."

My mind was going in a hundred directions. That meant anyone who had access to Clarissa likely had access to the boxes and photos, Clarissa included.

"Thanks so much for calling, Jess. That helps a lot."

"Sure. I hope Whitney is found or comes home soon."

"Me, too."

I hung up the phone and tapped my pen against my desk, then wrote down more notes. Clarissa's name kept coming up. She was so entangled in all of this, I just didn't know how. I couldn't nail her down on any issue and when I asked questions, she always had an excuse. I'd toyed with this idea, but the boudoir photoshoot made me wonder if Clarissa had a secret Fanzy page as well. Did other women in Branson Falls and no one knew about those yet? Was Clarissa running some sort of Fanzy account management business?

I went on Clarissa's social pages and looked for any links

that might lead me to a Fanzy page of her own if she had one, but didn't find anything. That wasn't a surprise though because the links were private and I still couldn't figure out how Whitney's link had been shared.

I dialed Hawke and explained what Jess had just told me and what some of my theories were. "I think if these pages exist, and I can find the links to them, it might give us more clues about where Whitney is. We know Clarissa had photos taken because Jess remembered her name. Searching for Whitney's link is difficult because it's so public now. But if Clarissa has a page, I might be able to do a search and find where the link has been posted."

"I agree. Let me look into it."

"Can you also look into Clarissa's finances? Maybe the money is going through her, and that's why we couldn't find it when we were looking under Whitney's accounts."

"Good thinking."

"Thanks for your help."

"One more thing, be ready for our Valentine's Day date at six tomorrow," he said.

"Do I need to wear something specific?"

"Something easy to take off."

My core tightened. "I'm glad you're not on speaker right now."

"Everyone already saw the pics of Puerto Rico so I'm pretty sure they already know."

"Exactly! We don't need to keep reminding them."

He laughed. "I'll call you when I find out something about Clarissa."

"Thanks," I said, and hung up.

"What was that all about?" Ella asked, coming into the room, all bundled up.

"A photographer took sexy photos of Whitney and saw the same pictures she took on Whitney's Fanzy page."

Ella nodded, her hat almost falling off as she did. "If I was gonna put my lady bits out for everyone to see, I'd want a professional photographer, too. They make all the difference."

Ella had a point.

"Where are you off to?" I asked, watching her pull on her gloves.

She grinned and wiggled her shoulders in excitement. "To a show, I hope."

I glanced at the clock. "It's a bit early for a play."

Her eyes sparkled with mischief. "I wanted to see more of those sexy dancers like the other night, but guys who look like that and know how to *move* are hard to find in Utah. Then I remembered some signs I saw on a buncha street corners advertisin' these guys, and decided it might be the next best thing!"

I stilled, wondering what she'd gotten into now and hoped it wasn't someone trying to scam or rob her. "What were they advertising?" I asked carefully.

"It's a movin' company! Hunky Movers!" She swiveled her hips in an excited dance. "I've got some hotties comin' over to move some furniture for me!"

I'd seen their signs and thought it was an interesting ad campaign, especially in a place like Branson Falls. I didn't think many husbands would be thrilled about their wives hiring attractive guys to come in and move their furniture.

"I bet they'll look just like the dancers the other night! They better be wearin' tight jeans and no shirts!"

"I'm sure that would be some sort of OSHA violation," I said dryly.

She ignored me. "I can't wait to see 'em and watch 'em lift heavy things!"

"I think you might be disappointed."

She scowled. "I better not be! I didn't even need my furniture moved so I'm payin' good money for this entertainment!"

At least she wasn't going to get scammed or hurt, but she probably would have been better off renting *Magic Mike*.

"You'll have to tell me how it goes."

"Don't you worry," she said, holding up her phone. "I'll take videos for my socials and tag ya!" Ella waved and walked out the back door.

I blew out a breath. Good grief. It felt like Ella was a preview of what my mom would be like in twenty years, except my mom got into far more trouble.

Right after Ella left, two women I'd talked to at 111 during one of my visits there, Becca Couch and Megan Jorgensen, walked in. They saw me across the room and Megan said, "Can we talk to you, Kate?"

"Sure," I answered, grabbing two chairs so we could all sit together.

Megan folded her hands in her lap. "We've been worried about Whitney."

"Is there something specific that's bothering you?"

Megan turned to Becca and tilted her head a couple of times like she was encouraging Becca to speak. "I was in the bathroom after a meditation session at 111 and overheard some women talking by the sinks. I was in a stall so I couldn't see them, but they said Whitney had been threatened."

My brows pushed up into my forehead. "Did they say who threatened her?"

Becca shook her head. "No, just that given the stuff Whitney was involved in, it wasn't a surprise that she'd be in danger and she'd be lucky to not get killed. With everything that's happened, I thought I should tell someone and knew you were investigating."

"Do you think the comment was related to her Fanzy account?"

"It sounded like it. I didn't put two-and-two together until after everyone started talking about the account. And another thing. Clarissa was there."

My mouth fell open slightly. "During the conversation about Whitney being threatened and killed?"

Becca nodded. "I've known Clarissa for a long time and I recognized her voice."

"What did she say?"

"She said it wasn't the time or place to be talking about things like that."

Maybe Clarissa was protecting Whitney, or maybe she was protecting herself.

"One other thing," Becca said. "I saw Shasta and Whitney fighting after church one Sunday."

"Recently?" I asked.

"About a month ago. I was walking to my car and heard raised voices. When I looked, Shasta was pointing at Whitney and told Whitney she was a b-i-t-c-h. Whitney just smiled and asked if Shasta was done, then Whitney got in her car and left." She shook her head as the memory replayed. "I'll never get used to those cars that are so quiet."

The wheels in my head were spinning on overdrive. "Do

you think Shasta knew about the cheating and Fanzy page at that point? Shasta seems pretty protective of her brother."

"She might have. The rumors about Whitney cheating and the photos had been going around then. But I thought you should know."

"Thank you," I said, grabbing my notebook and taking some notes.

Megan leaned forward next. "I got this message on my voicemail. It was weird. It says it's from Whitney, but it doesn't totally sound like her."

She pulled out her phone, put it on speaker, and played the voicemail. "Hi! It's me. I know people are worried about me, but I'm fine. Thanks for caring, but you don't need to look for me. I'll be back soon."

My eyebrows pinched together. "That's odd." It was definitely a woman, but the message was incredibly generic. "She didn't even use your name. Does it sound like her?"

Megan wrinkled her nose. "Kind of."

"When did you get this?"

"This morning."

I wrote that down too. "Can you send that to me?"

"Sure."

I took a few more quick notes based on what they'd both told me. "Thanks for coming to me with this information. It gives me more leads to work on."

"You're welcome," Megan said. "Let us know if you need anything else."

"I will."

They left and my mind was racing with everything Megan and Becca had told me. The voicemail felt like a break in the story somehow.

I texted Hawke:

> Call me when you get a few minutes.

If Megan had gotten a message, maybe other people who knew Whitney had as well. I called Cory. "Have you heard from Whitney yet?"

"Nothing yet. I'm going out of my mind worrying."

Damn. "Okay, keep me posted if you hear anything from her."

"Why," Cory asked. "Did you find something out?" His voice sounded hopeful and heartbroken at the same time.

"Not yet, but I'm working on it. Keep me posted."

I hung up the phone.

It was strange Megan would get a message, but not Cory. Then again, Whitney was divorcing the man. The only other person I could think of who might have received a call was Clarissa, who had been in the bathroom when threats were made against Whitney. I called her next.

"Did you get a call from Whitney?"

Clarissa paused like she was surprised I knew about it. "I actually did."

"Did it sound like her on the other end?"

Clarissa considered it. "I think so."

"What did she say?"

"She said she was fine, that people don't need to worry, and she'll be back soon."

That was exactly what the message on Megan's voicemail had said.

"I have a source who tells me some of the 111 clients were in the bathroom and said they overheard people talking about

Whitney being threatened. They said you were there. Is that true?"

Clarissa took a deep breath on the other end of the phone. "Partially. I came in from the back room while they were talking."

"What was the threat about?"

"I don't know. They stopped talking as soon as they saw me, but I overheard them say they heard she'd been threatened."

"How long was this before she left town?"

"A few weeks."

"And you're still not concerned that something happened to her?" It seemed like Clarissa should be beyond worried at this point.

"Her retreat ends soon. She's supposed to be back tomorrow, and she just called me," Clarissa justified, her tone defensive.

"When she doesn't show up, will you be concerned then?"

Clarissa's tone sounded defensive as she answered, "Absolutely. I'll be the first to call you and start looking for her."

I'd hold her to that.

The seductive tones of "Play Me" started coming from my phone. "That was fast," I said.

"Only when it comes to my job."

I could attest to that.

"What do you know about voice recognition software?"

"I know enough."

"Friends of Whitney's came to the *Tribune* to tell me

Whitney had been threatened by someone. They don't know who. Whitney left one of them a message on their voicemail this morning. It sounded incredibly generic, and they said that while it sounded like her voice, it didn't sound like her. I called Clarissa, who said she also got a call from Whitney and she answered it. She said Whitney told her the same information that was left as a message on the other friend's voicemail."

"Do you have a copy of it?"

"Yeah." I texted it to him.

"I'll go through it and see if I can glean anything from the recording."

"Is there a way to tell if it's someone mimicking her voice to try and get people to stop looking for her?"

He thought about it. "Inflection is key. Robots aren't great at that, or showing emotion with tone. They're getting better every day, but they aren't sophisticated enough yet."

"Is that the only tell?"

"It's hard to pin down with a voicemail. Anyone can download the software to replicate a person's voice and even their image in video. If you've ever been interviewed, or posted a video with your voice or image on social media, someone could copy your voice and say anything they want using it. It's one of the more devious cons because criminals will utilize the tech to replicate the voices of someone's kids or grandkids and make it seem like their loved one is in danger and needs money. It's easier to debunk if you're actually talking to the person on the phone."

"How?" I asked.

"Security consists of three things. One: What you know. For example, a password. Two: What you are. For example, a fingerprint. Three: What you have, for example, a key. If you have two out of three of those things, the information you're trying to access is generally considered very secure. If I were on the phone with Whitney, I would ask a lot of questions. A criminal replicating her voice might sound like her—what she is. But they won't know answers to specific things—what she knows. Ask personal questions that wouldn't have answers available anywhere online. Stuff that only Whitney and the person she was talking to would know. If she can answer the questions, I would be more likely to believe it's her. If she can't answer them, I would think something else could be going on."

I blew out a breath. "It would be helpful if more people knew that information, especially the people she's apparently calling." I paused. "What about her phone records. Could you look at those and find out where she was making the call from?"

"If you have the number, I can. But that will take some time."

"Meaning it's illegal?"

"Situational ethics," he answered.

I was glad one of us had them.

"I'll text you the number."

Chapter Seventeen

Spence came in with a late lunch for us both. He'd texted to ask what I wanted and I'd chosen an Oreo milkshake and fries. I needed Whitney finding fuel.

I took a bite of the shake and closed my eyes. "This is perfection."

Spence laughed. "I've seen that expression before. In the pictures in Puerto Rico."

I flashed him a wicked grin. "I had that expression a lot."

"Does Hawke know you're comparing him to ice cream?"

My lips slid into a sly smile. "He'd probably make a comment about being licked."

We both took a bite of our food, and then I got up to grab some water to wash it down.

"Do you think it was really Whitney who called Megan and Clarissa?" Spence asked.

I'd filled Spence in on my earlier conversations, and my discussion with Hawke. "I don't know. It's odd she told them both the same thing. I wish we had the recording of her call with Clarissa as well."

"You've done more to try to find her and unravel her disappearance than anyone," Spence said.

That was kind of Spence to say, but I still didn't feel like I was any closer to finding her. "I don't know. I feel like I'm missing pieces. I wish I knew who had called in with the tip about Whitney being seen at the ski resort. Or that Whitney would call me. I just want some confirmation that she's been seen, and she's alive and okay."

"Have you looked at her Fanzy page?" Spence asked

"I've looked at the areas I can see. But I can't access her direct messages, chats, account information, or billing info. All of that would be helpful."

"Hawke can."

"Yeah, he's already working on it, but Fanzy is hard to hack into with his usual sorcery."

"What about Shasta?"

"I think she's involved in all this, but I don't know how. She might just be an angry and protective sister, or she might have taken Whitney somewhere, or even hurt her. Every interaction I've had with Shasta has been unhinged."

"She was in the video Annie showed us of Mrs. Olsen preaching to Whitney about divorce at church, wasn't she?"

I blinked. "I'd totally forgotten that! She lives across town from them so she's not in Whitney and Cory's ward."

Spence nodded. "It's weird she just happened to be there that day."

I agreed. I pulled out my phone and moved next to Spence so we could watch it again. Maybe I'd missed something the first time, and two sets of eyes were better than one. As Mrs. Olsen's speech hit its crescendo and the camera panned the crowd, I saw Shasta with her head turned, staring toward where the camera was about to land on Whitney. The camera kept moving and stopped on Whitney, her mouth hanging open. But it wasn't Whitney I was watching; it was the couple behind them. A woman, her arms folded across her chest and her lips pressed into a thin, angry white line. Her husband was sitting next to her. They were both staring directly at the back of Whitney's head, but her husband's expression was one of adoration, maybe even love. I recognized one of them because I'd been sitting next to her at the sound bath and knew she wasn't a fan of Whitney. Stephanie Gress. "Holy shit."

I knocked on Stephanie's front door and given the noise coming from inside the house, it sounded like they might be testing missiles in there. Stephanie answered and looked at me with a confused expression as kids ran up and down the hall behind her. "Kate, what are you doing here?"

"I was hoping to ask you some questions about Whitney."

One of the kids screamed at a pitch so high I thought it might break glass. "It's not a great time."

"It won't take long."

She pressed her lips together and then smiled and gestured with her hand for me to come inside. She pointed to a living room right off the foyer. The house had been built in the last ten years and had light wood floors, a blue rug, and dark grey sofas with a plethora of throw pillows. She left for a few minutes to tell the kids to go play outside. They grabbed their coats and gloves, discussing their snow fort plans in detail.

"How can I help you?" Stephanie asked as she settled into the couch across from me.

"At the sound bath, you indicated you weren't Whitney's biggest fan."

Her lips puckered like she'd eaten something sour. "I'm not."

"Because of her Fanzy page?"

"Among other things."

"Do those things have to do with your husband?"

All of the color drained from Stephanie's face. "I…I…I don't know what you're talking about."

I cocked my head to the side, watching her closely. "Let me take a stab at this and you can tell me if I'm wrong. Your husband was looking at Whitney's Fanzy page and was a little obsessed with her. You caught him and blamed Whitney, instead of your husband, for wronging you. You then released Whitney's Fanzy page link so everyone could see what she'd been doing and you could shame her for it."

Stephanie ground her teeth together.

"Am I close?"

She shifted in her seat and put her hands in her lap. "Nate was cheating with Whitney's page and kept it from me for months. It affected our relationship, and threatened our eternal family. And he wasn't the only one doing it. She was cheating with thousands of men, a lot of them right here in Branson Falls, and breaking up families all over the place. Someone needed to expose her and I don't regret doing it."

"I'm sure that was a difficult thing to deal with," I said, trying to extend grace that Stephanie hadn't offered to anyone else. "Is it cheating though? Whitney had photos on a page publicly accessible to anyone with the link. She wasn't in an actual relationship with him."

"Wasn't she?" Stephanie argued. "He created a whole story

about them in his head. In his mind he was in a relationship with her. He was thinking of her instead of me and wishing she was his wife."

When she put it that way, I could see why she was so upset. But blaming Whitney instead of her husband wasn't right. It's probably what she'd been taught, but still wasn't fair. "He was in a relationship with her photos and videos. She wasn't present. A relationship requires two consenting people, and this didn't go both ways."

"It affected my relationship because he thought they were in one."

It was a tricky line. In this day and age of social media and influencers, people became their brands. But they were still people. Putting the blame of a relationship failure on a photo or presence online was a grey area. But I could understand how seeing someone else's life, and being attracted to them, could lead a person down a path to make them believe they were unhappy in their own relationship. It could also be used as a way to improve their relationship and make it better, provided the couple could communicate about it.

The front door opened and Stephanie's husband, Nate, walked in. He was tall with thinning brown hair, but his baby face and button nose made him look younger than he was. He was wearing a white dress shirt, dark blue sports coat, and tan pants. He saw us both sitting there and Stephanie turned to him, her eyes hollow. "You should probably come in here for this."

Nate's brows pinched together and he came in, putting his bag down next to the chair.

"Hi, Nate. I'm Kate Saxee, editor of *The Branson Tribune*."

"Nice to meet you," Nate said, sitting down on the couch. I

noticed Stephanie and Nate kept a whole cushion and a country of unexpressed emotions between them.

"I have some questions about Whitney Hatch for you."

His face paled. "I don't know how I can help you with that. I don't really know her."

Stephanie gave a derisive snort. "She already knows everything, Nate. Just answer the damn questions."

My eyes widened slightly at Stephanie's swear. I turned to Nate. "Where did you first hear about Whitney's page?"

He closed his eyes and blew out a long sigh. "From some friends. The link was being shared with lots of guys."

"Do you know where your friends found the link?"

His gaze shifted up to the ceiling like he was trying to remember. "It was being posted in some online chat forums. I could send you the forum links if you want."

"That would be great," I answered. Maybe I could find more information there. "What was the subject of the forums?"

"Men's groups, mostly. A lot of men in the groups were from Utah."

"Was Whitney specifically targeting Mormon men when she shared the link?"

He drew his brows together, thinking. "A lot of Mormons were in the group, but the group members were broader than that. It was men from all over who were looking for a place to connect with other men and talk about shared perspectives."

I'd researched enough stories over the years to know that sounded like the Manosphere. I would run fast and far from any man involved with that dumpster fire of misogyny and entitlement.

"So, you got the link and started subscribing to her page?"

"Yeah. She posted photos and sometimes videos. She chatted with people a lot in the chat room. She said that with her schedule, it was easier to respond to chats."

"Were the chats public?"

"Some of them were. It actually kind of made me uncomfortable because some of the men in the chats were really obsessed with her."

That caught my attention. "Obsessed how?"

He shifted like he was uncomfortable talking about it. "They wanted her to go on dates with them in real life. They offered her money, and cars, and whatever she wanted. One guy was especially creepy. He kept telling her he wanted her to be his sugar baby and that if she were his, he'd never let her out of his sight."

That sounded creepy. "How did she respond?"

"The same way she responded to anyone hitting on her. She would brush it off, or make some flirty comment and then keep going."

I wanted to find out more about these guys Nate thought were sketchy. "Can you still see the chats?"

"No. You pretty much have to be online at the same time they're happening. The logs only go back for twenty-four hours."

Users might have to be online and watching in real time, but I wondered if the chats were archived for the page owner.

"Is there anything else you can think of that you might want to tell me?" I asked.

Nate shook his head.

I gave him my card. "Please call me if you remember more."

He nodded and looked at Stephanie, who seemed to be on

the verge of angry tears. I thanked them both and showed myself out.

As soon as I was in my Jeep, I called Hawke and told him the latest developments, then asked, "Do you think Whitney's disappearance is related to Fanzy and someone who was following her, took her?"

"We're going to find out," he said.

I'm not going to lie, his matter-of-fact confidence was a turn on.

Another call came through. "I have to take this, but let me know if anything comes up," I told him.

"I will."

I hung up and answered the other line. "Hey, Bobby. What's going on?" Maybe my mom's witches were totally nude now.

"You need to come to the police station. Ella's been arrested."

I had to pick my jaw up off the floor before I could answer. "For what?"

"Vandalism."

What the… "I'll be there in five minutes," I told Bobby, and sped down the road to the Branson Falls police station.

Another officer was waiting at the front and escorted me to a back room. Ella was sitting at a table, her eyes narrowed and lips puckered like she was contemplating vengeance via murder. Her hair was a hot mess, and her pants looked wet and muddy. She was also wearing handcuffs. I took my earlier statement back. Ella seemed to be trying to surpass my mom for getting into trouble.

"What happened?" I asked her, my tone shocked.

"Injustice, that's what," she snarled.

The door opened and an officer escorted Keanu into the room. Keanu was a local kid who was often either drunk, or high, or both. He looked, and sounded, like he'd stepped out of a 1980s movie. He'd helped on a lot of my investigations since moving back to Branson. He was quirky, but I liked him. He sat in a chair in the corner and waved at me, his cheeks getting rounder with his smile. "Hey, reporter lady!"

"What are you doing here?" I asked him, confused.

Keanu's eyes went wide and he pointed at Ella. "I was helpin' granny!"

Bobby came into the room then. He was holding some yard signs that he put down on the table. The first sign showed moving boxes and furniture. The name "Hunky Movers" had a photo of cartoon biceps next to the H in the name. Scrawled across the sign in thick black marker was the word 'LIARS!!!!!' in all caps.

Another sign looked the same, but 'NOT TRUE!!!!!' was scribbled across that one. Also, in all caps.

"Most people upset with a company write a review and put it up on the internet. Ella, here, decided to take her opinions to the streets." Bobby waved a hand across the contents of the table.

My mouth fell open. "*You* did that?" I pointed to the signs.

"It was false advertisin'!" Ella insisted, shoving a finger toward the signs and pointing at the biceps. "I paid for a show and thought I was gettin' one! I expected some Drake and Hawke look-a-likes in my livin' room, movin' my furniture. Instead, I got some men almost as old as me, complainin' about hemorrhoids and talkin' about their daily fiber supplements. If I wanted that, I could go down to the nursin' home!"

I blinked, totally stunned. "Did you kick them out?"

She tried to fold her arms across her chest defiantly, but was impeded by the handcuffs. She glared at the cuffs, then at Bobby for putting them there. "No, I let 'em finish movin' things because I wanted to see how the couches looked with the new layout. But as soon as they were done, I called the company to complain."

"What did you say?" I asked.

"I told them their ad lied, the men weren't hunky at all, and I wanted a refund. They refused because they said the movers had moved things and they'd done their job."

I agreed with the company about that.

"As soon as I hung up, I got in my car and went around to all the signs I'd seen advertisin' Hunky Movers and I made some accurate adjustments." She picked at some mud on her pants, completely unapologetic.

"What happened to your hair and clothes?" I gestured to the mud and the mess on her head.

She screwed up her face like she was smelling something unpleasant. "It was windy and my wig came off while I was bendin' over to fix the signs. I had to chase it down the street and got mud all over my pants."

"Your hair performed a prison break?"

She looked at me from under her lashes, her expression pinched as she tapped her foot.

"That's where I came in!" Keanu grinned and lifted his hands to give himself a high-five.

Ella glanced at him, her eyes softening slightly. She was still irritated as hell, but appreciative of Keanu. "He was able to run faster than me and he saved my wig from traffic."

"Good thing, too," Keanu said, a note of seriousness in his tone. "It went flyin' down the sidewalk and almost hit a pedestrian. They thought it was a bird either attackin' or dyin'. They started wavin' their hands and pushed it away from them. Another gust picked it up and sent it straight into the street. A bus almost ran it over! But don't you worry, I jumped in front, grabbed her hair, and rolled back to safety."

I shook my head in disbelief at the entire situation.

Bobby pressed a hand to his forehead and leaned against the table. "You can't just go around markin' graffiti on advertisements you don't agree with, Ella."

She looked affronted. "Of course I can! They lied, and I didn't want anyone else to get bamboozled!"

I looked to Bobby, and Bobby just shook his head.

Ella's furious glare settled on Bobby. "I can't believe you arrested me!" She pointed a finger at him and wiggled it a little like she was trying to hex him. "Your days of getting' pies are numbered, Bobby Burns!"

She only gave him pies as a bribe to get out of speeding tickets so I wasn't sure that was her best threat. Maybe promises of more pies and bribes would have worked better.

"I'll have to take my chances," Bobby said. "You better hope the company doesn't decide to press charges."

I looked at Bobby. "Is she free to go?"

"Yeah, but stay around town 'til I know what the Hunky Movers management wants to do next."

He turned to Keanu next. "You too. You're a witness."

Keanu's grin spread even wider. "Right on!"

I nodded to all of them and took Ella to the scene of the crime to pick up her car. She grumbled about her rights, her duties as a good citizen, and injustice the whole way there.

After I dropped Ella off, I called Drake.

"Do you know anyone associated with the Hunky Movers?"

Drake paused. "The moving company that says they use hot guys to move your stuff?"

"Yeah."

He paused again. "If you need something moved, I'm happy to help next time I'm there."

Visions of Drake lifting heavy things made me glad I hadn't started driving yet. "Not me," I explained. "Ella's in a bit of a legal situation. She hired them to move some furniture and thought she was going to get a side show of stripper magic. She was upset when they arrived and the men didn't meet her hunky standards. So, she vandalized the company's signs and called them liars."

Drake laughed for at least fifteen seconds. "I'll see what I can do."

Chapter Eighteen

Hundreds of flowers of all kinds were standing in buckets. Each flower was wrapped in its own plastic, with a little plastic filled water container covering the stem. It was Valentine's Day, and love was in the air, even at the high school.

Brad Rose, a high school junior, had saved up money from his job to buy every girl a flower for Valentine's Day. It was adorable, and the community taking care of each other was one of the things I loved about a place like Branson Falls.

I took some photos of Brad standing in the middle of all the buckets of flowers.

"How did you come up with this idea?" I asked him.

He lifted his shoulder, bending down to grab a flower from the buckets. "I used to see how sad my sisters would get on Valentine's Day if no one gave them anything, and I didn't want other girls to feel like that. I wanted to do something to let them know they matter."

That was so cute my heart almost burst.

He started handing the flowers out and the reactions were

priceless. Some women were ecstatic, others were shy, but they all had huge smiles. "This is the sweetest thing," one girl said, thanking Brad. "I've never gotten a flower on Valentine's Day before."

And that's how it went with every girl he gave flowers to. I had no doubt that he'd be on top of every list for every Girl's Choice dance for the rest of high school.

I stayed a little longer to take photos, and talk to some of the recipients and teachers before I left to go back to the office. On my way to my car, my mom texted.

MOM

You forgot to leave Gandalf's medication for tonight.

Dammit! I had. The pills were still in my Jeep.

KATE

I'll bring it by after work.

MOM

Okey dokey!

Then she sent me twenty-three emojis, careful not to include the poop with hearts that she still maintained was actually happy chocolate ice cream.

I walked into the office and could hardly see my desk, or anything around it. At least two dozen deep red roses, the blooms heavy and petals like velvet, were sitting in a vase that was as big as a small child.

"We're taking bets on who they're from," Spence said,

coming out of his office. I had to look around the flowers to see him.

"I think Hawke," Ella said from the other side of the vase, and I jumped because she was short enough that I couldn't see her there.

"I think Drake," Spence said. "What's your guess?"

I looked at the flowers, gorgeous, long-stemmed red roses. They were romantic, traditional, and expected. "I think," I said, grabbing the card, "they're probably from Drake."

I read the card:

Nothing could be as beautiful as you, but I told the florist to try. Happy Valentine's Day. - Drake

"Well?" Spence asked.

"Yeah! Don't leave us hangin'! I've got a milkshake ridin' on this!" Ella said.

I laughed. "They're from Drake."

"Dangit!" She fisted her hand and moved it in front of her in an aw-shucks gesture. "If those are from Drake, I can't wait to see what Hawke's getting' ya!" Ella said. "Hopefully it's him naked, holdin' the bouquet. And hopefully someone gets pics!"

I rolled my eyes, though I didn't mind the visual. I just didn't want to share it with others.

"Brother Love's Travelling Salvation Show" started playing on my phone.

"Happy Valentine's Day," I said when I answered.

"Happy Valentine's Day to you, too," Drake said. "I wanted to make sure you got the flowers."

"I did, and they're absolutely gorgeous. The vase is so big I'm going to have to move them to the treat table while I work. Ella might try to steal them, but the vase is bigger than she is so I don't think she could carry them out the door."

I saw Ella stick her tongue out at me and I smiled.

"Tell her if she does, I'll get her arrested for a second time."

I laughed. "Thank you. They're really beautiful."

"You're welcome. I wanted to tell you thank you for the chocolates. They taste amazing."

"You're welcome. They're from a shop in Belgium that I love. I would have given them to you in person if you were here."

"Give me a couple of weeks, then we'll have our Valentine's Day date and make up for it."

"I'm looking forward to that," I said, and genuinely meant it.

"I have to get to a meeting, but I'm glad I got to hear your voice."

"I am too," I said, my fingers trailing over the velvety petals of the stunning flowers.

I hung up the phone and jumped again when Ella poked her head out from behind the flowers. I was going to have to move them or I'd have a heart attack by the end of the day.

"What did ya get Drake?"

"Chocolates," I answered. And something else, but I wanted to give it to him in person.

"What did you get Hawke?"

"I can't tell you that because he doesn't even know yet."

She put her palm to her chest, affronted. "You think I'd tell him?"

I arched a brow. "I think you'd tell *everyone*."

She shrugged. "Okay, you're probably right."

I wasn't going to lie. It was weird buying Valentine's Day gifts for two guys. I wasn't sure how polygamists and dudes with secret families survived. Trying to juggle two men and make sure they were happy was exhausting, let alone more than two partners, and kids. It seemed like a lot of work.

I moved the giant-sized vase off my desk and turned on my computer. I had an email from Nate Gress with the links to the men's group forums he'd been part of. I clicked through and started reading some of them. It was exactly what I'd thought. A lot of manosphere anti-feminist verbiage with post after post about men's rights, and how women should do as they're told. The posts also focused on how women needed to stay in traditional roles and their place was in the home. They should be barefoot, pregnant, and subservient, and they needed to be kept that way.

Every post was a reminder of the childhood, religion, and culture I'd grown up in where women weren't given power. They were dismissed, and when they threw a big enough fit, they were given small victories, which later taught them to accept crumbs as progress and be happy about it. They were trained to not only accept abuse, but be grateful for it.

One post, from a user called MightyMen, explained that women were basically car models. And they all had different features and upgrades and you should be able to choose what upgrades you wanted. Other people commented under that post, expressing similar views. Then MightyMen posted Whitney's photo and said she was the Ferrari of women, but had an independent streak that needed to be tamed. Several men commented heinous ways they would do that, and the MightyMen poster then dropped the link to her Fanzy page.

I'd heard a lot about Whitney over the last few weeks, and I couldn't imagine this was Whitney advertising her page here. Whitney, who valued her independence and cared deeply about her career and being able to take care of herself. Someone else must have found her page and turned her into the perfect trad wife ideal in their head, then posted links about her.

I tried to get information on the MightyMen screen name, but didn't find a name associated with it. Though, I did find them on other boards spouting the same nonsense, and sharing Whitney's link.

I wondered if maybe Shasta, or one of the women who thought Whitney was cheating with their husbands, had been pretending to be a guy and shared the links in these forums. Some of the responses were beyond scary and made me even more concerned for Whitney's well-being.

I was scrolling through more forums and posts when the bell on the front door jingled and Hawke walked in wearing a grey winter coat, jeans, black boots, and a t-shirt so tight he might as well have not been wearing it at all. I let my eyes linger and he grinned, catching his tongue between his teeth. He walked to my desk, said hi to Spence on the way, then noted the massive arrangement of roses on the table across from me. His eyes narrowed slightly, the only indication he'd had a reaction to seeing them, and remembered I was dating two men on a holiday celebrating love.

"Happy Valentine's Day," he said, leaning against my desk.

I smiled and leaned closer to him. "Happy Valentine's Day to you, too."

"It will be happier in about six hours when we leave for our date."

"I'm looking forward to seeing what you've planned."

He angled his head and crossed his arms over his chest. "Some of the surprises are already waiting for you, you just haven't found them yet." He gave me a wink and my stomach clenched in anticipation.

"Hot dang! A sexy scavenger hunt!" Ella said, clapping her hands as she came in from the back room where I was certain she'd been hiding behind the door and spying.

The corners of Hawke's lips quirked up. "Something like that."

"The kid at the high school bought hundreds of flowers for all the girls so you've got a lot to live up to," Ella warned him.

"Hopefully I'll measure up," he said, his eyes sparkling.

I'd seen him naked and he measured up just fine, in all the ways.

"What are you working on?" he asked, glancing at my computer screen.

"I've been looking at the forums that Nate Gress sent me showing the posts with links about Whitney. I really do think someone from Whitney's Fanzy page, or even these forums, might have taken her," I said.

"Why?"

I showed Hawke some of the posts and watched him cringe harder the more he read. That he found it as disturbing as I did simply reinforced my opinion that Hawke was one of the good guys, despite what Drake liked to tell me about him.

"This ties into what I was coming to talk to you about," he said. "I got into Whitney's Fanzy account."

My eyes went wide. "What did you find out?"

"Whitney's business is Love and Light Holdings, and is

registered to her. The business tied to her Fanzy account is called 111 Holdings Inc."

My mouth fell open. "111 Holdings Inc., like 111 Healing and Crystals? That could easily be Clarissa."

Hawke nodded. "I already checked and 111 Holdings Inc. was created in Delaware, so it's not tied to a person or social security number."

"Of course it's not." I still felt like it was too much of a coincidence to not be a clue though.

"I also looked into Clarissa's finances. There's nothing strange going on in her personal or business accounts, and no signs of large deposits, or money from Fanzy."

My shoulders slumped and I dropped my chin. I felt like Clarissa was involved in this somehow, and was counting on her finances to help me figure it out. "Damn. I was hoping that would give us some answers."

Hawke rolled his head from side-to-side, stretching his neck. "We still don't know who owns 111 Holdings Inc. It could still be Clarissa."

He was right. I tapped my pen on my desk, thinking. "Since you were able to get in, can you also check the Fanzy chats? Nate Gress said there were some guys in the public chats that seemed scary and wanted Whitney to be in a relationship with them. He said the chats happen in real time and aren't kept for people to read back through, but I wonder if the account manager has access to them. I'm also sure there's a private message section that some of these guys might have tried messaging her at."

"I'll look into it."

"Thank you. Did you find out anything else while you were searching around?"

"Not about Fanzy, but the voice recognition software wouldn't work on the voicemail recording to tell us if it was Whitney, or a robot. The recording was too unclear. But even if the recording was crystal clear, we still wouldn't know unless we could have a conversation with her and ask questions only she would have the answers to."

That's what he'd told me earlier too, but I'd still been optimistic. "Damn. I was hoping that would be a lead."

He tilted his head to the side, considering. "It still could be, because I searched her phone records and she hasn't made any calls from her number in the last three weeks."

"Nothing?" The surprise was evident in my tone.

"No. So I don't think the voice on Megan's voicemail was hers, and whoever Clarissa was talking to, it wasn't Whitney."

I thought about it for a few minutes. "She was at a 'no tech' retreat so maybe she just used someone else's phone to call them."

"It's possible, but most people barely remember their own phone numbers now, let alone the numbers of friends. Phone contact lists have all of that information now and few people commit numbers to memory."

"That's a good point."

"The records show the last place her phone was used three weeks ago. It was in Branson Falls."

I stared at him. "Clarissa said Whitney's been at the retreat since then. Clarissa also said she's talked to Whitney, and gotten texts from her. She showed them to Bobby."

"Maybe," Hawke said with a shrug, "but not from her regular phone."

My mind was spinning. "If the last place her phone was used was Branson Falls, she either turned her phone off before she left Branson and didn't make any calls or use her phone on the way to the retreat, or she turned her phone off and never left."

"That's the conclusion I came to as well."

Could Whitney really still be in Branson Falls? And if so, was she here because she wanted to be, or was she being held captive by someone?

"I'm going to talk to Clarissa and see what she says. Maybe I can get the number Whitney called her from and you can trace it."

I went to 111 Healing and Crystals, possibly also 111 Holdings Inc., and Starr was working at the front. She had a star shaped earring that went from the top of her earlobe to the bottom like her ear was being impaled. It was pretty cool. "Hi, Starr! I like your earring."

She flashed a bright smile. "Thank you!"

"Is Clarissa here?" I looked around the store, hoping I could manifest her.

Starr frowned sympathetically. "No, she's out of town."

That was unexpected, especially since Whitney, and Clarissa's best friend, was supposed to be back any day. "Do you know where she went?"

Starr shook her head. "Nope, she just said she was taking a last-minute trip and she'd be back in a day or two."

The timing felt very convenient.

"Do you know when she left?"

"This morning."

I told her thanks for her help and called Hawke.

"Clarissa took a last-minute trip somewhere. Can you check her phone and see where she might be?"

"Yep, give me a minute."

I drove back to the office while he did his magic.

"Her phone was last used in Branson Falls yesterday."

I narrowed my eyes. "So, she either left her phone in Branson Falls, or turned it off." I paused. "Or maybe Whitney and Clarissa were taken by the same person." I still had my suspicions about Clarissa, but now I didn't know what to think. Maybe Clarissa was the one holding Whitney and she turned her phone off so she couldn't be found.

"Those are all possibilities."

"Okay, thanks for your help. I'll see you in a few hours."

"I hope I get to see *a lot* of you around that time as well."

I smiled and blushed at the flirting. "The feeling is mutual."

I pulled into a *Tribune* parking spot, thinking about Whitney and Clarissa. I needed to figure out a way to track them. There had to be something.

I grabbed an apple from the treat table because I needed something sweet, but also needed to look amazing in my Valentine's Day dress tonight. I caught Spence up on everything that had happened.

"I never realized how hard it was to track down an adult. With all the technology we have now, it seems like it would be easy."

"It probably is if your phone is on." I said the words and then stopped with my apple halfway to my mouth. I dropped the apple back on my desk and woke up my computer.

"What are you doing?" Spence asked as I pulled up a page.

"Checking on a hunch." I typed some things into my background search. "Wendy mentioned that Whitney's car was quiet as she drove away. A car that's quiet is most likely an electric car."

Spence furrowed his brow. "What does that tell you?"

"A lot of electric vehicles have an app that includes GPS tracking information for where the car is located. And if Whitney had to charge the car at a pay station, there would be a paper trail record for it because it's all done through credit card."

The search results populated. Bingo.

I called Hawke. "Whitney has an EV that tracks her location."

Hawke was silent for several seconds. "That makes her, or her car at least, much easier to find once we get into the system."

I gave him the make, model, and VIN I'd found from my search.

"We should have the info by tomorrow at the latest," he said.

"You're pretty handy to have around."

"Just wait until later," he said, his voice practically a purr.

I hung up, and went to drop off Gandalf's meds to my mom and dad.

I knocked on the door and went inside, calling out hello. The house smelled heavenly. I walked into the kitchen, decorated with stone countertops, hardwood floors, and stainless-steel appliances, and saw my mom decorating heart-shaped sugar cookies. "Those look amazing," I said, picking one up and taking a bite before I remembered about the dress. I debated it for about five seconds and decided the dress could handle a sugar cookie.

I put Gandalf's meds on the counter and heard a rumbling coming from down the hall. I watched as Gandalf tore into the kitchen wearing a little bowtie made from the same pink sequins the witches were wearing. A tiny little bell hung from the middle of the bowtie.

Pocket followed Gandalf, but at a slower pace. She was wearing a little skirt made of pink lace and black tulle.

"You're really trying to use up those sequins and lace, aren't you?" I said to my mom. "Why is Gandalf wearing a bell?"

She spread some icing over a cookie and answered, "So Pocket can find him easier and not run into as many walls. She's getting used to our house, but they can play better when Pocket knows where Gandalf is."

"That's adorable," I said, bending down to pet them both and then snap a photo.

"Isn't it cute?" my mom said. "They're on a little Valentine's date!"

I rubbed both their tiny heads and they closed their eyes like they were in heaven—or high. "Are they going to watch the witch strip show in the front yard for their date?"

She slapped me across the butt with the towel on her shoulder. "It's not a strip show! And don't be silly. The puppies aren't interested in witches. But I've made them a very special Valentine's dinner of boiled chicken and vegetables, with puppy cakes for dessert."

"Hopefully these cakes aren't shaped like bones." Her recent attempt at dog cookies had left the end of one side of the cookies broken off and the remaining cookies looked like they should be outside with the stripper witches.

She glared at me. Hard. "They're on the counter over there so the frosting can set."

I looked at the adorable tiny cakes and started to laugh.

"What's so funny?" my mom asked.

"Was this a new frosting recipe?"

She nodded as she continued her frosting and decorating. "Yep. It's yogurt frosting. I tinted it with beet juice so it would be light pink, and made a little red heart in the middle with cherry juice. I wanted something special for their date."

"I'm not sure the ingredients worked out that well." I picked at the cakes, grabbing some crumbs for the pups.

She frowned and put her frosting piping bag on the counter before coming over to look at the plate. She gasped. The pink frosting covered the top of the cupcake, but the red heart hadn't set correctly and had leaked out of its edges and formed a circle. With the pale pink background and the darker pink middle that was now a circle it looked a lot like puppy cake boobs. It felt kind of perfect for Valentine's Day, actually. My mom grabbed the plate from me, shaking her head. "I don't understand how this happened!"

"Maybe it was one of the ingredients? Or maybe they were too hot when you frosted them?" I discreetly dropped the crumbs in front of Gandalf and Pocket.

She stared at them and I watched as her expression turned from horror to determination. "It's fine. I have more frosting and can cover it up. No one will ever know."

I snapped a photo.

She whipped her head around to me and pointed. "You delete that right now, Kate Saxee!"

I put my phone back in my purse. "The good news is that you now have dick cookies and boob cakes under your belt, and it's only a matter of time before you can open an erotic bakery."

Her eyes were slits and her lips pinched together. She tapped her foot on her hardwood floor for several seconds before responding with, "You're lucky I love you."

I gave her a huge smile, trying to get her to think I was too cute to harm. It had worked for me a lot as a kid. "I love you, too," I took another bite of my cookie. "Speaking of your bakery, we need to come up with a question we can ask each other in case someone ever calls trying to pretend to be us and we need to be able to prove it really is us."

She moved more cookies from the cooling rack to the frosting and decorating area. "Why would we need that?"

I grabbed a glass and got some milk from the fridge as I answered. "I'm investigating Whitney Hatch's disappearance and Hawke told me that voices can easily be replicated. One of the new scams is to duplicate a person's voice and call their family members asking for help. The family member thinks it's their loved one because it sounds like them. We need a secret code in case that ever happens, and it needs to be something someone else doesn't know."

"Like psychics who contact dead people and get answers only the dead person knows!" She was so excited that she squeezed her piping bag and some of the frosting came out—which, like her puppy boob cakes, was also appropriate for Valentine's Day.

"Something like that. I was thinking that if we're ever in

that situation, we can ask each other what your dog bone cookies turned into."

If looks could kill, my mom would have murdered me.

"That won't work," she said.

I put my glass of milk down. "What do you mean? It's perfect! No one else knows it happened!"

She went back to her frosting. "It won't work, because I won't answer the question." She refused to look at me as she said it.

"Then I guess I'll just think it's a scam and won't be able to rescue you."

"I'll come up with something else to ask."

I shook my head, envisioning the whole thing already. "This is going to be you saying: tell me what I made you wear for the Christmas parade when you were fourteen and me refusing to answer, and me asking about the dog bone cookies and you refusing to answer, and both of us will have no idea if the other one is actually in need of assistance."

"Don't be silly. You were an adorable bunny and Drake still remembers it. I did you a favor."

I stared at her, and felt like she should really be studied by a professional for her justification skills.

"I'll come up with a list of secret questions you can choose from," she helpfully offered.

"Okay, but the questions better be as entertaining as dick cookies and boob cakes."

She mumbled something under her breath that sounded like pseudo-swears.

I picked up the plate of cookies she'd made for me.

"Grab that one, too," she said, pointing. "It's for Hawke."

"None for Drake?"

She dropped some pink sprinkles on the cookies she'd just frosted. "You're not seeing Drake tonight."

"How do you know that?"

"Because Hawke told me you're going out with him. You have a lot of talents, but even you can't manage them both in one night, and Drake's not even in town. I'll give him his cookie plate the next time he stops by."

Good grief! She talked to them more than I did! "Why is Drake coming over?"

She lifted her towel holding shoulder and gave me a look like she thought the question was odd. "Because he always stops by when he's in town. He's busy right now though because of the legislature."

I narrowed my eyes, irritated. "I'm aware. It sounds like you see him more than I do."

She nodded her head. "Probably. But neither one of your boyfriends are whisking me off on vacations to Puerto Rico, so I must be doing something wrong."

I pointed my last bite of cookie at her. "Make them some boob cakes," I said, popping the bite in my mouth. "That might help."

She rolled her eyes. "Have fun tonight and don't make me a grandma. I'm not that old yet."

Sheesh! "Neither am I!"

I petted Gandalf and Pocket and told them to enjoy the boob cakes, then took the cookie plates and left to go back to my house and get ready.

♥

Several people were standing in my yard, trying to peer through the fence slats as I drove over the patches of ice in my driveway and parked my Jeep in the garage.

"Hi," I said warily to the group as I got out of my Jeep and went around the corner.

"Hi, Kate," my neighbor, Silvy, said with a smile. She was one of the people who had been finding creative excuses to stand at her window and watch Hawke shovel.

"Hi, Silvy. What's going on?" I gestured to the handful of women around her.

"Oh, well, we didn't mean to pry, we've just been watching them work all day and were curious. We couldn't wait to see the final results."

I pulled my brows together, trying to figure out what they were talking about. "Final results of what?"

Silvy and a few of the other women there gave a knowing smile and gestured to the backyard.

Phyllis came running out of her house, waving her arms in the air. "Wait! I wanna see the reveal too! I've been watchin' 'em take stuff back there all day!"

I had no idea what they were referring to, but clearly people had been at my house all day doing something in my yard. I moved around the women, opened the gate, and gasped.

My backyard had been turned into a secret garden. Stunning hot pink and ice white roses dripped from a square trellis that had to be at least eight feet tall. The middle of the trellis was rounded to create an arch opening. The roses covering the trellis and arch were woven between white twigs and emerald greenery. The greenery and pink and white accent flowers continued down, flowing over shelves on either side of the arch. Pots of roses in various shades of pink were placed on the shelves, and the hot pink rose and greenery train dripped down the shelves like a floral blanket. The flowers pooled on the ground, and hot pink rose petals were scattered across the snow, creating a rose petal path to the fence gate. The arch faced the back of my house, and was perfectly centered so I would see it every time I looked out my kitchen window.

Silvy put her hand to her chest in awe and whispered, "I've never seen anythin' like that!"

Greta, one of the other women, fanned herself even though it was about thirty degrees outside. "Is it a proposal? Is he in there somewhere?" She poked her head from one side to the other, standing on her toes like she might be able to see him. "Maybe you should go look!"

"The bigger question is who did this for ya?" Phyllis said.

Silvy pointed to a stone bench placed under the arch. A card was sitting in the middle of it. "That might tell ya!"

I didn't notice the bench at first because I was so distracted by the flowers. I didn't even need to look at the card to know it was Hawke, and he'd turned my backyard into a stunning garden escape that smelled like romance and joy. I walked across the petal path to the bench.

"It's Hawke, isn't it?" Phyllis asked, dancing back and forth on the balls of her feet with excitement.

I picked up the card, noting Hawke's handwriting on the outside, and nodded. I couldn't wipe the smile off my face, and had a feeling it would be there all night.

Phyllis sighed. "He's so dreamy!"

Silvy put a hand to her heart and looked like she might swoon. "What would it be like to be young again?"

The women left, gushing about the few men who still knew how to be romantic.

I sat on the bench, taking the flowers in and breathing their sweet fragrance. I opened the card.

236

A sexy fire and ice themed rose garden for my favorite fiery Valentine. Happy Valentine's Day. - Hawke

Chapter Nineteen

Hawke knocked on the front door. I opened it, and debated whether we should even go to dinner, or straight to dessert in my bedroom. He was wearing a black suit that perfectly draped over his broad shoulders. His dress shirt was also black, and his tie was solid silver. His freshly shaved jawline was a temptation, but not nearly as tempting as his full lips, or the emerald eyes that took me in from head to toe. Slowly.

My hair was down in loose curls that framed my face. My lashes were long and black and my lips a deep scarlet. I was wearing a dark red satin evening dress with a neckline that plunged almost to my belly button, and showcased my chest and cleavage. The dress was form fitting from my chest to where the fabric ended at my mid-thigh, and one side had a slit that went up my leg about four inches. My shoes were strappy silver stilettos.

"I hope your suit has breakaway Velcro or I might rip it off," I mused, wondering how long it would take to get it off without damage. It looked designer and expensive.

"It's a good thing that slit in your skirt is there and the

fabric can be easily pushed aside because I might not even try to take the dress off of you."

I licked my lips and his eyes followed the movement.

"Thank you for the gorgeous roses and flower display," I said, inviting him in the house.

He smiled. "You're welcome. They sent me a photo of the finished project and I was pleased."

"It's absolutely stunning." I motioned for him to follow me to the back. "Truly, one of the most incredible things I've ever seen."

We stood on the back porch, taking in the beautiful floral art.

He leaned in and whispered, "It's a clue."

"A clue?"

"For your Valentine's gift."

My eyes widened. "*That's* not my gift?" I asked, gesturing to the massive floral display taking up a significant amount of square footage in my backyard that had to have cost him thousands of dollars.

He shook his head and his lips curved up. "No, it's not."

"Now I'm going to spend the rest of the night trying to figure out what that could hint at." It was pretty enough to get married under, but we hadn't even had a DTR discussion.

"You won't have to wait long," Hawke said, looking at his watch. "Speaking of that, we should probably go."

I sighed and followed him inside, kind of wanting to stay there. "I'm sad I won't be able to enjoy them for more than a few days." It was way too cold for the flowers to survive.

"You will. The team is coming back to build a greenhouse around them tonight. I hope that's okay. The roses on the trellis and arch are climbing roses, and the flowers in the pots are potted roses you can cultivate all year. On our trip, you mentioned how much you loved the flowers in Puerto Rico and that you enjoy gardening. The snow makes that difficult for half of the year, so I wanted to fix that. If you don't like it or think it takes up too much space later, they can take it down."

I stared at him, absolutely stunned, and then threw my arms around his neck and kissed him, hard. He wrapped his arms around me, his tongue twisting with mine as he pulled me closer. I breathed in his scent and reached my arms around his back, letting my hands slide down to his perfect ass.

Hawke pulled back slightly. "I'm not opposed to saying to hell with our plans, but we have a luxury suite in the mountains tonight after dinner that I think you'll want to experience."

I bit my lip, grateful for the permanent-marker-like lipstick I was wearing that wouldn't smudge even in case of Hawke. "We should get there fast then."

He grinned, picked up my overnight bag, and took my hand to help me through the snow to his truck.

We'd driven for about an hour and were now standing in front of a fifty-foot-tall slab of granite with a black door carved into it. The LDS church has a vault built into the side of a mountain in Salt Lake City. I'd wanted to get into it for years, but it had security that I didn't think even Hawke could bypass. This looked a lot like what I imagined the vault looked like, though.

"If this is the Church's Little Cottonwood Canyon mountain vault, that would be an incredible present because there's a great deal of information in there that I'd like to get my hands on, but I'm not sure I'm dressed for that."

He flashed a wicked grin. "I could get you undressed any time."

"Don't tempt me," I warned.

Hawke gave five knocks on the door in a special pattern. When the door opened, a woman wearing a soft pink dress that fell to the middle of her thigh was standing there. "Password?" she asked.

"Too sweet," Hawke answered.

She smiled and let us in, then said, "Follow me."

We followed her down a dark hallway that was lit with white candles in black gothic holders. The walls were stone, granite likely, and a deep red and black rug ran down the middle of the hallway. After a few minutes, we came to another solid black door that the woman had to open with a key.

When she did, we followed her into a large room with red, silver, and pink metallic balloons covering the tall ceiling. Tiny lights were strategically installed on the ceiling to look like stars, and crystals dangled several feet, reflecting the light. Private booths were carved into the mountainside, almost like rooms, and the woman in pink led us to one with a bottle of wine chilling in a bucket next to the table. "This space is yours, Mr. Hawkins and Ms. Saxee."

I sat, scooting into the round booth. The seats were soft and the fabric that covered them was black velvet. Hawke sat next to me, draping his arm over my shoulders as the woman picked up the wine from the bucket, uncorked it, and poured us both a glass. "Enjoy your meal," she said with a wink.

I picked up my glass and Hawke picked up his.

"Here's to romantic dinners and new experiences," Hawke said.

We clinked our glasses together and each took a sip of our drinks.

"I haven't heard someone use your real last name in a long time."

He swallowed and I watched the Adam's apple bob at his neck. "There are times when even I require a surname."

I laughed and looked around the gorgeous room. I was totally stunned and had never experienced anything like this. "What is this place?"

Hawke glanced around as well, though I had a feeling he'd marked every entrance, exit, and threat from the moment we stepped inside. "An old speakeasy. When prohibition was going on, it was one of the places people went to get alcohol."

"You mean the alcohol people in Utah weren't supposed to be drinking anyway because it was against the Word of Wisdom?"

"One and the same."

A server came and took our order and before long, we had appetizers and were enjoying the most amazing food I'd ever eaten.

My mom's comment earlier had made me wonder what Hawke wanted his future to look like. I'd had a very sexy time in Puerto Rico with him, but that's all it had been. Sex, and relaxing, and trying to recover from the mayhem of the housing development story and the notoriety that came with it. We'd talked, but hadn't gotten into any deep or important subjects. Now seemed like a good time to start. "Do you want a family?"

He answered without hesitation, "Yes, I want a partner and everything that goes with that."

I nodded. "What about kids?"

He thought about it. "I'm still undecided. My job would make parenting difficult. I would want to be there to actually be a dad to them and be present in their lives. That's not a possibility right now because my schedule is too unpredictable."

"That's the truth. I wouldn't even know how to find you when I was ovulating to get pregnant."

He laughed. "But my job could also change in the future, so maybe kids would be more of an option then."

I turned, angling my body toward him so I could see him better. His gaze fell on the bare strip between my breasts. "So, you don't have a deep yearning desire to have kids?"

"I definitely like that act that makes kids, but a deep desire to be a father? No, not really. What about you?"

I'd thought about it a lot and didn't have an answer. "I'm not sure. I'm young, my career is going well, and I don't want to give that up. If I had kids, I would need a partner who could actively help so I could keep working because my job is important to me." Maybe Hawke could be that person…at some point, which was fine because I wasn't in a hurry to decide. I also wasn't sure if I was what he was looking for long-term, either. There were a lot of unanswered questions.

"We've got time to figure it out," he said.

The server brought our main dishes, and refilled our wine.

"Thank you for the gift," Hawke said, referring to the Valentine's Day gift I'd given him earlier.

I inclined my head toward him. "I thought about giving you a test drive in a supercar, but you have two Ferraris I've never seen, and a whole garage full of supercars that you've probably already been trained to drive like someone's trying to kill you. I tried to find a test drive for a Smart Car, because I figured you'd never driven one of the those, but there's not a lot of demand for that, apparently."

The grin he was trying to hold back broke into a laugh.

"So, I thought you might enjoy a little piece of our beach instead." I'd given him moving sand art made from the sand I brought back from our beach in Puerto Rico.

"I love it. I already put it in my bedroom so it can remind me of us every morning and night."

I smiled at that, my finger trailing around the rim of my wine glass. "I also thought you might like strawberries and chocolate." I'd given him those, too.

"I do."

But I hadn't given him all of his gifts yet. "I thought you might enjoy it even better on me."

Heat flared in his eyes. "I would."

"Your other gift isn't visible right now."

Hawke's gaze turned predatory. "It's dark in here, so it could be."

I licked my lips. "It's worth the wait, trust me."

He handed me another black metallic box wrapped with hot pink ribbon. I opened it and found a black satin blindfold. "Is this for me to wear, or you?" I asked.

He cocked a brow. "Maybe both of us at one point or another."

I felt something else under the blindfold. I lifted it and

found a metal figurine of the Eiffel Tower. I looked up at him, confused. "What is this?"

"Your present. Pick a week"

All of the gifts clicked together in my head. The spa robe, the wine glasses and French wine, the flowers. "The flower arch represented the Arc of Triumph?"

His lips curved. "Yeah. I was trying to be subtle."

My mouth went slack and my brain felt like it was processing too much at once. "You're taking me to Paris?"

He put a hand on my thigh and electricity flowed straight up my dress. "I'd like to. We can fly into Paris and stay for a few days before going to a beautiful estate in the French countryside with wine tours. I'd really enjoy doing that with you."

I shook my head in disbelief. "I'd love that, too, but this seems like a lot. Especially after you just took me to Puerto Rico."

"It isn't."

"I didn't give you something like this." I felt strange to be the one in the relationship who couldn't give as much. It seemed unbalanced.

"You did. You gave me something meaningful. You've given me so much more than a trip. I love your humor, your fire, your ambition," he paused, "your ass." I smiled and shook my head before he continued, "There was a long time in my life when I didn't have anything to look forward to. I tried to fill that space with things. But what I look forward to the most now, is you. My job is lucrative, but it keeps me busy and I don't get to see you as much as I wish I did. I have the resources and I just want to spend time with you."

Well, that was incredibly romantic. I still felt unbalanced, but I could work on that.

He put his palm against my cheek and moved closer to me, his lips pressing into mine and his other hand took advantage of the slit in my skirt and started moving up. His tongue traced my lips and then he caught my bottom lip between his teeth and bit gently. His hand was still working its way up my thigh and I wondered if the booth was big enough for me to climb over and straddle him.

My phone started to vibrate.

It was a holiday and everyone knew I was out with Hawke, so I wasn't expecting any calls. I grabbed my phone from my purse and pushed my brows together. "It's a number I don't recognize, but maybe it's Whitney." I'd put her number in my phone just in case she called me after I left my message for her at the ski resort where she'd been sighted. I'd also tried calling her several times over the past couple of weeks and hadn't gotten an answer but I'd left voicemails. Maybe she was calling me from someone else's phone just like she'd called Megan and Clarissa.

"Put it on speaker," Hawke said.

I answered. "Hello?"

The connection wasn't great and it sounded like it was cutting in and out for several seconds, but I heard a woman's voice softly say, "Your Whitney needs help." And then the line went dead.

Chapter Twenty

Hawke was on his phone asking someone to trace the phone number and location before I even put my phone back in my purse. I signaled for the server to bring our check, but Hawke had already taken care of it.

He took my hand as we swiftly exited the romantic and unique speakeasy that I hoped we could come back to some-time and take full advantage of the booth.

"I'm still expecting to see my gift at some point," Hawke noted as we rushed out the door.

"I'm still planning to show it to you at some point," I promised, and we got in his truck to try and find Whitney Hatch.

Hawke's phone rang. He answered it and since it was connected to his truck's Bluetooth, it was on speaker. "Talk to me," Hawke said.

A female voice answered. "The call cut out, but we have

the location it was made from. It's just a question of whether or not she's still there. He might have moved her."

"Understood," Hawke said. "Send me the address." He hung up and the address popped up on his truck's GPS and started navigating us there.

"*He*," I asked, surprised. "Do you have a suspect?"

Hawke sliced his head down once. "Several, based on you asking me to check Whitney's Fanzy chats and private messages. There were a couple of concerning people commenting on Whitney's chats and sending private messages to her. She was engaging with some of them so I had an associate track them down. The one we're most concerned about was a guy named Rick Baden. My associate is still working on finding out more."

"Why was Rick Baden more concerning than the others?"

"He was actively pursuing Whitney, trying to get her to meet up with him, and going to places she was at. He mentioned in the private messages that he was in Branson Falls on several occasions looking for her."

I shuddered. "That's creepy."

"After you mentioned Whitney's car, we found her EV location. It's at the same mountain resort where you stopped to look for Whitney after someone reported a sighting of her."

"So, she's there," I said.

He glanced at me and gave a slight shake of his head. "Her car is there. Whether she's there or not is another question. Based on the address we just traced her phone to, I'm guessing she's not."

"Do you think Rick followed her to the ski resort and took her?"

"I think it's a possibility."

I tapped my hand on my leg, trying to get rid of nervous energy and think. "Could this be a human or sex trafficking situation?"

Hawke paused. "I never say no because anything can happen, but I'm very familiar with trafficking, and this feels more like an obsession that morphed into an abduction."

Interesting. I put that trafficking information down in my file of things to research about Hawke that might give me more answers about him.

We pulled into Rick Baden's neighborhood in an older area of the city. We slowed down as we drove past a house with yellow vinyl siding and white trim around the windows. It had the house number we were looking for, an attached garage, and the snow had been cleared from the sidewalk. Hawke parked down the street.

"Stay in the truck," Hawke said, grabbing a gun from his glove compartment.

I scoffed. "Absolutely not."

He took a deep breath and rolled his tongue along the inside of his cheek. "Situations like this can become volatile really fast. Police will tell you no call is more dangerous than a domestic call, and I'm treating this like one. From my team's search, we know that Rick is a gun owner and has several firearms. I don't want you to get hurt."

I nodded in agreement. "And I don't want *you* to get hurt. So, let's come up with a believable story that will get us both in the house so you can disarm him and then we can look for Whitney."

Five minutes later we were standing on Rick's porch wearing our fancy Valentine's Day coats, clothes, and shoes, and ringing his doorbell. He opened the door after a few minutes. He was in his fifties at least, with a receding brown hairline, and a beer belly.

He took us both in from head to toe. With our clothes, we probably looked like we'd accidentally wandered off the set of a dance-related reality show. "What do you want?" Rick asked, his voice gruff.

Hawke flashed him a winning smile. "I'm so sorry to bother you. My truck broke down and my phone is dead. I was wondering if I could borrow your phone to call a tow truck?"

Rick's eyes tracked from Hawke to me, and then back to Hawke with suspicion. "Why don't you use her phone?"

"I didn't bring it," I said, deliberately trying to sound ashamed and apologetic, like everything was my fault. "He told me I'm on it too much and I needed to leave it home and focus on him." Thank the goddesses for the part of "chorus member" in my high school musical because pretending to be a woman who did what she was told was taking some serious acting skills.

Hawke reached his arm around me and pulled me to him, his hand resting just under my right breast. Rick tracked the movement, his gaze holding there, and I wanted to take my very pointy heels and kick him directly in the balls.

"Gotta keep the little lady in line," Hawke said, throwing in a bit of the Utah accent where all the words ran together and none were properly enunciated.

Rick's eyes sparked at finding a kindred misogynist spirit. "Sure do. Come in out of the cold and I'll grab my phone."

"Appreciate it," Hawke replied, guiding me inside while also shielding me from anything unexpected that Rick might do.

"Thank you so much," I said. I started bouncing from foot-to-foot. "Would it be possible for me to use your bathroom? We're not from here and it was a long trip. It looks like we'll be waiting in the truck for a while."

"Sure," he said. "It's down the hall."

He led the way on old tan hardwood floors, and I counted two doors on one side and three doors on the other. A stairway that led down was near the end of the hall. "You have a lovely home," I said, my tone oozing sugar.

"Thanks, I grew up in this house." He pointed to the door closest to the stairway. "Here it is."

"Thank you again," I gushed. "You're a lifesaver!"

I went in the bathroom and pulled out my phone, checking the floorplan of the house that I'd pulled up before we came in. The house was older so the basement wasn't required to have windows. I guessed that if Whitney was in the house like Hawke's people thought, she was down there. I took off my heels and left them in the bathroom so they wouldn't click on the hardwood floors.

I could hear Hawke talking in the other room, gathering intel and keeping Rick interested as I crept down the stairs. It was dark except for one sliver of light coming from under a door. I moved toward the door and turned the knob slowly, but it was locked. I decided to chance it and whispered, "Whitney?"

No answer.

"Whitney?" I said again, a little louder.

This time, I heard a voice. "Yes! It's me! I can't get out!"

Adrenaline rushed through me and I took a breath to try and center myself. "This is Kate Saxee. I'm bringing help," I said, and crept back up the steps. I grabbed my high heels and put them back on, flushed the toilet, ran the water in the sink, and then came out of the bathroom and back down the hall. "Thank you," I said to Rick. "I feel much better."

"You're welcome."

"Is the tow truck coming to save us?" I asked Hawke, giving him our pre-arranged question that would let him know I'd found Whitney.

He sliced his head down once in acknowledgment that he'd received my message, and also in answer to my question. And he did it right as my phone rang in my purse, belting out the exciting chorus to "Brother Love's Travelling Salvation Show."

I saw Rick process the realization that I had my phone. His face turned red with anger and he lunged in my direction, but before he could reach me, Hawke had him on the ground, his arms pinned behind his back. He folded like a fish. Hawke grabbed a zip tie from his pocket and tied Rick's hands, then called the police giving them an efficient summary of the situation. The police arrived in less than five minutes, and five minutes after that, Whitney was released from the basement room she'd been locked in.

The EMTs were on the scene checking Whitney over, but said she seemed fine. "Do you want to go to a hospital?" I asked her.

She shook her head. "No. You got here in time. He didn't hurt me physically."

He'd certainly hurt her psychologically, and I hoped that she'd get the help she needed to process through that. "I tried to contact you several times and we tried to locate you, too. But your phone hadn't been turned on for weeks."

She took a deep breath and closed her eyes, putting the meditation and breathwork classes she taught to good use. "Because our phones were taken when we arrived so that we could be present and not worried about social media, work, or any of our other stresses. I was honestly looking forward to the break."

I could understand that.

"Clarissa got texts and voicemails from you, and Megan got a voicemail, too, a few days ago."

"The voicemails weren't from me."

"Who were they from?"

"Rick. He used videos of me online to replicate my voice. Then he looked in my phone's contact list to find out who to call."

Just like Hawke had explained.

"How did he see your contacts if you didn't have your phone?"

"I had another phone that most people didn't know about. It wasn't connected to the internet, but I kept it with me and checked in with Clarissa a couple of times while I was away. Since I had it with me, it was the phone Rick used to call people who were listed in my contacts and recent calls. Clarissa was the person I contacted most. Megan was also someone I spoke with a lot. He picked those two."

"Why did he call?"

"He'd been watching local Branson Falls gossip and he knew people were looking for me. He also knew that my friends and family were saying they knew where I was and they weren't worried about me. He thought that would be a good cover since the only person saying I was missing was Cory, the man who's about to be my ex-husband, and was angry I'd asked for a divorce. Rick made the calls because he wanted to reassure people I was fine, and he didn't want anyone else looking for me."

"How did he find you?" I asked. We'd been trying to find her for weeks, but like she said, the people who knew where she was weren't worried because the whole point of the retreat was for her to not have contact with anyone—and since she had the second phone, she'd still had contact with some of them anyway.

"I didn't know it at the time, but Rick had been stalking me in Branson Falls and followed me to the retreat. He joined the retreat and befriended me. Three days ago, I was out for a walk and took my burner phone so I could text Clarissa. Rick saw me, and asked if I wanted company. We walked and talked a little and even got a drink at the bar. The next thing I remember is waking up here."

"He drugged you?"

"I believe so. I had my burner phone with me at the time so he had access to that phone and the contents, and he was able to keep in touch with people who might have been concerned if they hadn't heard from me after the retreat ended."

"How did you know to call me?"

"I got your note at the front desk when I got back from a group activity one day. I knew the situation I was in could be dangerous, and the fact that you were looking for me gave me some sense of security. I figured you'd be able to get help if I needed it. I put your number in my burner phone just in case."

"How did you get your phone back from him?"

He wanted me to send him some of my private photos. I

told him they were on my phone in a password protected folder so he'd have to let me use it. While I had the phone, I hit send on your number. As soon as I saw that it connected, I said my name so you'd know it was me. When I said, "Your Whitney needs help" it was because I knew he would take that as me asking him for help, and I hoped that you'd also get the message that it was me and I needed help."

I was impressed. "That was quick thinking on your part."

"Thank goodness you got here when you did. The more time went by, the braver he got. I think he would have been capable of anything."

Hawke came up behind me. "We're cleared to leave. If the police need anything else, they'll call us, and they have your numbers, Whitney, in case they need to talk to you."

She looked exhausted and like she needed to sleep for days. "Do you want us to take you back to Branson Falls?" I asked.

She thought about it. "No. My things are at the hotel, and my car is there. I don't want to face all the questions I'll get when I go back, and I definitely can't go back to my house and deal with Cory right now. I really want to shower, eat, and get some sleep. Then go back to Branson Falls tomorrow."

I nodded in understanding and put my hand on her arm in reassurance. "We're staying in the city tonight so we can follow you back tomorrow if you want."

"I'd like that," she said.

"I'll have someone outside your room all night so you feel safe and know there's nothing to worry about," Hawke said.

She looked relieved, and considering the ordeal she'd just been through, I didn't blame her.

We got Whitney back to the hotel where she'd been

staying for the retreat. Her bags were still in her room because she'd paid for a few extra days to stay a little longer, if necessary. It was necessary.

"You just carry zip ties in your pocket?" I asked as we walked back to Hawke's truck.

He threaded his fingers between mine, and warmth rushed through me at his touch. "You never know when you might need one."

I guess he was right, and we'd needed one tonight, but still. "I'm not sure whether to be unsettled by that, or turned on by your preparation skills."

"I always vote for turned on."

I shifted my head from side-to-side. "It's probably a little of both."

We got to the parking garage and took the elevator down. "You played that part well. Who knew you could pretend to be docile and submissive?" he mused.

I screwed up my face in disgust even thinking about it. "I'll probably need a dentist appointment next week because I ground my teeth off doing it."

He threw his head back and laughed. "It's good it was just an act. That kind of woman is not for me."

"What kind of woman is?"

He took his other hand and placed it under my chin, lifting so our eyes met and said, "You are."

Butterflies started a synchronized dance in my stomach. Hawke made me feel special, and it wasn't the trips, or gifts, or things he gave me, it was the realization that I mattered to him not for what I could do for him, but because of who I was. He felt like a partner and that was something I hadn't had in any of my past relationships.

The elevator dinged and we walked to the truck where he opened the door for me. When he got in the driver's seat, he turned, giving me his full attention. "When your phone rang at Rick's house—whose ringtone was that?"

I cringed and wondered if it would ruin the night if I answered with the truth. I also didn't want to lie to him. I pressed my lips together, took a breath, and answered, "Drake's."

Hawke snorted a laugh and his smile lingered long after he finished. "I bet he *loves* that. What Neil Diamond song is mine?"

It made sense he didn't know because he'd never been around to hear my phone ring when he'd called. I was suddenly embarrassed by the song choice and thought about lying to him about that as well. I finessed the truth instead, hoping he wouldn't press. "One of Neil's ballads."

He thought about it for a minute. "Which one?"

So, he'd pressed, and I wasn't going to lie. "His song, "Play Me"."

Hawke ran his tongue over his lips, as they stretched into a grin. "You would definitely be my preferred instrument."

I arched a brow, the movement an invitation. "Oh yeah?"

His grin turned predatory. "Yeah. Why don't we go back to our hotel for the night and I'll show you."

And he did.

Chapter Twenty-One

After a very satisfying night with Hawke, we met Whitney at the resort and followed her back to Branson Falls. We got her settled in her hotel room in town, paid for under Hawke's name so that Whitney could have some solitude and privacy for as long as possible. If people knew she was back, they wouldn't leave her alone. She wasn't ready to see Cory, and she needed some space of her own so she didn't want to stay with friends.

Hawke left to get her bags from her car. I hadn't broached the Fanzy subject with her yet because she hadn't been in the right headspace for it, but I needed to discuss it with her. "I don't want to push, but I have some other questions for you when you're available."

She nodded and sat on the edge of the bed, the crisp white linens wrinkling. "There's a lot to tell you about. Let me get settled here and then I'll call you and set up a time to talk."

"That sounds good. Maybe Clarissa will be back by then. Honestly, I kind of expected to find Clarissa with you yesterday because she left suddenly."

It might have just been the lighting in the room, but it seemed like Whitney lost some of the color from her face. "When did she leave?"

I thought about it for a beat. "Yesterday morning. I went to 111 to try and talk to her about you, but Starr said she had left and wouldn't be back for a day or two."

Whitney pursed her lips. "I'm not sure where she is, but I'll make some calls and see if I can find her."

The door opened and Hawke came in with Whitney's bags. "I'll have someone watching the hotel again so you don't have to worry."

Whitney's appreciation for the safety Hawke offered was evident in the way her shoulders relaxed. "Thank you."

We left her hotel and drove the few miles to my house. Hawke took my bags inside, put his arms around my waist, and gave me a long kiss. When he was done, I licked my lips, and his eyes followed the movement. "I have to check on some things, or I wouldn't leave."

"I have to do the same, or I wouldn't let you."

His eyes sparked with anticipation. "Later, then," he promised.

Hawke left and I unpacked my bag, thinking of everything that had happened since yesterday. Whitney's reaction to the news about Clarissa being gone set off alarm bells. Whitney hadn't given me any details about her relationship with Clarissa beyond the fact that she'd called Clarissa a couple of times on her burner phone. I couldn't tell if Whitney was worried that Clarissa had left, or possibly worried that

Clarissa might find her. I still had so many unanswered questions.

I grabbed my laptop and pulled up Whitney's Fanzy account that Hawke had just given me access to. He'd sent me some of the chats he'd been concerned about, and directed me to the private messages folder. My stomach tightened as I read Rick Baden's messages; they were beyond disturbing. I wondered why Whitney hadn't tried to report him. There were other completely inappropriate messages as well, but none as concerning as Rick's.

I read through some of the chats and several things the users on Fanzy were saying seemed familiar. I pushed my brows together as I flipped over to the Manosphere forums and recognized similar posts. The way things had been phrased in the Fanzy chats and in the comments on the forums was almost identical. But different users were saying them. A lot of the users were probably just spouting talking points they'd heard from other people in the community, but several of the posts were almost verbatim.

Whitney had been advertising her page on these forums, so it would make sense that some of the users would have gone to the Fanzy page and tried to chat with other users who had similar perspectives. The way some of these guys talked though was contrived—almost like a bot was posting using AI or something. Maybe the forums were like other social media sites and the more people engaged with it, the more the algorithms recognized that the page was popular and promoted it. The bots would make sense if that was the case.

I scrolled through some older messages in Whitney's Fanzy inbox, trying to figure out when the page had been started. That's when I came across a message from Clarissa. It said, "You'll regret this. I'll make sure of it."

I scrolled through to see if there was any other communication in the account from Clarissa. I couldn't find any. I tapped my fingers against my thigh. I needed to talk to Whitney whether she was ready or not. I grabbed my purse and keys, and left to go to Whitney's hotel.

Hawke called while I drove. "Whitney left."

"Do you know where she went?"

"No, but I'm tracking her phone."

My phone buzzed with someone else trying to call at the same time I was talking to Hawke. "I have another call coming in. Let me know if you find out where she's going."

"I will," he said, and hung up.

I clicked over to answer the other line. "Hello?"

"Kate, this is Jacey." Her voice sounded frantic and kind of hushed. "A friend is in trouble. Can you meet me?"

"Sure, what's going on?"

She didn't answer my question and instead said, "I'll send you the address."

She hung up, and thirty seconds later, an address came through on my phone. I pulled over, clicked on it, and also sent it to Hawke with a short text explaining what Jacey had said. Then I let my GPS navigate me there.

I pulled up to the Old Mine Mercantile, an abandoned building by the river that, like most old abandoned buildings, was rumored to be full of paranormal activity. Aside from being used as a haunted house around Halloween each year, it was rarely occupied by anything other than the alleged spirits, rats, and teens looking for a place to make out. However, if the cars outside were any indication, today it had a lot of visitors.

Hawke had texted me with Whitney's phone location, and this was the same address.

I moved up the stairs and through the open front doorway. I heard voices, and followed them until I got to an area that opened up into a bigger space. I crept around the corner, into the room where I was hidden from view, but could clearly see Clarissa sitting in a chair across from Cory Hatch and Harry Bracker. They were sitting next to each other on a couch that looked like it had seen a lot of things and should probably be set on fire.

I took in the area, marking all the doors and windows. As I did that, I noticed Jacey across the room, hidden behind an alcove. Her phone was on a stand, recording Clarissa, Cory, and Harry.

Clarissa sat with her legs crossed at the knees and her back straight. "Do you know the history of this place?" She asked Cory and Harry, gesturing around her to the room with high ceilings and Georgian architecture that had surely been stunning when it was built.

Cory squinted, his mouth turning down in a frown like she'd lost her mind. "It's an old building."

Clarissa angled her head to the side, considering his description. "An old building, but one that has a lot of stories. It was used as a brothel by a famous madame named Queen Belle, who helped run the Red-Light district in Salt Lake City before it was disbanded. When that happened, she moved to another location that catered to high-end clientele." Clarissa put her hand out, gesturing to the room like she was revealing a magic trick. "Here."

Harry crossed his arms over his chest and rolled his eyes like this was the most ridiculous thing he'd ever heard. "The history lesson isn't necessary. You said you'd tell us where Whitney is. Just do it so we can let the police know."

"She might be in danger," Cory added, a little more desperate. His shoulders were tight and he was wringing his hands in his lap.

Clarissa pushed her lips out in an exaggerated way like she was playing dumb. "Why would she be in danger?"

Harry's jaw was moving like he was grinding his teeth. "You know why."

Clarissa crossed her hands at her wrists over her knee and leaned forward like she was very interested. "Why don't you spell it out for me, Harry and Cory. Why would Whitney be in danger?"

"Because people were looking for her," Harry ground out. "Stalking her."

Clarissa lifted her shoulders in a little shrug. "That seems strange. Why would they be doing that?"

Cory threw his hands in the air. "Because of her Fanzy account! Now tell us where she is!" Cory yelled. He was unhinged, a completely different version of the Cory I'd seen and talked to before.

A soft voice came from around the corner. "I'm right here," Whitney said, stepping out from behind a pillar. I was relieved to see her. She was the epitome of calm and collected. Like she hadn't fled Branson Falls for her mental health and then been abducted by an insane person and just released yesterday. I wasn't sure what she was doing here, though.

Relief washed over Cory's face and he raced over to her with his arms wide like he was going to give her a hug. She held up her hand an arm's length in front of her, and stepped back. "Why don't you have a seat, Cory."

Cory's expression crumpled into one of hurt and disappointment, but he went back to the couch.

Clarissa's attention shifted from Cory to Harry like she'd caught two mice in a trap. "So, people were looking for Whitney, and stalking her, because of the Fanzy account you didn't know about until a week ago? Yet you were trying to get her disappearance investigated since she left three weeks ago."

Cory pressed his lips together and a vein started pulsing at Harry's temple.

"Why were you so worried about where I'd gone," Whitney asked Cory.

"Because you're my wife." His eyes were glassy, but his tone betrayed the emotion he was trying to present. He was angry, not worried about her.

Whitney tapped a finger against her chin and looked speculative. "That's an interesting word. Wife. To some people, it means love, loyalty, support, and true partnership where couples take care of each other. To others, it means prize, servant, assistant, and control." She took her hand and pointed first to Cory, and then to Harry. "You and your friend, Harry, fit in the second category."

Cory's fists were clenched on his legs, and despite the cold weather outside and the lack of heating in the abandoned building, a sheen of sweat broke out on Harry's forehead.

Whitney walked closer to them both, pacing back and forth. "Before we got married, we talked extensively about our hopes and dreams. You knew I wanted to continue my career and build my business. I never hid that. When we got married, everything changed. You tried to control my friends, my job, and you used the church and your place as the priesthood holder as a weapon to do it. You told me often about how you had the God-given authority and power in our relationship, and I didn't.

"You used coercive control and manipulation on me daily. You made me question my own lived experiences and the abuse you were inflicting on me. You asked me to submit when I'd told you before we were even engaged that I would never marry a man like that. You knew exactly what I wanted from a spouse and made sure to be that while we dated. You presented yourself as kind and loving until we got married, and then your personality change gave me whiplash.

"I tried everything I could to make it work. To make you happy. But eventually, I realized that your happiness would only come at the expense of my own, and that was a price I wasn't willing to pay. And all of that happened long before I found out you opened the Fanzy account with my photos without telling me and without my permission."

My mouth fell open in complete shock. Whitney hadn't known about the Fanzy account? I'd known something fishy was going on with the account, but I'd thought Clarissa was the mastermind and Whitney was part of it. Now Clarissa and Cory's mutual hatred of each other made more sense, and Clarissa was absolutely validated.

Whitney shook her head and stared blankly at the wall above Cory and Harry like it might offer up some clarity and advice. "You acted like my divorce request was a shock. In the community, and at church, you played the part of victim and loving husband, and let people, including your own family members, drag me, and my name, through the mud because I'd asked for something as horrible as a divorce. The image you projected to everyone else was all an act. You didn't support me in my hopes and dreams, and not only that, you tried to hold me back. And when you realized you couldn't, your jealousy became a weapon that you used against me."

Cory was fervently shaking his head, his eyes pleading. "I didn't."

Whitney gave him a knowing smile that said I-know-you're-lying-and-I'm-disappointed-in-you. She stopped pacing directly in front of Cory. "Those photos were taken for you. As an intimate, private, and personal gift for my husband. Not only did you take the pictures and post them online for anyone who wanted to pay you to see them, you also took videos and photos of me that I didn't know were being taken and posted those, too."

I had to cover my mouth to stop my gasp from alerting them that I was there. There were a lot of forms of betrayal, but as a woman, this one was high on my list. If I were Whitney, I would have been so livid that I'm not sure what I would have done.

Whitney moved her legs, hip width apart, and squared her shoulders letting Cory know exactly who had the power in this situation. "I wondered what was going on when you were suddenly making money after you'd been laid off. You told me you'd gotten a job, but it didn't come with benefits or anything else, and you never left the house or talked to people on the phone. I brushed that off because a lot of contract positions don't have benefits, and a lot of jobs are remote now and communication is over messaging software. But you were making *a lot* of money. A lot more than you had in the past, and you gloated about it constantly, telling me I now had no excuse to keep working and I needed to stop my silly little hobby—the *hobby* that had kept food on our table and kept our mortgage and bills paid while you were out of work—and start staying home and having kids. But you didn't have a job at all. What you were really doing was using *my* personal images, without my permission, to run a Fanzy account without telling me about it. You like to talk a lot about gender roles and what a husband and wife should be. Is this what a husband does? Exploit and lie to his wife?"

A chill ran through me hearing Whitney's explanation and I felt horrible for her and what she'd been through.

"A husband takes care of things," Harry interjected with a tone of malice. "And a wife should hearken to him and submit. If he wants to use her photos for his business, it's his right."

"Oooo," Clarissa said, warning in her tone, "the law is not on your side there."

At that, Cory quickly turned on his friend. "It wasn't my fault. I didn't want to do it, but Harry came up with the idea."

"How," Whitney asked.

Cory ran his hands up and down his thighs like his hands were sweaty. "We were on our LDS missions together. It was common knowledge in the mission field that the better the missionary you were, the more *blessed* you'd be when it came to finding a wife, having kids, and getting a better, high-paying job. I was a *great* missionary and got rewarded for it. With you."

That was so vile I felt like I was going to throw up in my mouth. Based on Whitney and Clarissa's disgusted expressions, they felt the same way I did.

Cory continued, "I had the wife I'd been promised, but you

refused to give me the kids, and then I lost my job. Maybe I'm an asshole, or maybe I was looking for validation, but I showed Harry the photos you'd given me to show off. All of the missionaries I'd served with on my mission agreed you were the hottest wife. I was discouraged because I couldn't find work. Harry said I could make a lot of money on Fanzy with photos like that, of someone who looked like you. I didn't feel good about it, but he took the USB drive with the photos without my permission, and made the account to prove it could work. It did. You had followers almost immediately, and the followers kept growing and paying. Harry took a percentage because he said it was all his idea. Once the money was coming in, I couldn't turn it down. I had to get more photos and videos of you so we had new content. That's when I set up secret cameras."

My stomach lurched as I thought of what that betrayal would feel like as well. My most intimate moments filmed without my knowledge and made public by the person who was supposed to love me more than anyone. I'd probably never be able to trust a man again.

Whitney was frozen in place, absolutely furious after hearing all of the details. Clarissa picked up the conversation, "The irony here is that you weren't making money through a business on your own merit. You were using your wife to do it, while condemning her for having her own job. And you were doing it in an incredibly personal, and illegal way."

"It was his right," Harry insisted again.

Harry was an ass.

Clarissa looked at Whitney, who was still seething. "I think this is a good time to get back to our story about Belle," Clarissa said, slapping her hands on her thighs. "She cared about women. The ones who worked for her, and the ones who didn't. The ones stuck in abusive situations, or with unsupportive husbands and family members. She taught these women that they were the ones in charge of their lives, their businesses, their finances, and their futures. And she taught them how to ensure they stayed that way. How to empower themselves, defend themselves, and become a success so they could live the lives they authentically wanted to live, not the lives they were told to. The women Belle helped were a force of nature—women always have been."

Whitney had composed herself and once again stood tall in front of Cory and Harry. "In case the subtext was lost on you, *I* am that powerful woman," Whitney said. "Clarissa is that powerful woman. Every. Single. Woman is a force of nature, and you'd be surprised at how many of us surround you. You will face the consequences for what you've done. And you will not take advantage of one of us again without facing our army."

My heart was beating furiously in my chest and I felt like I'd just been given some kind of rallying cry I didn't know I'd needed.

Harry's takeaway was different. He scoffed and shook his head like he couldn't care less. "You can't prove anything."

Clarissa's lips slid into a slow smile. "Oh, we can prove everything. We're women. You really shouldn't underestimate us."

Harry scoffed. "How?" he asked, squaring his shoulders. "There's no paper trail. It's your word against ours, and I hate to break it to you and your little women's empowerment speech, in this state, a man's word counts more."

Whitney grabbed her phone, opened a document and held

it in front of Cory and Harry as she scrolled. "We know who you all are. We have the names and addresses of every person who visited my Fanzy page, we even have the personal information of the people who commented in the forums you were advertising my page on."

Cory and Harry's faces both paled. Sweat broke out on Cory's forehead, and I could see a vein sticking out on Harry's neck as the panic set in. They both looked like they were going to be sick.

Whitney gave a thoroughly satisfied smile. "You thought you were in charge. You weren't, and you still aren't."

Sirens wailed in the distance and got closer.

Harry looked like he'd made some kind of decision. He stood, his face stoney, and moved toward Clarissa. "I didn't want it to come to this, but I'm not going to let you ruin our lives over something as dumb as a website and some photos." He moved toward Clarissa and tried to attack her. She turned into him as he rushed, grabbed his arm, and flipped him over her shoulder. Whitney handed her some zip ties and Harry's hands and legs were quickly immobilized.

Clarissa got up, brushing the hair back off her face. "You underestimated your opponent. Twice. Didn't we just give you a whole speech about that?" She frowned and gave a frustrated shake of her head as she immobilized Cory as well. "I didn't want it to come to this, but I'm not going to let you ruin Whitney's, or anyone else's lives, over something as dumb as a website and some photos. That's why by tonight, Whitney's Fanzy page will be taken down and replaced with a detailed account of what you both did."

"In the meantime, the police should be here any minute, and we can explain all of this to them."

Right on cue, Bobby came in the door with a few other officers, and Hawke followed. They looked at Cory and Harry, zip tied and furious, and Whitney and Clarissa told them what the men had done.

Bobby finished with Whitney and Clarissa and on his way out, mumbled about all the paperwork he'd have to do. The other officers took a resigned Cory, and a red-faced, furious Harry, to the squad car.

Hawke stood next to me, his hands in his coat pockets as he watched the police put them both in separate cars.

"Does everyone carry these now?" I asked, pointing to the zip ties hanging out of Clarissa's pocket.

Hawke snorted.

"They come in handy," Clarissa said with a grin.

"Where did you learn to fight like that?" I asked.

"I studied Krav Maga growing up. You don't want to mess with me," she said with a wink.

A smile tugged at Hawke's lips.

"Come back to 111," Whitney said, putting a hand on my arm. "We'll tell you everything."

Chapter Twenty-Two

"I wasn't expecting you to show up," I said to Hawke as we walked inside 111 Healing and Crystals.

"The address you texted me was the same one Whitney went to," he said, kicking the snow off his shoes. "I thought the situation might require some backup, but I was wrong."

I wondered if that made him feel bad. "Does that bother you?" I asked, curious. Hawke was used to being the hero and he was good at it.

He shook his head as we both took off our coats. "Not at all, I admire independence and people who can take care of themselves as much as I admire people who know they need help and ask for it."

We heard voices coming from the salt cave and stepped into the room. Whitney and Clarissa both greeted us with smiles and waves. Jacey did as well. Wendy was also there, and to my complete surprise, so was Stephanie Gress and Monica Pack. But some of the other women were giving Hawke the side-eye.

Whitney noticed and stepped in, gesturing toward us.

"Everyone, this is Hawke. When I was taken captive by Rick, Hawke showed up at Rick's house with Kate to rescue me. I don't know what would have happened without them both."

They still looked at Hawke warily, and one woman with curly hair and a stunning smile said, "How do we know you're not part of the problem and you're not going to tell everyone about us?"

Hawke's brow furrowed. "Tell on you?" he said, his voice going up a bit at the end of the question. "I might want to recruit you. You're clearly all talented women to pull this off."

"Recruit us for what?" she asked, still suspicious.

"To work for me. I was recruited and trained before I started my business, and you're just as talented."

I tried not to get jealous of the compliment. I wasn't successful, but I tried.

"What exactly is your business?" she asked.

I gave her a silent high-five because I had the same question.

"All kinds of things," Hawke said with a wink, and I heard half the room sigh.

Whitney motioned to chairs in the ground up salt area. We both took our shoes off and sat in the circle of intentional women.

My gaze floated around the room, taking in each one of them. "I've been investigating Whitney and her disappearance for a couple of weeks. I have some of the pieces, but need the rest. It's clear you all orchestrated this plan, so tell me everything, from the beginning."

Clarissa and Whitney looked at each other and Whitney angled her head toward Clarissa, who answered, "We all found out about Whitney's Fanzy page after Stephanie Gress caught her husband, Nate, on the page. Stephanie was shocked and told some of the other 111 women about it. I overheard them talking about it in the bathroom one day and we all had a meeting. They were upset and confronted Whitney."

That must have been the situation Megan and Becca told me about when they stopped to talk to me at the *Tribune*.

"Other women in the 111 group did some spying and found out their husbands were also subscribed to Whitney's page."

Whitney shifted uncomfortably in her chair as she relived the memory. "I was absolutely horrified," she said. "I was also furious, and felt completely betrayed. I'd taken those photos for Cory for our anniversary. At first, I didn't believe Cory had done it. I thought maybe someone had stolen the USB drive with the digital copies and made the page."

Clarissa continued, "We knew whoever was running the Fanzy page had to have access to Whitney's photos. She checked and her USB drive containing the photos was still at their house, and so was the photo album, so it wasn't a leap to think Cory was involved."

Whitney dropped her chin to her chest and I couldn't tell if she was ashamed or simply exhausted. "I didn't want to believe he'd done something like that, and even argued with Clarissa about it when she suggested it was him."

That also explained why I'd had reports of Clarissa and Whitney arguing and Whitney looking like she was crying.

"How did you find out he'd done it?" I asked.

Whitney shifted on her chair and took a breath. "Cory had been depressed since losing his job, but about six months ago, he had a personality change and started acting like he was an alpha male again, just like he had when we first got married—but worse. He kept trying to tell me what to do, and that didn't go over well," Whitney explained. "He wouldn't stop harassing me about kids and not following the gospel. I didn't tell him I never wanted kids. I said I didn't want them right now. And when I do have them, I don't want to give up my business or what I've built, so I want a partner who understands that and wants to help take on the load of raising a family. He wasn't interested in that."

"He fought with her over the business, kids, and her responsibilities as his wife at 111 one day," Clarissa said. "And he became even more controlling of her. We put a tracking device on Cory's car and Elaine," she gestured to the curly-haired woman who'd been skeptical of Hawke, "followed him to a restaurant where Harry and Cory met to discuss the Fanzy page."

Elaine took over the story. "The men made a lot of inappropriate references about Whitney, and talked about how they'd be paid for their parts in her Fanzy page scheme. Harry had already set up the business, and made sure it couldn't be tied to either one of them. He's a sneaky scheming ass, and even named the business so it would sound like something Whitney and Clarissa would have called it, 111 Holdings, Inc. just in case they were ever caught."

I nodded as that puzzle piece fell into place. "I knew about 111 Holdings Inc., and wondered if it was part of 111 Healing and Crystals, or Whitney's business Love and Light Holdings."

Elaine shook her head. "Not at all. Harry did that on purpose. Aside from being in charge of the money, he was also in charge of marketing and getting the word out about the page. He also handled the business side. Cory was in charge of helping with the marketing, and getting more content from Whit—which he did secretly. As soon as I knew the details, I came back to 111 and had a meeting with Clarissa and all of the women who knew about the Fanzy page to figure out what to do next."

Jacey put a hand to her heart and let go of a deep sigh. "We were horrified," she said. "Absolutely gutted for Whit."

Wendy spoke up next, "Whit wasn't the only one who had sexy photos taken. We decided that if these jerks could do this to Whitney, they could do it to any woman, and we weren't going to stand for it, so we came up with a plan."

I wondered if more of the women who had boudoir photos taken were involved. It seemed they thought of it, too, and made sure they wouldn't be.

"Obviously, I couldn't stay married to someone who would do this to me," Whitney said.

"But no one knew," I pointed out. "Everyone except the 111 women thought you'd started the Fanzy page."

Her eyes twinkled deviously. "We knew people would assume that, so we let them. It played into our plan."

That was impressive. I didn't think I'd be able to handle the scrutiny. "What was the plan?" I asked.

Clarissa leaned forward to explain, "We knew the town would support Cory because he's lived here for so long; and despite it being more common now, divorce is still looked down on and discouraged in the church, Utah, and especially a small town like Branson Falls. We knew that as soon as she asked for the divorce and it became public, people would turn on Whitney. We wanted to use that fuel to fan the flames and make Whitney and Cory the subject on everyone's lips. That's one of the reasons we came up with the idea for Whit to leave.

Not only would her disappearance after the divorce announcement make everyone in town curious and keep them talking, it would also allow Whitney to not have to deal with the backlash while we were setting all these things in motion. It kept her safe from Cory and Harry, too."

"We helped Whitney disappear, and stoked the disappearance rumors," Jacey explained. "We also got you an anonymous tip that Whit had been seen at the mountain resort and was staying there. We knew you were getting frustrated that Clarissa wouldn't tell you where Whit was and we needed you to stay engaged."

So that's who had left the tip. "I wondered who that was." I tapped a finger against my lips as I thought back to some of the puzzle pieces I was still trying to put together. "Someone was seen helping Shasta put the photos of Whitney up."

Monica gave a sly smile. "That was me. Shasta is one of those people who reacts first and thinks later—and sometimes doesn't think at all. She's very protective of Cory, so we sent Shasta the link to Whitney's Fanzy page to get her angry. She confronted Cory about it and Cory pretended not to know what was going on and acted devastated that Whitney had a Fanzy page. I know Shasta, so I suggested Shasta post the photos, and even suggested trying to put the photo in the newspaper as an ad."

So, Monica was responsible for Shasta. "I remember. She was very upset when I said the *Tribune* wouldn't run the ad."

Monica nodded. "We wanted you to know about the rumors so you could cover what was going on and investigate as well. We knew your work could back up our claims when we went to law enforcement. We also *wanted* Whitney to look bad because it would make the fallout so much worse for

Cory, Harry, and anyone who was subscribed to Whitney's Fanzy page when the truth came out. Anyone who had previously supported Cory would turn on him."

My gaze tracked from Stephanie to Monica. "I talked to you and Stephanie a couple of times," I nodded in both of their directions. "You seemed to be on Cory's side and didn't indicate you were fans of Whitney."

Stephanie smiled and answered, "I pretended to be pissed at Whitney, but I was the first woman in our community to know about the page, and I'm the reason Whitney found out about it when she did. I was pretty sure Whitney wasn't at fault, and even if she had a Fanzy page, it was my husband who chose to look at it. He was responsible for that choice, not Whitney. Nate got nervous after you stopped to talk to us, Kate. Based on the questions you asked, he thought something was going on with Whitney. He told the men in the forums he was in, and on Whit's Fanzy page, that Whitney might really be missing. Which Cory and Harry already suspected because of the messages they were getting on Fanzy."

"Did you and the rest of the 111 women have something to do with the messages as well?" I asked.

"Some of them," Clarissa admitted. "But definitely not all." She nodded towards a few of the women in the group. "We had women posting the link in the forums, and also posting threats to Whitney on the Fanzy chat to freak Cory and Harry out. That made both of them even more worried—not about Whitney, but about their crimes being discovered. That's when we dropped the Fanzy link all over Branson Falls using an unknown number to text as many people as possible. Cory and Harry lost it. They already thought Whitney might be in danger, and they knew if something happened to her, they could be implicated. Prison scared them more than their complete lack of morals. They started getting sloppy and trying to do anything they could to distract from Whitney's story while they attempted to find her. We helped them along by instigating events that could be tied back to Whitney's story," she said with a wink.

"The porn protest that was really an anti-Whitney and anti-male revue protest?" I asked.

Clarissa grinned. "We scheduled the male revue show and leaked it to the men in town after the fact to rile them up about women and purity—two things they love to regulate. That caused the protest with The Ladies leading it instead because men in our culture are so used to having women organize and manage events. The Ladies participation was disappointing, but not a surprise since some women are still stuck being complicit in their own subjugation."

"Then there was the boob crossover bag ban debate," Wendy said, laughing. "That was a favorite. One of the husbands complained about the issue and his wife encouraged him to post about it knowing full well that it would cause drama, and the reminder about Whitney and sexuality could be brought back in. Some of the 111 Women responded to the comment."

My eyebrows flashed up and held as my lips spread into a wide smile. "I saw that," I said. "I was managing the post on the *Tribune*'s page and was proud of the women clapping back."

"It was fun to rile them all up, but it served another purpose as well," Clarissa said. "The protest, male revue, and boob crossover bag ban was all to try and draw out the other men involved by making them angry enough to talk about it, show up at the protest, post publicly about the boob crossover bags, and complain in general. We knew Cory and Harry were running Whit's Fanzy account, but wanted to know who else was involved, and who had joined the page to look at Whitney's photos."

"Were you able to get the information you needed that way?" I asked.

Clarissa threaded her hands together and leaned forward. "We were able to confirm the information we already had."

My brows pinched. "How?"

"Through the link to Whitney's Fanzy page that we posted on the men's forums."

Hawke blew out an impressed whistle.

"Monica got her degree in computer science and she's a computer genius," Whitney explained.

Monica blushed at the compliment. "I haven't been allowed to work because my husband doesn't agree with a woman having a job outside the home, but I've kept my skills sharp and learned how to do all kinds of things like hack computers, perform man-in-the-middle attacks, and install malware. The link that was placed on the forums had malware that I designed to be installed when someone clicked the link. I programmed it to scan all the files on a computer, and send me anything that looked like a home address and names associated with the address. I also parsed the data to find Branson Falls names and addresses specifically."

Hawke's eyes bulged, impressed, and he was not an easy person to dazzle. "How did you get around anti-viruses and their heuristic analysis?"

She grinned and seemed excited to be able to talk shop with someone who understood that world. "I wrote the malware to crawl their system slowly in the background and send the data back to us in small batches while they were making another web request. This disguised the information as just another request from their browser. Computer security isn't on the top of most people's minds, especially in Branson, so they wouldn't have noticed anything suspicious."

Hawke stared at her for several seconds. "I really might offer you a job."

Monica's grin got wider. "I might take it. Secretly, of course."

Even I was impressed, and I didn't have a full understanding of everything she'd done. "If you were planning to expose the data you had, all of the people involved, and also expose Cory and Harry, why wait so long to bring Whitney back to Branson?"

Clarissa answered, "We kept Whitney's disappearance going because we knew the more it was talked about and the longer she was gone, the more worried and frantic Cory and Harry would be about the Fanzy threats. We knew that as the threats increased, Cory and Harry would become desperate and would be more likely to make mistakes. We just weren't counting on Rick the dick actually abducting Whitney."

Whitney and several of the other women smirked and giggled at 'Rick the dick'.

Clarissa continued, "Whit was supposed to be back before Valentine's Day so we could confront Cory and Harry. We'd been coordinating using a burner phone and I couldn't reach her. Then, your questions about the phone call I got from Whitney made me worried. I went to the retreat to find her, but no one had seen her for a few days. I thought Cory and Harry had found her, so I came back to talk to them and find out where she was. That's when I heard from Whitney about Rick the dick, your and Hawke's help, and found out she was back in Branson Falls. We decided to keep our original plan and confront Cory and Harry together."

"He was a bit of a wrinkle," Wendy said, her tone still perky and optimistic, "but you helped take care of that problem and got Whit back safe!"

I waved my hand in front of me like it wasn't a big deal. "Whitney thought fast and was able to get us the information to find her. For the rest, I didn't do it alone. Hawke helped with the investigation, and got us in the door at Rick's so we could verify that Whitney was there."

"Not that it matters, but I do think Cory was truly concerned about you while you were gone, Whit," Wendy said.

Whitney shook her head. "He was concerned about his cash cow being gone. He says he loves me, but I don't think he even knows what love is. That made it easier, and more satisfying, to confront him tonight."

"Why didn't you just turn Cory and Harry in when you first found out about the unauthorized Fanzy account?" I asked.

Clarissa answered, "In the past, I'd worked with a nonprofit that provides legal counsel for women. I gave the attorneys some hypotheticals to get advice."

"Family Law Consultants?" I asked.

She gave me an intrigued look. "Yes. They said we needed as much evidence as possible. We needed to know who was involved, and as many of the players as we could find. We also needed Cory and Harry to admit to it if possible. They'd covered their tracks well, so there was nothing tying Cory and Harry to the Fanzy account. Just like Harry mentioned tonight, they could have gotten away with it all and blamed it on Whitney. We needed an admission, and solid proof. Now we have it because they fell for everything we did, and admitted to it all on camera."

"And you were there to report it all from a neutral perspective," Jacey said with a smile.

"Why not just ask me to help?" I wondered. A lot of things would have been easier for me if they had, and if they'd given me the information they knew.

Clarissa's chin dropped and she looked up at me from under her lashes, her features apologetic. "I'm sorry about that. We've read your work, and think you're excellent at your job. We knew that once you started to learn Whitney's story, you would keep investigating. We also knew it would make our case stronger if we had another investigation coming to the same conclusions we did. We thought you'd probably be able to find out even more, and you did. Not only that, but your persistence saved Whitney from Rick the dick and that was not something we anticipated." She put a hand to her chest and her eyes started to shine. "So, thank you, from all of us." The other women nodded in agreement, some of them wiping tears.

Initially, I'd felt kind of used, but now that I understood their reasons, what they'd done made sense. And I was touched that they'd wanted my help and made me a part of their plan. "I understand, and appreciate the explanation. I was glad I could help, and I hope all of the evidence we've gathered will make a difference." I grinned and shook my head, still stunned at the whole story. "You're basically a gang of badass women I didn't even know existed in Branson Falls," I said, genuinely impressed.

Whitney looked at me, her eyes bright. "And you're one of them."

I felt like I'd been given a hug with words, and felt humbled she thought of me that way. "That means a lot. Thank you."

"We all have different talents and one of our goals with 111 is to give women a place to showcase those skills," Whitney explained. "Clarissa teaches self-defense classes; Monica teaches coding and scripting; Elaine teaches finance classes that women often aren't taught because their husbands manage that. And we're going to keep adding classes." Whitney put her hands in her lap. "We sell crystals, but the healing comes first, and that means healing in a lot of different ways."

"What about you," I asked Whitney. "It's your story that helped to empower all of these women. How did you end up in a relationship with someone like Cory?"

Whitney shook her head. "Coercive control made me question everything, and always take the blame. He lied to me about who he was leading up to the marriage. When we were dating, he was cocky, but he was fun, supportive, and kind. He changed once we were married in the temple and eternally bound, though. He had different friends and people influencing him, and telling him who and what he should be, and what I should be as his wife."

"Did you discuss those expectations before you got married?" She'd mentioned it a little when she was talking to Cory and Harry, but I felt like there was a bigger story behind that.

She moved and crossed her legs under her in the chair, trying to get comfortable. "I absolutely did, because of my own upbringing. I wasn't raised in Branson Falls, but I *was* raised in a small town. My mom had a job because they couldn't get by without her working, but all of her money went to support the household, and my dad made more than she did so she was still reliant on him. She started college, but followed church counsel to get married and have kids as soon as possible. She never finished school. She once told me that it was one of her biggest regrets.

"My dad hated education because he'd never gotten one. It affected his worthiness wound, and made him feel ashamed. His ego couldn't handle people being smarter, or making more moncy than him, and he'd constantly talk about how dumb people were for wasting their money going to college. Meanwhile, my mom was scrimping, saving, struggling, and trying to find a way to keep food on the table. Every time my dad said something derogatory about getting a college degree, my mom would quietly take me aside and talk to me about the importance of an education. Next to church doctrine, there was nothing she drilled into me harder than the importance of going to college, being able to support myself even in a marriage, and having my own money. I didn't forget it. Now I have a bachelor's degree, I'm the part owner of a successful business that's growing, and I have my own bank accounts."

My heart hurt for her younger self. Hearing her story made me realize how much privilege I'd had in my own family where both of my parents had gone to college and not only supported my decision to get a degree, but felt it was their responsibility as parents to help me do it. "I didn't know that, Whitney. I'm sorry you had a dad who was so unsupportive."

Her gaze dropped and when it lifted again, her eyes were watery. "I am too. But I get to choose how to live my life and luckily, I knew my dad's opinion was bullshit because I saw how miserable my mom was. I'm grateful for those lessons."

I got up and went over to Whitney to give her a hug, and Clarissa, Jacey, Wendy, Monica, Stephanie, Elaine, and all the other women followed. It was a blanket of feminine energy and as I stood there, I realized there wasn't much that was more powerful than this.

Hawke got a call and had to leave, but I stayed and talked a bit more until the women began to disperse.

"What's next for 111 Healing and Crystals?" I asked Clarissa and Whitney after everyone else had gone.

"Once the divorce is final, we can change the business articles to give Whit her fifty percent share in a more formal fashion," Clarissa said.

"Do you plan to stay in Branson Falls?" I asked them both.

"Absolutely," Whitney said. "We've built a community here. There's a deep need for empowerment and connection among women. We're not leaving, or cowering, especially when I was the victim of this situation."

"Good for you," I said, meaning it.

"We'll keep building community, and I hope you'll be part of it," Clarissa offered. "We don't have an intrepid reporter in our ranks yet, and we'd like one."

I smiled, thinking of what it would look like to have a

bigger community for myself in Branson Falls. It was a small town, but not a place where I felt like I had a lot of close friends other than Spence, Ella, Phyllis, and Annie. Most of the friends I was close with were from college and lived out of state. "I'd like that."

"We're a small army of women right now," Whitney said, her eyes sparkling, "but we're growing. I've found that when women finally get fed up, they're unstoppable."

I grinned and grabbed my phone. "I'm going to make sure that line is highlighted in the story."

I gave them both a hug.

"I'll let you know when the next full moon release ceremony is," Clarissa said as I turned to leave.

I grinned. "I'll make sure to let Bobby know we're not conjuring demons."

Clarissa and Whitney laughed and I waved as I left.

Chapter Twenty-Three

Ella came into the main office, her eyes wide. "Saw the website." Her lips were stretched to show her teeth in a grimace. "That's a whole lotta tea. The Ladies have been pourin' over it all mornin'."

Like Clarissa and Whitney had warned Cory and Harry, the site had gone live last night as soon as the meeting at 111 had ended. It explained the basics of what had happened to Whitney, and listed the names of every man in Branson Falls who had visited Whitney's Fanzy page through the link. It also directed people to check out the *Tribune*'s coverage for more information. I'd been working on the story most of the night and today so we could get it out in the next weekly issue, and had posted a shorter version on the *Tribune*'s website and socials.

Whitney's Fanzy page now had a logo on it that looked like flames and stars and directed people to the website explaining what had happened to Whitney, and telling people how to protect themselves if something similar happens to them.

"That site is really something," Spence said.

I took a break from writing and stretched my arms above my head. "They did a good job."

Spence looked at the site on his phone. "Nice of them to drop the *Trib*'s name. They must have appreciated your persistence and that you really did end up having to rescue Whitney."

I closed my eyes, and sagged into the back of my chair. "I'm just glad she was okay. I'm still floored with the level of strategy they put into their plan. It was beyond impressive."

"They should offer their services for a fee," Spence said.

"I heard the Rick guy tried to attack you and Hawke was on him like fry sauce on fries!" Ella said.

I laughed. "I'm not sure how you heard that since we were the only ones there."

Ella tapped her index finger to her temple. "I've got my sources."

I laughed. "That's not a bad idea. I should have this article for you to look over and provide edits on shortly."

He nodded and walked over to the fridge to get a drink.

Ella came over from where she'd been making a plate of donuts and getting a glass of milk from the fridge. "What happened to Cory and Harry last night?" she asked, sitting in a chair at one of the correspondent desks and arranging her snacks.

"They're in jail as far as I know. The prosecutor is probably still trying to decide what to charge them with."

Ella's face puckered in anger. "Throw the book at 'em!"

I shook my head. "Distribution of an intimate image is only a Class A Misdemeanor in Utah for a first offense. That's just a fine of $2500 and up to a year in jail."

She slapped a hand on her thigh. "You've got to be kiddin' me," she said, outraged. "Cory and Harry probably made more than that in a day on Fanzy usin' her photos! He should be in prison!"

"I agree. The fact that Whitney was abducted and her life was threatened because of it might make it more serious, but we'll have to wait and see what Cory and Harry are charged with."

Ella tapped her fingers on her glass of milk. "How long will it take Whitney to get that divorce?" she demanded. "She should've been outta that marriage yesterday!"

I raised a brow. "That's quite a change of opinion. *Yesterday* everyone was on Cory's side and saying Whitney deserved anything bad that happened to her."

Ella put her hands on her hips. "Well, we didn't have all the info yesterday!"

I pressed my lips together and nodded. "So maybe in the future everyone in Branson, and especially The Ladies, will refrain from rushing to judgment before you have all the information?" I asked, knowing full-well they wouldn't.

Ella scrunched her nose up. "Maybe, but I wouldn't count on it from everyone."

"I bet Shasta feels pretty silly," Spence said.

I'd heard from the 111 Women about that actually. They'd added me to their group text thread. "I have it on good authority that Shasta is pretty pissed at Cory, but will probably find a way to make it Whitney's fault shortly."

Spence snorted sarcastically. "It's always the woman's fault in a place like this."

Wasn't that the truth.

"What about Stephanie and Nate?" Ella asked.

Stephanie had said they were trying to work through things with the help of a therapist, but I didn't want to give too much information that wasn't mine to share. "I'm not sure what will happen with them in the long run, but I think they're trying to work through things."

Ella sighed and shook her head. "I hope they can figure it out. Men just don't know how to communicate what they want, especially in the bedroom."

"It doesn't help that women in this culture aren't taught to nurture their sexual side because that's a sin," I pointed out. "They're supposed to go from thinking sex is almost as bad as murder, to having it for the first time on the same day. There's no normal progression of a relationship over time where sexual exploration happens in stages. They go straight from kissing to sex literally overnight. It creates a lot of dysfunction and misunderstanding. If couples would talk, they could alleviate a lot of problems."

Ella listened and nodded. "I guess I never thought of it that way, but I can see it. What about all the other guys who were lookin' at Whitney's photos and listed on the site? Are they in trouble too?"

"Not legally, but I imagine their wives aren't happy."

Ella's eyes bulged and she pressed her lips together before saying, "Some of The Ladies husbands were on the list. It's been a poop storm of gossip today!"

"Who knows," Spence said. "Maybe there will be a lot more divorce announcements. Mrs. Olsen will have to make a schedule for Fast and Testimony meetings."

I laughed at that, pretty sure Mrs. Olsen was likely to be censored the next time she got up to the microphone. "These

111 Women are pretty badass," I said, turning to Ella. "You might want to reconsider your Ladies membership because a new and improved group of women are in town."

Ella tapped a finger on her chin, thinking about it. "The Ladies will always be around, but I hope more 111 Women rise up. We need that."

I couldn't agree more.

Ella popped the last of her donut in her mouth. "What's with the greenhouse in your backyard?" she asked around her bite.

I narrowed my eyes. "How did you know about that?"

She moved her shoulders from side-to-side as she tried to figure out how to answer. "Saw some pics."

I sighed, leaning against the back of my chair. "I really need to get some taller trees."

Ella wiped her hands against each other to get rid of the crumbs from her food. "It's in the same place as the wedding arch Hawke built ya."

I closed my eyes and shook my head. "It wasn't a wedding arch; it was a floral display. Hawke had the greenhouse built around it so I can keep enjoying the flowers, and garden during the winter."

"But it's not see-through," she said, like it should be.

"What does that have to do with anything?"

She lifted her hands, palms up. "We can't see what's goin' on inside!"

"Good!" I hadn't thought of doing anything illicit in there, but now I would just because I could.

Ella stomped her foot. "That's not fair."

"My life isn't a reality show, Ella."

She wrinkled her nose, annoyed at the little bit of privacy I was grateful for.

I stifled a yawn. It had been a long few days and I was ready to pick up Gandalf and go home and relax. I sent the draft of my article to Spence and grabbed my coat and bag.

On the way out the door, I remembered a question I'd been meaning to ask Ella. "What happened with your arrest for the vandalism of the Hunky Movers signs?"

She lifted a shoulder. "Drake took care of it. I just had to pay for the signs to be replaced." She scowled, thinking about it. "I was pretty opposed to that on principle. He said I can't say anythin' bad about the company anywhere, or tell my opinion about their false advertisin' online. So, he's basically makin' me lie. But I'm not goin' to jail so I'll deal."

I laughed at her explanation. "I'm glad I won't need to visit you in prison."

"To be honest, gettin' arrested was on my bucket list so I'm kinda excited I got to check that one off. But Bobby's still on pie probation for puttin' me in jail!"

I laughed and told Ella and Spence goodbye, then got in my Jeep to go retrieve my dog.

When I arrived at my mom and dad's house to get Gandalf, two kids, probably around twelve, were on the front lawn by the witches. My mom was pointing and giving them instructions. Hawke was standing there as well with his arms crossed over his chest, overseeing the whole situation.

"What's this?" I asked, walking up to my mom and Hawke.

My mom turned. "Hawke was nice enough to do the job the police wouldn't, and find my witch vandals. It's no wonder he's so successful in his business; he's *great* at apprehending criminals!"

I didn't have all the information about Hawke's job, but knew it consisted of things a lot more serious than finding mischievous kids.

Hawke's lips curved in an amused smile. "Thanks, Sophie."

I watched the kids trying to move one of the witches. "Valentine's Day is over. Shouldn't you be taking the love-spell-stripper-witches down for the year?"

She glared at me for the stripper comment, and put her hands on her hips. "Don't be silly, Kate! Love is always in season!" My mom's attention turned back to the kids and her eyes narrowed. "No, not that way, Porter. The spell stick needs to be angled," she said, walking over to show him the proper degree to lean the cauldron-stirring-stick-stripper pole.

The kids were trying not to laugh, and so was Hawke.

I shifted toward him, taking in his black winter coat that covered far too much of his jeans. "How did you know it was the kids who turned the witches into strippers?"

He nodded toward a grove of trees. "The day the witches were vandalized, I saw two teenagers watching us from behind those trees. One looked terrified, the other was laughing. I talked to them after everyone left and asked some questions."

I raised a brow. "Questions, or did you add some threats?"

His lips curved in a half smile. "Maybe a little of both."

That sounded like him. "Why did they do it?"

He angled his head toward a red brick house across the street. "Because they were paid to by your mom and dad's neighbor, Gladys."

I couldn't hide my surprise. "How did she even find someone to hire for that? Did she go on the dark web and ask for some vandalizing bandits with a creative flare for crafting?"

He snorted a laugh. "They said she saw them beating a bush with a stick and thought they'd do a good job with the witches."

I shook my head. "I can't believe this war between them is still going on. It's going to be a feud until one of them dies."

Hawke grinned. "If Gladys had never said anything, your mom probably would have taken the witches down after Halloween and not thought of them again until next October."

"Probably. I'd like to say lessons were learned, but I don't think they were."

We watched the kids continue cleaning up their mess with my mom's supervision, and I filled Hawke in on the information from after he left 111 last night.

"I saw the website," Hawke said with a tone of approval. "I'm impressed with how organized they were. They had a plan for almost everything."

"Women in the church are raised to be experts at organization, planning, strategy, and events. I'm pleased they've turned their talents to taking down assholes."

The corners of his lips quirked up.

"How did your work go? You had to leave suddenly last night."

He folded his arms across his chest. "Good. I'm working on something and needed to do some reconnaissance."

My ears perked up. "Care to tell me what it is?" He'd helped me on a lot of investigations, and I'd helped him on a few, but I never got as much information about those cases as I wished I did.

He licked his lips. "Not yet, but I might need your help in the future."

I lifted my chin in interest. "I'd like that." One of my concerns about a relationship with Hawke was how much he wouldn't be able to share with me. Secrets are relationship killers and as a journalist, I was far too curious for that to work long-term. But if we could find a way to work together on things, that would solve the problem.

"How are the flowers?" Hawke asked.

"Beautiful. The greenhouse is amazing and I love it." I'd already been out there, planning what I wanted to do next. I was excited to grow some flowers I could cultivate and bring inside so I'd always have fresh arrangements.

"Good. I was hoping it would work out."

"It's pretty warm in there. And smells incredible. I even took a blanket and some pillows out so I could relax on the bench and read."

He raised his brows. "Do you want some company?"

I grinned. "I was hoping you'd ask."

We grabbed Gandalf from the house and waved to my mom who was still directing the kids and fussing with some of the sequin hearts.

"No grandkids!" she called as I walked to my Jeep and Hawke walked to his truck.

I rolled my eyes. "You already have a grandpup! That's all you need!"

She gave me a thumbs up.

Hawke arched a brow. "Grandkids?"

"Don't ask."

He laughed and followed me to my house where we put Gandalf inside with his dinner. We spent the next few hours in the greenhouse—which, thanks to Ella's warning, I knew was not see-through—with takeout, a bottle of wine, and not many clothes.

It took two more weeks, but Drake was finally done with the legislature and we were able to go on our make-up Valentine's Day date. I was wearing a deep pink strapless satin dress that pushed my cleavage up. A belt the same color as the fabric wrapped around my waist and created a cascade of ruffles around the hem. The back of the dress went to the floor, but it had a slit in the front by the belt that went up to the middle of my thigh. It was gorgeous. I wore my brown hair down in soft waves, and my makeup was light, but with a shimmery bold pink lipstick.

A knock sounded on my front door and since Gandalf was staying with my parents for the night, there wasn't the usual barking to notify me.

I opened the door. Drake was holding a massive bouquet of red roses and he looked like sin. He wore a midnight black suit, a crisp white shirt, and a black tie. His hair was messy in the way that made me want to run my fingers through it, and he had a slight bit of scruff on his chin, which was unusual for him. He was the consummate good boy politician and priesthood holder, and was almost always freshly shaved. I appreciated the scruff that made him look more human, and sexy as hell. As I took him in and then met his eyes, it felt like a jolt zinged through me and I realized something about him felt different, too. "I like the beard," I said, stepping aside so he could come in the house before all my neighbor ladies watching from their windows fainted at how hot he was.

"Thought I'd try something new," he said roughly, taking me in from head to toe. His gaze heated at my chest, and turned fiery when he got to the slit in my dress that led up. He met my eyes again, his voice strained, "You look incredible."

"Thank you," I said, and blushed a little at his perusal. I wasn't a woman who needed validation, or a man to survive, but I did want a partner to share my life with, and I wanted us to have a mutual attraction to each other. It was nice to dress up sometimes and feel desired.

He handed me the roses and I went to the kitchen to put them in a vase. When I came back out, he was standing in front of my wall, looking at photos. "These are all from when you were reporting outside of Utah?"

"Yeah. That time was meaningful to me. I got to experience a lot, and learned even more."

"Would you do it again?" he asked. "Leave Branson Falls to go report somewhere else?"

I lifted a shoulder. "I guess it depends. If the right opportunity came up, probably."

He nodded like he was thinking that through.

I took a box from the table and handed it to him. I'd put a lot of thought into this, and hoped he liked it. "I sent you the chocolates on Valentine's Day, but I wanted to give you this in person."

He gave me a quizzical look as he took the box from me and opened it.

He glanced up at me as he pulled the tickets from the box. "Box seats to a Jazz game?"

The corners of my lips curved up. "I thought it would be fun to watch a game with you."

He grinned, his eyes sparkling as he reached a hand toward my face and brushed my hair from my cheek. "I'd love that."

He put the box down on the table.

"I have something else for you, too," he said.

I lifted my brows, wondering what it could be. He'd already given me flowers, twice.

He pulled a red shiny box from his pocket that was the size of a greeting card and about an inch thick. It was wrapped with a black ribbon. He handed it to me.

I undid the ribbon, took the lid off the box, and gasped as my lips parted. Inside the box was a black silk tie with a hot pink lipstick print on it. The last time I'd seen it, the soft silk had been sliding over my mouth, and then my wrists as they were tied with it, and it was being used as a prop for performative sex at the male revue.

My heart started to race and my skin tingled. I looked up at him, speechless, as the dance replayed in my head—and not for the first time. He leaned in, putting his hand on my waist to pull me closer, then he whispered in my ear, "Find me later..." his voice trailed off.

My breath was ragged as I tried to process what he'd said. I stepped back so I could search his eyes. "That was you," I breathed.

He held my gaze as he sliced his head down once and in a deep, gruff voice said, "It's always been me, Katie. Now let me show you the rest."

The End

Watch for *The Devil Buys Lottery Tickets*, coming in 2026!

Books by
Angela Corbett/Destiny Ford

<u>Kate Saxee Mystery Series</u>

The Devil Drinks Coffee

Devilishly Short #1

The Devil Wears Tank Tops

The Devil Has Tattoos

The Devil Shops on Sunday

Devilishly Short #2

The Devil Gets Divorced

<u>Tempting Series</u>

Tempting Sydney

Chasing Brynn

Convincing Courtney (Coming Soon)

<u>A Dude Reads Romance Series</u>

A Dude Reads Romance-Tempting Sydney

A Dude Reads Romance-Chasing Brynn

<u>Hollywood Crush Series</u>

A-List

<u>Fractured Fairy Tale Series</u>

Withering Woods

Scattered Cinders

<u>Emblem of Eternity Trilogy</u>

Eternal Starling

Eternal Echoes

For special sneak peeks, giveaways, and super secret news, join Angela's newsletter!

https://mailchi.mp/6ce29309302a/newsletter-sign-up

If you enjoyed reading *The Devil Gets Divorced*, please help others enjoy this book too by recommending it, and reviewing it on Amazon, Barnes and Noble, Google Play, iBooks, or Goodreads. You can also review it in my author store at www.angelacorbettshop.com. If you do write a review, please send me a message through my website so I can thank you personally! www.angelacorbett.com

xoxo,
    Ang

About the Author

Angela Corbett is a *USA Today* bestselling author, and a graduate of Westminster College where she double majored in communication and sociology and minored in business. She has worked as a journalist, freelance writer, and director of communications and marketing. She lives in Utah with her extremely supportive husband, and their sweet Pug-Zu, S'more. She loves classic cars, traveling, puppies, and can be bribed with handbags, and mochas from The People's Coffee. She's the author of Young Adult, New Adult, and Adult fiction —with lots of kissing. She writes under two names: Angela Corbett, and Destiny Ford.

http://www.angelacorbett.com/

Join my newsletter to get a free book!
https://mailchi.mp/6ce29309302a/newsletter-sign-up

facebook.com/AuthorAngelaCorbett

x.com/angcorbett

instagram.com/byangcorbett

tiktok.com/@authorangelacorbett

www.ingramcontent.com/pod-product-compliance
Lightning Source LLC
Chambersburg PA
CBHW041745010726
47507CB00008B/289